I0603811

LUANN K. EDWARDS

An Odd Request

LuAnn K. Edwards

All scripture is from the New International Version.
ISBN: 978-1-0882-4459-3

Dedication

To women who support others in ministry.
Thank you for your dedication to the Lord's work.

A story of building trust and love.

Take delight in the LORD, and he will give you the
desires of your heart.
Psalm 37:4

One

Early January
Pleasant Springs, Tennessee

My best friend, Jill Drake, entered my home without knocking, laughed, and handed me *most* of my mail. "Your mail carrier gave me this instead of putting it in your box. Must have thought I was you. After all, we're almost twins."

Her long, dark hair and tanned skin looked nothing like my fair skin and strawberry blonde hair. Not to mention my freckles—lots of freckles.

"They think you live here because they see your car here all the time." I chuckled and glanced at the standard-sized envelope she still held. "What's that?"

"Someone was in a hurry or had lousy handwriting. Who do you know in Orlando? Bim Pibersan?"

I took the envelope from her, checked the return address, and squinted. "That's just Ben Peterson, the Missions Pastor from Hart Fellowship. He's raising money for his church's next trip. He's sent me letters before."

"Isn't he the pastor whose wife died in a fire a couple of years ago in Chattanooga?"

I nodded and frowned. "While she visited her mother there. Annie and her mom both died. Tragic." I tossed the envelope into the mail pile on the end table, along with the utility bills and junk mail.

"Aren't you going to open it?"

"Why should I?" I rubbed my chin. "He's only requesting money as usual."

She smirked. "But what if he's not asking for a donation?"

I shrugged. "No big deal. I'll read it later." I smiled and rubbed my palms together. "Ready for hot chocolate?"

Jill and I met most Saturdays at her house or mine to knit and crochet toboggan hats, mittens, and scarves for the kids at Creekside Children's Home. On that early January afternoon, I'd prepared hot chocolate and snickerdoodles and started a fire in the fireplace in the front room of my tiny bungalow.

We didn't need to walk far to enter my kitchen—a few steps to the left of my living room. To the right was the bathroom, bedroom, and my washer and dryer, which stood behind a set of bifold doors in the hallway. That was it. Not a tiny home, but almost.

We stepped into the kitchen and gathered our treats.

"You liked Ben and Annie, didn't you?" Jill took a bite of her cookie.

"I loved them both."

"And you have a lot in common with him?"

"I suppose." I narrowed my eyes. "Why do you ask?"

She took a sip of her hot chocolate. "You should find

out if he's dating anyone."

"You realize he lives 600 miles from here." I crossed my arms and sneered. "I can't call him and ask him for a date."

"But you can take a trip to Florida, spend time in Orlando, and ask him to show you around. Discover if there are any sparks."

I shook my head. "Sparks are my middle name according to Michael."

She laughed. "Yep. Fiery and feisty. But you've mellowed out since then."

"Losing the love of your life can do that."

Jill agreed. "If Ben lived here and wanted to date you, would you be interested?"

I stared out the kitchen window. "The opportunity for full-time ministry again?" I grinned at Jill. "Yes."

~

Folks might call Jill and me spinsters. But the term didn't fit either of us. We were both too young to be considered old. Years ago, age thirty-five fit that description, but no longer. And although neither of us were married, we both were at one time. My husband, Michael, died five years before when he fell off a ladder while he cleaned the church's gutters, one of his many jobs as the pastor of a small church. Jill's husband died seven years ago while deployed overseas.

My job as a CAD Technician at an engineering firm in town kept me busy. Jill was a civil engineer at the same company. Our employer may have been small, but we won a good share of major projects—a benefit of being the only firm in the county. Our biggest competition came from the larger firms in Chattanooga located fifty miles southeast of Pleasant Springs.

On Wednesday evening, Ben sent me a message through social media: Did you receive my letter?

He must have really needed the money.

I typed out a quick response. Yes. Will pray and get back to you.

He responded with a thumbs up.

After I completed chores around the house, I prayed over how much money I should give Ben toward his trip and grabbed my checkbook. I sent him a message: Check ready to mail. Verify your address. Return on envelope hard to read.

The following morning while at work, I received another message from Ben: What check? Did you read my letter?

I cringed. Weren't you requesting money for a mission trip?

No. Read it and get back to me.

Sure thing. I'll read it when I get home.

An hour later, Jill and I went to lunch.

After I told her about my strange messages from Ben, she invited herself to my house after work. She wanted to be there when I opened and read his letter.

~

Jill arrived at 6:00 p.m. "Have you peeked inside yet?"

I frowned and shrugged. "I can't find the envelope."

She scurried to my end table and picked up pieces of mail lying there. "Where did you put it?"

I stomped my foot. "I told you, I don't remember."

"Where have you looked?"

"Everywhere. The kitchen, my dresser drawer where I keep my bills, even the trash can."

"Go check your room again, and I'll check the kitchen."

I darted to my bedroom and checked my drawers, closet, and under my bed. Nothing.

"Found it." Jill hollered from the kitchen. "With some other mail. How did it end up in your junk drawer?"

When I returned to my living room, I joined Jill on the sofa. "I threw everything in there when my parents called to say they were on their way over Sunday afternoon and then forgot about it."

I snatched the envelope from her hand, tore it open, and pulled out the folded letter.

"Read it aloud. I want to hear what he has to say." She wiggled in her seat and clasped her hands under her chin. "He may want to date you."

I placed the letter on the sofa next to me on the opposite side from Jill and wrinkled my nose. "He can't want to date me. We haven't seen each other in years."

"And why is that?"

"After Michael graduated from college in Chattanooga, he attended seminary for three years. By the time we came back to Tennessee, Ben and Annie had moved to Orlando."

Jill sighed. "Why didn't you stay in touch?"

"Annie and I did by email, and Michael and Ben did too. But never Ben and me."

She nudged my elbow and reached across me for the letter. "Hurry and read it. You're not getting any younger."

I shook my head, took it from her hands, and read aloud.

Dear Rebecca,

I hope you are doing well and your

new year is off to a good start. Please pray over my request. Annie has been with the Lord now for two years. I'm still at a loss over her death. Her passing has affected my ministry, professional and personal relationships, my attitude, and caused me difficulty with people in the church. I'd like to remarry, but the thought of dating brings me overwhelming anxiety.

Jill drew her eyebrows together. "Poor guy. He doesn't want to date."

"No. But it sounds like he's requesting prayer. We were a real foursome all those years ago when he was an associate pastor in Chattanooga, and we prayed for one another often." I glanced at the letter and continued to read aloud.

Will you be willing to become my . . .

"What?" I wadded up the letter and threw it across the room. "I refuse to read any more of this nonsense."

Jill jumped up, retrieved the letter, placed it on my end table, and smoothed out the wrinkles with her fist.

"What's wrong with him?" I stood and tried to snatch the letter from her hands.

She held it over her head, her eyes wide. "Whoa, forget the dating."

I shoved her onto the couch. "Give it to me."

She read, *. . . my wife without doing the*

dating thing?

I plopped onto the floor, sat with my back against the sofa, and pouted.

Jill continued to read.

Consider this letter my offer of marriage. I've prayed over this decision for the past few months and believe we will make a great ministry team.

Sincerely,

Benson E. Peterson

She squealed. "The letter includes his phone number."

I spoke in an annoyed tone. "He's crazy. Annie's death turned him into a lunatic." I twisted toward Jill. "Who in their right mind would send a letter and propose marriage to a woman he hasn't seen in twelve years?"

"A man who thinks you will make the perfect wife for him?" Jill beamed. "Give me your phone. I'll text him for you."

"Oh, no you won't." I jumped up, grabbed the letter from Jill's hands, and paced. "Don't you see? There's nothing personal here except my name. He probably sent it to fifty women hoping one would respond."

"Fifty? But he messaged you too."

I stopped and stared at Jill. "Along with how many others?" I waved the letter in front of her face. "How tacky can you get?"

She rose from my couch. "How are you going to respond?"

"I'm not." I flung the letter across the room and

placed my hands on my hips. "He doesn't deserve an answer."

~

After Jill left, I reread the letter from Ben. Marry him? The man had problems. Mental ones. And because of him, I had a terrible headache.

While getting ready for bed, I received another message from Ben. Are you in?

The nerve of some people.

In what? A harem? Then picking out your bride? A modern-day Esther story? You are out of line, Ben. What's happened to you?

He responded within five minutes: No. A harem? Seriously? You are the only woman I contacted. Pray before you turn me down like I'm crazy.

I plopped onto my bed. He said I was the only woman? Should I give him a chance? But he didn't want to date. How could I give him a chance?

Pray like he asked.

Instead, I found a piece of stationary and carried it to my kitchen table. I wanted to be gentle when I let him down.

Dear Ben,

I understand the pain of losing a beloved spouse, and I'm sorry you have had a challenging time.

Michael and I thought the world of you and Annie. You were instrumental in our coming to know Christ while we were in college and an inspiration to us before we married. We counted you both as dear friends and mentors during our four years together in Chattanooga.

I'm flattered you considered me as someone with whom you would like to do ministry. But my experience is tiny compared to the megachurch you serve in. I doubt I'm qualified for such a position. For the past five years, since Michael's death, I've done little in serving except to teach a ladies Bible study and pray for those in need.

I've spent time over the past few months asking the Lord to direct me to where He wants me to serve Him, and I sense it's here in Pleasant Springs. Not Orlando. I appreciate your contacting me, but I cannot accept your offer of marriage.

Sincerely,

Becca Hill

I included my phone number and sent Ben this message: I'm responding to your request by snail mail. Blessings.

Two

I dropped the letter in my mailbox before I left for work on Friday. We worked long days on Monday through Thursday, but only four hours on Friday, which became my afternoon for errands around Pleasant Springs.

Often, I walked at a nearby park or hiked a trail that led to beautiful springs and waterfalls. I loved the rolling hills that surrounded Pleasant Springs and spent time outdoors as much as possible when weather allowed.

After work, and before I arrived home from the grocery store, I received a message from Ben: Check out this video.

I put away my groceries, sat at my kitchen table, and clicked play. What a cute guy. He had aged well, and the video brought him to life. Much better than staring at his profile pic on social media.

"Hi, Rebecca. I'm recording this message for the tenth and last time. I suppose, because you felt you needed to send me a letter, your answer is no. My request must be the oddest one you've ever received. But to be more effective in ministry, I need a wife. If you'll listen to me, perhaps you'll recognize it as something good for you too."

"Yeah, right." I smirked and shifted in my seat.

"I remember the wonderful times Annie and I shared with you and Michael back in Chattanooga. What would it be like to share them again?"

I paused the video. We did have great fellowship together, but we'd need Michael and Annie to enjoy that again. I pressed play.

"I promise to care for and respect you, offer you stability, and to be attentive to your needs and supportive in your endeavors. In return, I'm asking you to assist me in ministry, be available when I counsel women, accompany me on mission trips and local outreach opportunities, encourage, and pray for me."

Sounded like a business proposition to me. One I wasn't willing to negotiate.

"Annie found me to be a good husband, and many ladies in the church describe me as a 'good catch' as I'm sure you'll agree within time." He shook his head and crossed his arms. "Sorry, now I sound arrogant and I'm not. But I refuse to record this again."

"You sure do sound arrogant." I chuckled at his discomfort.

He dropped his arms to his sides. "Pleasant Springs must be a wonderful place, but Orlando has much to offer too. Many ministry opportunities await you here. This will be a rewarding arrangement for both of us. I can offer you a life of ministry with me as we serve the Lord together. If ministry is what the Lord called you to do all those years ago, and what He still has planned for you, please do it with me."

I paused the video again. He appeared sincere, but it made no sense to me. There was no need to continue watching. I peeked at the time, 1:30 p.m., placed my phone face down on the table, and stood to prepare my lunch. After I fixed myself a peanut butter and jelly sandwich, I glanced at my phone and mumbled. "Guess I can listen to whatever else he has to say." I flipped over my cell and clicked play.

"Either you're attracted or not to full-time service for the Lord, which is all I can offer you, except for the things I've mentioned. If you're interested, text me and I'll contact you to discuss this further.

"I hope to hear from you soon. I have prayed about this and believe I'm being led by God to ask this of you."

The video ended. No mention of the expectation that love would come in time.

"Go away, Ben."

~

Jill stopped by my home later that afternoon. "I can't wait to see this video you got from lover boy today."

"Stop the silly talk. If I'd known you'd be this excited, I wouldn't have texted you." I tucked my hair behind my ear. "He's not giving up."

"And why should he? This could be your chance to have the children and family you've always wanted." She smiled. "And if that's not enough, he's offering you the full-time ministry you've been yearning for since Michael died. Why are you fighting this? You loved serving the Lord as a pastor's wife."

"I'll show you why. Follow me." I led her to my kitchen table where my computer sat and pulled up Hart Fellowship. "Look at that auditorium. How many people do you think attend there?"

Jill scrunched her nose. "A few hundred?"

"Do you need glasses? Must hold 5,000. And they

have three services every Sunday." I crossed my arms. "What can I offer a church that size?"

Jill opened her mouth and closed it again. She glanced from me to the computer screen and back to me. "So, it's not marrying the guy that's got you uptight, it's his enormous church?"

"I teach a Bible study with five ladies. What if I'm asked to teach one with five hundred?" I clutched my chest. "I can't do that."

"Excuse me a moment. Aren't you the one who told me that God equips those He calls?"

I frowned and rolled my eyes. "Don't get all spiritual on me. Crowds scare me. I'm fine in a small church like ours, but not a megachurch in Orlando."

"You can do whatever God calls you to do." Jill took a seat and pulled the computer over to her. "Now show me the video of Pastor Ben."

I brought it up on my computer and hit play.

Her eyes lit up, and she fanned her face with her hand. "He *is* a cutie. How much older is he than you?"

"Six years, I think. Maybe eight."

When the video ended, she rose from her chair. "I've never been a pastor's wife, but I'd become one for him."

"Time for you to go home. Don't you have a dog to feed?"

"Marry Ben. I'll move to Orlando too. Maybe he's got a pastor friend for me."

"You're impossible." I led her to the living room and pointed to the door.

"No wait. What did you tell him? Are you meeting soon?"

"I sent him a letter this morning. That's all the response he needs."

~

On Saturday, Ben called me at 1:05 p.m. Where did he get my cell number? He couldn't have received my letter that fast. I let the call go to voicemail. Hearing his voice, and if he talked all soothing and caring like, I might cave. A huge mistake. Besides, he was on the edge of stalking me.

When I listened to his voicemail, I was sure of it. He greeted me and said, "Will you allow me the opportunity to visit you next weekend? I can be in Pleasant Springs on Friday evening and stay through Sunday afternoon. You know my intentions, which will make dating bearable for me, if that's what you prefer. I'd like to meet with you in person to discuss this further to decide if we can make this arrangement work. Orlando is a wonderful place to serve the Lord."

I raised my voice at my phone. "Give it up, Pastor Peterson." I sent him a text within minutes and with little thought: Where did you get my phone number? I can't do this. Stop contacting me.

You included your number on a sympathy card. Said not to hesitate to call if I needed you.

That's absurd. I didn't mean for him to call if he needed a wife.

A minute later, I received another text from Ben: I'm here if you change your mind. Praying you will.

Change my mind? An emptiness simmered inside of me. He offered me something I'd prayed for during the past four years. Full-time ministry, including mission trips. *Is this your answer, Lord?* I shook my head.

16

Three

During the following week, I reread Ben's letter and messages and watched the video from him over and over. What if this was the Lord at work? Had I hindered what God wanted to accomplish through me?

Jill and I talked often, and she joined me in prayer. We talked about how weird it would be to marry someone and not be in love with them. How long would it take for that to happen? And what if it never did? And did Ben want a wife or an assistant? A cook and housekeeper? Was the relationship a superficial one or an actual marriage? If superficial, I'd never have the family I dreamed of having. I needed to ask these embarrassing questions before a wedding could take place.

And what did Riley think of this? She must be in college by now. Did she know what her dad was up to?

After a week of intense praying and no further contact from Ben, I stared at a text I wrote: **You may visit. When will you arrive?**

~

Relief washed over Ben when he received Becca's text. He was sure he'd understood God's plan and Becca was his future bride, but he endured doubt throughout the week while he waited on her to contact him. He sent a return text with his tentative plans: Arrive in Chattanooga at 4:00 p.m. Friday and return home Sunday afternoon.

After he made his airline reservations, he bowed his head and offered thanks. *May everything go well on this visit, Lord. I can't offer her my heart. That will come later. But I can offer her a good life and years of service to You.*

~

On Monday morning at 10:00, Ted Bailey, my boss, called my desk phone and invited me to his office.

His door was open, and he motioned me inside. "Take a seat." He frowned and lowered his voice. "Are you okay?"

I glanced at the opened door and back at my boss. "Did Bob say something?" He was one of our top engineers.

Ted nodded.

"I didn't sleep well last night and have a lot on my mind. Major decisions to make." I covered my mouth to hide a yawn. "I'm almost done with your plan set and will finish Bob's this afternoon."

He clasped his hands behind his neck. "This isn't like you. Bob's plans held priority. You should have known that. Do you need this afternoon off?"

"I'm fine. But sleepy. May I have a fifteen-minute break to take a walk and clear my head? The nippy weather should wake me up."

"Sure should. It's freezing out there." He pecked keys on his computer. "Wait until after 10:30. Calendar shows Bob will be in a meeting. He's anxious about this project and has been taking his frustration out on everyone. I don't want him to see you leave."

Ted was a good boss. "Thanks. I'll do that." I returned to my cubicle and peeked at my watch. Twenty-five minutes. Enough time to finish Ted's plans before I slipped out for a quick break.

~

A walk was what I needed, but as soon as a blast of cold air hit my face, I jogged two doors north to Mama Lou's Café. I ordered a hot chocolate for me and a coffee for Ted. He'd appreciate my way of saying thank you, and I wished to stay on his good side.

Ted wasn't in his office when I returned, but I set the cup on his desk. I shot him an email and told him the coffee was from me. Since I'd finished his plans, I worked on Bob's and ate a granola bar for lunch.

I sat back and smiled when I finished everything before quitting time. Would have been earlier if Bob hadn't stopped by to check in with me five times throughout the afternoon.

At home that evening, I relaxed in a hot bath in hopes it would help me get a better night's sleep. At 9:30, when I crawled into bed, my phone pinged. A text from Ben: **Looking forward to spending time with you.**

I stared at the ceiling for what seemed like hours.

~

The rest of my week went by too fast. In a normal work week, the days drag on. But when I hoped for a long week, Friday came early.

I left work at noon, drove home, and prepared a meatloaf for supper to bake after Ben arrived. A quiet evening in front of the fireplace sounded nice. I didn't know what Ben had planned and wanted to be prepared to stay indoors because of our recent chilly weather. Not likely that we'd take a stroll at the park nearby.

Ben sent me a text before he left the Chattanooga airport: Be there around 5:30.

Already nervous, I became a shaky mess while I waited. He rang my doorbell at 5:35. Why had I agreed to his visit? Was I as crazy as him? I opened the door and stepped aside for him to enter.

"Whew. Thirty degrees colder here than at home. I doubt I brought warm enough clothes." He thanked me for allowing him to come. "I hope you won't regret your decision."

With his smile and smooth talk, I regretted it. "Good to see you, too, Ben. Let me take your jacket." I invited him to have a seat on the sofa, carried his coat to my room, placed it on my bed, and took three deep calming breaths. When I returned to the living room, I sat in the chair opposite him. There weren't a lot of choices of where to sit in my living room. I owned little. A couch, chair, end table with a lamp, and a television mounted on the wall made up my décor with knick-knacks thrown in. Enough clutter for one small room.

After I asked if he'd like a hot drink, he suggested dinner.

"I have a meatloaf ready to bake. Should be ready in forty-five minutes."

He twisted his mouth to one side.

"Are you okay?"

"May we go somewhere instead? I drove by a café in town."

"Do you think I'm a terrible cook? Did Michael tell you that?"

He leaned toward me. "I'm sure it's delicious. But I

don't want another meatloaf. Women at the church bring them to me all the time, and I can't eat another one. Already had two this week."

I chuckled and covered my mouth to hold back a full laugh. "I understand. But I had it much better. The single men from our church brought me plenty of smoked pork and chicken."

"Now, that I'd like." He asked again about the café, and I told him that or pizza would be fine. He opted for Mama Lou's.

Our short drive was filled with silence. I expected Ben to take the lead and talk first because he'd come up with this crazy idea.

Years before, when he taught or preached, he could talk for hours and keep our small group's interest the entire time when he shared from God's Word. But I'd never spent time alone with him without Michael or Annie present. Did Ben feel as awkward about being with me as I did with him?

At the restaurant, an outgoing hostess with the cutest southern twang greeted us. My drawl from growing up in Chattanooga wasn't as strong as those from Pleasant Springs, which was one of the things I loved about this small town. That and their country charm along with the friendliness of the people.

She seated us at a table for four in the center of the café.

After Ben ordered the chicken fried steak, and I selected the pot pie, it was time to forge ahead with my interview. I had questions that needed answers.

Four

I gnawed on my lower lip and peered at Ben. "How's Riley?"

"Great. She's a sophomore in the business program at the University of North Florida in Jacksonville. Her focus is on marketing." He smiled. "She has her mother's personality."

"She'll do great." I looked toward the counter where my boss had taken a seat. "Does she know you're here to visit me?"

"Not yet. I'll tell her soon."

I glanced at Ben. "How do you think she'll take the news that you're shopping for a wife?"

He released a heavy sigh. "I'm not shopping. I've found her in you. No more looking."

I peeked over at Ted. He saw me and waved. I grinned and faced Ben.

Ben's eyes narrowed. "He a friend of yours?"

"My boss."

Ben stared at the table and fiddled with his paper placemat. "Do you date much?"

"Not at all. Like you, the thought of dating makes me nervous."

The server delivered our meals and freshened our

drinks. After calling Ben dawlin' and winking at him, she slipped away. I rolled my eyes, but her attentiveness didn't seem to faze him. He bowed his head and offered a quick prayer.

"What are you hoping to find in a wife?"

"For starters, someone to watch out for me. Remind me of my appointments, review my teaching notes, and that type of thing."

"Don't you have an assistant for that?"

He cut his meat into bite-size portions. "We have several, but they're busy. Doris Clark is the best, but I don't involve her unless I have to."

"So, you need someone to be your personal assistant." I bounced my knee. "Cook and housekeeper too?"

"I cook a little and have a biweekly cleaning service." He reached across the table but didn't touch me. "I don't need a wife for those things. I need your prayer support and help in ministry. Didn't I make that clear in my letter and video?"

"You did. I wanted to verify that I understood."

He relaxed back in his chair. "Do you eat here often?"

I responded in a haughty tone. "We have more important items to discuss than where I eat."

He straightened his shoulders. "Like what?"

"Like, how soon are you hoping this wedding will take place?"

"If it's up to me, next weekend will be good."

"Next weekend?" That came out much louder than I'd intended, which caused Ted to glance our way.

I smiled at my boss, lowered my voice, and clenched my teeth at Ben. "You want me to make a major decision like this today so we can marry next weekend?"

"Since you invited me to come, I presumed you'd decided."

I crossed my arms. "That's crazy."

"Let's discuss this back at your place. I have data I wish to share with you to help you with your decision regarding our arrangement."

"You keep calling this an arrangement." I wrinkled my forehead and frowned. "What do you mean by that?"

His eyes flitted around the café before they landed on me. "That's something we need to talk about in private."

"Let me ask you a few questions as a friend. When I lost Michael, there were several hurdles to cross. I stopped taking care of myself as I should have. Are you eating well?"

"Sure. Those meatloaves are amazing." He smirked. "And women show up with crock pots, so I have to return them."

I grinned. "What did you say in your video? The ladies find you to be a 'good catch?'" I opened my eyes wide and nodded. "They know what they're doing."

He looked away. "I'm eating well."

"Exercise?"

He eyed me and deepened his voice. "Are you asking to see my guns?"

Warmth spread up my neck. "What about rest? Do you take time out to do things you love and find time to relax?"

"I'm off all weekend and here with you."

"You can't relax on this visit. Admit it, you're as uneasy being here with me as I am with you."

"I enjoy your blushing." He set his fork on his plate.

"That helps me to relax."

"Moving on, what about friendships? Do you have a good friend to confide in? Hang out with the guys and do something fun?"

"Why are you asking me these questions?"

"To determine if you'll be honest with me." I tapped my index finger on the table. "You're failing."

He shook his head. "I cook sometimes and do a lot of takeout." He sighed and leaned back in his chair. "Have a membership at the gym, but don't use it, and jog three or four times a week. For relaxation, I drive to Cocoa Beach most Mondays, my day off, and have lunch, and I play racquetball with a friend often on Saturday afternoons."

"That's great. If I marry you, will you take me to the beach on Mondays?" I waggled my eyebrows at him. "I love the beach."

He tried to hide his grin, but the corners of his mouth curved upward. "Perhaps on Saturdays too."

"How's your sleep? You look tired."

When he didn't answer, I told him how it was for me. I lost twenty pounds because I wouldn't cook for one person. Hid myself from everyone so I wouldn't have to talk about the pain. And slept clinging to Michael's pillow to inhale his scent until his scent faded away.

"You understand." His features softened, and he picked up his fork and knife. "I've experienced all that too."

"My help came from my friend, Jill, who got me outdoors to walk every afternoon. She came to my house to cook with me and taught me how to crochet. She helped and encouraged me to return to work at the engineering firm after a three-month leave of absence."

"Sounds like you found a good friend." He nodded. "That's what I need you to do for me."

But what about my needs? "Okay. Tomorrow I'll teach you how to crochet."

"I meant get me out of the house and encourage me. Except for my jogs, trips to the beach, and racquetball, I'm a homebody now that Annie's gone. My motivation died with her."

"But what about Jill? She's a widow, too, and we've become like sisters." I folded my hands in my lap. "I'll have a tough time leaving her because she needs me, and I need her."

"Does she have family in the area?"

"Her parents moved back here a few months ago, and her sister lives in Chattanooga."

"And your family?"

"My parents live east of there, and my brother is in Nashville." I stared at my hands. "I'll miss them too."

He cleared his throat. "Does this mean you're leaning toward saying yes?"

~

Ben sat back and enjoyed another blush rise on Becca's cheeks. He remembered how Annie and he had commented on Becca's blushing and freckles. Adorable. He must win her over. In time, he could love this woman. But until then, sharing his ministry and being seen with her would be enough. Perhaps the concerns at the church would die down and his coworkers would lighten up on him.

Five

Ben grasped a manila file folder from the backseat of his rental car, a dark gray Nissan Versa, and we hurried into my home to escape the near-freezing temperature. I asked him if he'd like me to start a fire.

He glanced at the fireplace and back at me. "I have information to show you, and it might be better for us to use your kitchen table. We won't be able to enjoy a fire."

"Okay. Follow me." I strolled into the kitchen.

We sat at the kitchen table after I prepared a cup of coffee for Ben and hot tea for me.

"What secrets lie in that folder, Pastor Peterson?"

"Stats and photos you may be interested in reviewing." He pulled out forms he'd brought. The first one he handed me included his credit score. "I want you to understand my financial position so you'll know I can provide for you." He then gave me a copy of his assets and liabilities and followed that with his latest pay stub. "You can work if you want to, but you won't have to get a job."

"Impressive." He could take on a wife and family. They must pay better at a megachurch than they do in a small town for a pastor.

"And here are pictures of the inside of my house.

There's four bedrooms, and I use one of those as my home office."

He showed me photos of the kitchen, dining area, living room, and his office. He then showed me the master bedroom and bath. "I'll let you have this one, and I'll take the guest room." He handed me another picture.

I expected this because of his use of the word arrangement. But it hit me hard. The realization he didn't want a wife in the full sense of the term. He wanted a companion. I stared at the master bedroom picture. "What happens when Riley comes for a visit? She'll wonder what's going on when we're not sharing the same room, won't she?"

"She's the only person I plan to tell. Everyone else will believe we're . . . you know."

"Jill knows the truth. She was with me when your letter came and saw the video you sent."

"Best if we don't let anyone else in on our arrangement. May raise questions."

We continued to chat about his home, church, and life in Orlando. A big city where I didn't want to live. And because it was late, I needed to send him on his way.

"Where are you staying for the weekend?"

"A bed-and-breakfast along the highway. The one with the cross on the mailbox."

"Maggie's Place." I shook my head. "Next time, stay at the small motel in town. Maggie Stone is a church member, but she's also a gossip. Be careful what you say in front of her. It may end up in her weekly blog post."

He thanked me for the advice, stood, and strode to the living room for his jacket.

After he left at 9:30, I paced throughout my house, called Jill, and told her about my evening. "This arrangement won't work."

"Sure, it will. The benefits of married life with a great-looking companion, but you don't have to worry about being brokenhearted if something happens to him like it did Michael. You're not expected to bare your soul to him or fall in love."

"That's one way of looking at it." I moseyed into the kitchen, cleared our cups from the table, and put Ben's in the sink.

"You're rewarded with stability and opportunities to serve in ministry for the Lord. That's a win if you ask me."

"What happens if I fall in love with him, but he doesn't reciprocate?" I refilled my cup with water and heated it in the microwave for another cup of tea. "Don't you think that could cause issues?"

"Guard your heart. Don't let yourself fall for him."

"Yeah, right."

~

On Saturday morning, Ben arrived at 9:00—the time we agreed upon when he left the night before. "I've made plans for us today if you agree. Are you ready to go?"

I peeked at my jeans and long-sleeve plaid shirt. "Do I look okay?"

He unzipped his jacket and showed me his shirt. "I'd say we're equally dressed."

I smirked. "If you say so." The faded, baggy green T-shirt did not suit him at all.

Within minutes, we headed to Chattanooga. Ben asked me if I'd like to visit the Tennessee Aquarium. We'd be indoors where it was warm, plus I hadn't been there in thirteen years. The last time was when Michael and I took Riley while Ben and Annie traveled to

Knoxville for a wedding.

"Sounds good."

We purchased our tickets and visited the Ocean Journey first. We didn't take time to pet the sting rays but watched the lemurs romp through the trees. The butterfly exhibit was one of my favorites. Ben took a terrible picture of me with a butterfly on my nose. And the penguins—what could be cuter? From there, we viewed various fish and sharks. After observing hundreds of jellyfish, we made our way to the River Journey.

The otters were fun to watch. But when I stopped to view the alligators, Ben told me not to waste my time. I'd see many when I moved to Orlando. I shivered. Ugly, scary creatures.

We wandered through the gift shop without making a purchase and returned to his car. Ben asked if I'd like to grab a sandwich at a restaurant two blocks away.

After we sat across from one another at a four-person table in the back corner, Ben ordered a burger, and I ordered the chicken salad.

"Do you have plans after lunch?"

"Will you help me buy a new shirt?" He snickered. "You stuck up your nose at the one I'm wearing."

"I did not." I grinned. "But you could use an addition or two to your wardrobe. The faded green is not a good look for you."

He leaned toward me. "Well, we'll find out if you can do better at picking out my shirts. Consider this a test."

I wiggled my head from side to side and pointed at him with my index finger. "You're on, mister." I chuckled. "And after we shop? What then?"

"Do you like museums? We can visit the Hunter Museum of American Art."

"Been years since I was there. I'd love to go."

The server brought our sandwiches to the table, and Ben offered a quick prayer.

I swallowed my first bite. "As your wife, what type of things would you expect me to do at Hart Fellowship?"

He picked up his napkin and wiped his mouth. "Accompany me to services and special events. Offer suggestions or your opinions at meetings that include our spouses. Take an active role in the prayer ministry. Things like that."

"Would I need to stand in front of the church and speak or lead a large Bible study?"

"Only if you want to take a leading role. No one will force you to do anything you're not comfortable with." He smiled. "But I will want you to help with mission trip planning and going on the trips with me. Is that okay with you?"

"I'd like that."

His eyes sparkled. "Then you're on board with this?" He scooted closer to the table. "Ready to commit to being my wife?"

"Whoa." I lifted both hands in front of my face. "Too soon for that."

"But I need to know. Are you in or not?"

"You're expecting an answer today?" I pressed my lips together.

"Or tomorrow."

"How long have you been praying about this?" I massaged my temples. "Shouldn't I get equal time?"

"Four months, and no." He scowled. "I don't have

that long."

"You don't have that long for what?"

"I need a wife now. I may lose my job if I have to wait four months."

How could a church fire someone for not having a spouse? Was that possible? I leaned toward him. "Explain your comment."

"People are talking. Making remarks that I should be in a relationship by now."

"Church people?"

"Other pastors. We have seventeen full- and part-time on staff."

I tried to relax and crossed my legs. "And your senior pastor? What does he say?"

"John Young? Nothing now, but he often called me into his office for counseling the first year after Annie's death because of my gloomy attitude."

"There you have it." I brought my hands together. "I'm sure you're not in any danger of losing your job, or he would talk with you about it now too. Wouldn't he?"

"His son-in-law, Keith Morgan, says otherwise. He's our youth pastor and my closest friend."

I smacked my palm on the table. "That's really stupid. How can someone tell you that you should be in a relationship after two years?" I tilted my head to the right. "We don't all grieve the same."

"That's what I said. But Keith says the rest of the staff don't agree. They say I'm grumpy, not doing my fair share of the work, and need a wife to keep me on track. As you know, without Annie, I can't buy decent clothing." He clasped his hands on both sides of his jacket at the zipper and pulled it open. "You'd be a perfect fit for me. Say, yes."

Six

After lunch, Ben drove to a department store. While he perused the rack for a good buy, I picked out two long-sleeved tees from a display table and carried them over to him. "Try these. They're extra soft for added comfort."

He grimaced. "Not my style. I like short sleeves, and I'm looking for yellow."

"You shouldn't wear yellow, and on days like today, you need long sleeves." I shoved the shirts into his chest. "Try them on." I raised my eyebrows. "I like them a lot."

"And you like these colors?" He held the two shirts.

I led him to the table. "There are others if you prefer, but the teal or chocolate brown will look fantastic on you with your sandy blond hair and brown eyes."

He took them both and strode back to the dressing room. When he returned, he wore the teal shirt.

"That's you." A great fit. He *was* one good-looking guy. "Do you like it?"

"Soft like you said." He shook his head. "But I'm not sure it's me."

I touched the sleeve on his upper arm and included a squeeze. "Nice."

He jerked his arm back and glared at me. "What are

you doing?”

"I . . . I . . ." What did he expect me to say? I gaped at him. He got upset because I touched him? I turned and zipped to the front of the store.

This would never work.

~

Ben hurried into the dressing room and put on his old shirt. Why had Becca touched him like that? Annie always squeezed his upper arm too.

And where did Becca run off to? He wouldn't win her over if he lost his cool with her.

He returned the shirt he'd tried on to the display table. A new shirt would need to wait. He started toward the front of the store and turned back. He'd better buy the shirt and compliment Becca on her taste.

And let her touch him again? He wasn't ready for that. But he needed to make amends.

~

I paced and fumed inside the store for two minutes but didn't want anyone to hear my grumbling, so I went outside to the sidewalk in front of the store. I continued to pace, looked upward, and raised my palms. *How can I marry someone I can't touch? Waiting to fall in love is one thing, but I need physical contact.*

Jill and I hugged each other, patted each other's shoulders, and joined hands to pray. Ben acted like I did something awful. Maybe sinful. He needed to go back to Orlando.

"Becca?" Ben caught up with me on the sidewalk. "I bought the teal shirt." He opened the bag to show me.

I kept my pace and scowled. I didn't care what shirt he did or didn't buy.

He remained beside me. "Are you ready to go to the

museum now?"

I stopped, stared at him, and spoke with irritation in my voice. "No, museum. I'm ready to go home."

"Okay." He pointed in the opposite direction. "We're parked over there." He led the way.

I climbed into his car and focused straight ahead. He was in for a long, quiet drive. I'd wait to tell him to get lost after we arrived at my house.

~

Ben needed to proceed with care. Becca wasn't too keen on this idea of his, and he had to exercise caution to not further alienate her. "Did you hear me say I bought the shirt you picked out? I'll wear it when the weather is cool back home." He glanced at Becca.

She crossed her arms and bounced her left knee.

He bit the inside of his cheek and rolled his neck. "I overreacted when you touched me."

She glared at him. "You think?" She turned her face toward the passenger side window. "You made me feel like the biggest loser of all time. Like my touch disgusted you."

He sighed and told her how Annie did the same thing. "My first thought was you shouldn't be touching a married man like you did. After years of being married, I sometimes forget I'm now a single guy."

Becca gazed at Ben, and her voice softened. "I understand that. When a man flirts with me, I think, don't they know I'm married?" Her shoulders drooped, and she clasped her hands together in her lap.

"Am I forgiven?"

She nodded. "But Ben, if you want this to work, I have needs too. More than a desire to serve in full-time ministry."

He squirmed and scrunched his nose. "And what are those?"

"For one, physical touch. Like hugs. In fact, tomorrow at church, you need to hold my hand from the time we exit your car until we return after service." She peered at him. "People will be watching. And if you hope to convince them that we're a couple, you need to prove it by your actions."

"I'm not ready." He slumped his shoulders and rubbed his face. "That implies intimacy, and we're not there yet."

She crossed her arms again. "Then there's nothing further to discuss. I'll attend church alone tomorrow."

Now what, Lord? She asked for more than I'm ready to give.

~

Part of me regretted what I'd said about attending church alone. Ben had grown on me. We had tremendous obstacles to climb, but my red flags weren't from the Lord. They were all from me and the fear that came with uprooting myself from this small community I'd grown to love. Pleasant Springs was my safe place. I didn't want to leave.

When Ben pulled into my driveway at 4:15, he asked if he could come inside to talk things over and afterward take me to dinner.

"We'll eat supper here. There's plenty of meatloaf." I smirked.

He twisted his mouth. "Sounds great."

We hurried inside, and I took our coats to my bedroom. When I returned to the living room, Ben sat on the sofa and patted the cushion next to him. He smiled when I took my seat, and he asked if I'd like him to start a fire.

"Sure. That sounds nice."

He piled on fresh wood and lit the fireplace before he returned to my side. "That will take the chill out of the air." He fidgeted and hesitated before he spoke again. "Do you want to practice?"

"Practice?" I narrowed my eyes at him. "What?"

He opened his palm and put his hand between us.

I stared at his hand in disbelief and placed my palm on his. When he closed his fingers around mine, warmth spread throughout my body. I raised my eyes to his. "Are you okay with this?"

He grinned. "I'm okay with you."

"And what about my meatloaf?" I nudged his elbow. "Are you ready to eat?"

"Can we sit here and enjoy the fire for a few minutes longer?"

I was good with that. And hopeful. Looked like church was on in the morning.

LUANN K. EDWARDS

Seven

When Ben arrived Sunday morning at 9:30, I dashed outside to save time. Our service started at 9:45, and it took six minutes to drive to the church. No need to be late. Everyone would want to meet my new friend, and I wanted to show him off.

I filled Ben in on my expectations while we drove. "Don't forget to hold my hand. More ladies than Maggie like to gossip. We'll need to convince them that we're a couple and have known each other for many years."

"Any other instructions?" He cut me a look and shook his head.

"And if I do or say anything we haven't talked about, understand that I'm looking out for you." I giggled.

"What are you planning?"

"Simple acting. Which may mean nothing at all. We'll discover how it goes." Could I pull this off? Part of me felt deceptive, but I expected fun and excitement too.

Ben parked the car at the church and told me not to move. He loped to my door, opened it for me, and offered his left hand to help me out of his car.

"That's unnecessary."

He kept hold of my hand and closed the car door. "But this is Pleasant Springs. I've observed other men doing the same for their wives or girlfriends." He grinned. "Playing the part."

"When and where did you see this?"

He nodded toward a couple in the parking lot.

I pursed my lips. "They've been married for sixty years, and she uses a walker." I chuckled. "Now remember, this is my turf. Let me do most of the talking."

"Ouch." He shook out his right hand. "I talk for a living, remember?"

"I remember a few times years ago when you said things from the pulpit that you shouldn't have. You made Annie blush more than once."

"I assure you that I manage myself much better now." He opened the door to the church, where two ushers and Maggie greeted us.

Maggie, who was close to my age, gushed and turned on the southern charm. "Why Pastor Peterson. You told me you were here to visit a special lady in town, but you never mentioned she was our very own Rebecca Hill."

I pretended to swat Ben's arm. "This silly man. Why do you suppose he didn't share that pertinent information?" I glanced at Ben. "Were you trying to keep us a secret?" I needed to remove ourselves from Miss Gossip as soon as possible. I linked my elbow with Ben's and tugged him toward another church member. "Risa McDonald, I'd like you to meet my dear friend, Ben Peterson."

Risa celebrated her eighty-second birthday in December but appeared much younger. She dressed well, wore perfect makeup, and got plenty of exercise.

Although she craved attention and visitors, she wasn't a busybody.

She stuck out her hand, welcomed Ben to the church, and hugged me. "Please stop by this week—been too long since our last visit."

We agreed to meet for lunch on Friday at Mama Lou's.

Ben and I made our way into the sanctuary and found seats in a pew halfway up on the left side of the church. He held my hand in a snug grip, which pleased me. He kept holding it after we sat.

I whispered. "We can abort the original hand-holding plan, because there's no one else sitting in our row."

He tickled my ear with his breath. "Are you okay with this? I kind of like holding your hand."

Ben earned a point or two with his comment. I opened my eyes wide and focused on Deacon Jones when he greeted the congregation to prepare for making the week's announcements. Maybe this arrangement could work out after all.

When Deacon Jones exited the front, Pastor Oldham took the stage, which wasn't the normal order of service. He strode to the microphone. "Ladies and gentlemen. Maggie brought it to my attention that we have a special guest this morning. A visiting pastor from Hart Fellowship in Orlando, Florida." He scanned the congregation. "There he is with our dear, sweet Becca." He pointed at us. "Pastor Peterson, come forward and greet our congregation."

I grasped Ben's arm before he rose and kept my voice low. "Be careful what you say."

He smiled. "Don't worry about me. I'll do you

proud."

How did our pastor know which church Ben was associated with in Florida? And what else had Ben told Maggie about why he was in town? My cue to pray.

Ben took the stage and owned it. He greeted everyone and shared how happy he was to be in Pleasant Springs and visit our church. Seeing and hearing him speak, brought back memories of the times he preached in Chattanooga. He loved to share in front of groups, and his charismatic personality shone when he talked about God's love. I'd admired him all those years ago, and that hadn't changed. He would always hold a special place in my heart even if I didn't agree to marry him.

Pastor Oldham said, "What brings you to town? Looks like you're here visiting a certain young woman?"

Ben waved at me. "Honey, why don't you come here and join me?"

Several people in the front rows turned and stared at me.

Honey? I waved back and shook my head, ready to crawl under the pew.

"She's bashful this morning." He faced Pastor Oldham.

"Tell us about that. She's kept you a secret."

"I'll be happy to fill you in."

I squirmed. *Lord, it's time for him to sit now. Please?*

Ben looked across the congregation. "I'm wooing Rebecca Hill to be my wife."

My pulse quickened. He didn't just say that did he? What would people think? I glanced at the exit.

Oohs, ahs, and stares flew my way.

"I'd appreciate your prayers. Seems she's kind of

stuck on all of you here in this great town."

Pastor Oldham patted Ben on the back and congratulated him. "Becca will make a fine pastor's wife. She comes with experience. Blessings to you, brother."

Ben thanked him and stepped off the platform. People applauded and grinned at me. I sunk into my seat. Would it have been wrong of me to hope Ben tripped on his way back?

He slid in next to me and spoke close to my ear with pride in his voice. "That went better than I expected."

I leaned away from him and glared. "Really?" I stood for the song service and put several inches between us. What was Ben thinking? A man comes to town to visit his lady friend. No one has ever seen him before. And he asked her to marry him? How did that work? Did he expect me to lie and tell everyone that I made secret trips to Florida?

I shuddered and glanced around me. We needed to slip through the side door as soon as Pastor Oldham said, "Amen."

Before the end of Pastor Oldham's message, someone patted my shoulder. Maggie spoke into my ear from the pew behind us. "I'd like to talk to you before you leave."

Ben squeezed my hand, and I pulled it away. He got us into a big mess. I needed to get us out. There was only one person who could help me. I looked upward.

When the service ended, Ben and I stood and turned back toward Maggie.

She tilted her head and smirked. "Bless your hearts. Have the two of you been having a secret online love affair? Because Pastor Peterson has never been to

Pleasant Springs before. Or have you, dear Becca, been traveling to Orlando for the past few months. How could you keep that from us? We see you every Sunday and often during the week."

I eyed Ben, who appeared speechless. "Ben and I have known each other for sixteen years." I told her how Ben and his wife had first talked to Michael and me about the Lord and how we all became close friends. I ignored her comments regarding this being Ben's first time in Pleasant Springs and secret visits to Florida. Let her surmise whatever she wanted, but I didn't plan to reveal any details.

By this time, well-wishers had formed a line, and I gave them my full attention.

Ben greeted each one as well. After fifteen minutes, we made our way to his car.

When inside, I lashed out. "I can't believe you told the entire church that you'd asked me to marry you. This is a small town. Now everyone, not only Maggie, will wonder how this all came to be and how we've been dating each other. What's your plan now, Mr. Wise Guy?"

"Let's discuss that over lunch at Mama Lou's."

"Lots of ears there." I faked a smile and peered at him. "I have leftover meatloaf."

He brought his hands together under his chin. His eyes drooped like a local hog farmer's bloodhound. "Please no. Let's order a pizza and take it to your place."

I crossed my arms. "You deserve meatloaf." I shook my head and smiled. "But pizza sounds better to me too."

Eight

We called in our order for a pepperoni pizza and drove to the Pizza Shack located across the street from Mama Lou's Café. Ben parked and we strolled to the entrance. Grizzly, a big old dog, lay just outside the door.

"Hey boy." I bent and scratched him behind the ears. "How are you today?"

"Does he belong to the restaurant owner?"

"The town adopted him. His owner, Mr. Jed, died two years ago." I straightened and faced Ben. "Grizzly always came to town with him and waited outside while he conducted business indoors. Now Grizzly roams from place to place looking for handouts." My voice cracked. "And I think he's still looking for Mr. Jed."

"That's sad." He reached down and patted the dog's head. "His name fits with his thick, brown coat and size. He's huge."

We went inside, picked up our pizza, and drove to my house. After lunch, we sat seven or eight inches apart on my sofa and strategized—at least we tried to. We didn't get far. Ben told me to tell people whatever was necessary to be honest, but not too open. He threw it back at me because I lived locally and would be the one bombarded with questions. He felt bad about it, so I eased up on him.

After we finished that topic, he said, "Would you like me to start a fire?"

"I'm good." I stood and asked if he'd like something hot to drink.

"What I'd like is for you to tell me what you're thinking about us."

I returned to my place on the sofa. "I need time to think, pray, and get to know you better."

"Will you be able to give me an answer next weekend?"

"If you want my answer next weekend, you'll need to work on your wooing skills."

He stumbled over his words. "But I . . . Haven't I? . . . What else do you expect me to do? I held your hand and built you a fire."

I bit my tongue to keep from laughing. "You keep calling this proposed marriage an arrangement. But I need to feel special no matter what you call it. You must convey in a tangible way that I'm the woman you want to be your wife." I scooted closer to him and held his hand. "I also need you to describe what's going on inside your head and heart with relationship to Annie so I can discern where you're at in the grieving process."

He stared at the fireplace. "How long did it take you?"

"I'm not sure. After five years, I still have tough days but not as often." I rubbed my thumb across his. "Do you believe Annie would approve of the way you're going about getting a wife? Wouldn't she want you to be happy and in love with the woman you ask to marry you?"

He shrugged. "I don't know what she'd want. Only

that I wish she were still here."

I did my best to encourage Ben to rethink his plan. He made it clear he wasn't ready to love another woman. He'd feel unfaithful to love someone else. I experienced that feeling, too, for a while after Michael died, but he'd want me to love again.

We chatted about assorted topics for another hour before he got up to leave at 3:00 p.m. On his way out, I reminded him that I needed him to woo me like he told the church members.

"I'm not sure I understand."

I tucked my hair behind my ear. "Google it. How to woo a woman."

He lowered his head. "But that's a part of dating I didn't want to deal with."

"Too bad. If you can't make me feel special and wanted, there's no reason for you to come back next weekend." The back of my neck prickled.

He sounded frustrated. "You're making this more than it is. I want an arrangement—companionship—not a real marriage. You knew that before I came."

"This isn't just about you."

He softened his tone. "What am I missing here?"

"I need assurance that an actual marriage is a future possibility."

He brushed his foot across my rug near the front door and sounded agitated. "So, if I do the research, I can return next weekend?"

I wasn't about to back down. "I'll pray and get back to you by Thursday evening."

~

During his return trip home, Ben had plenty of time to mull over Becca's demands. He hadn't expected her to manipulate him like she had. She wasn't the same woman he remembered.

Had he known that about her, he may have considered a second choice. Who was he kidding? There was no number two. Ben felt certain the Lord had confirmed Becca for his wife. He didn't need to look elsewhere. She was the one.

But why couldn't she be happy with companionship? At least for the next year, while he dealt with his grief. She wanted a husband who loved her. How could he do that to Annie?

~

Monday morning at work, I placed my purse in my file drawer and turned on my computer. Four emails awaited me from coworkers.

The first said, "Marriage? Does that mean you're moving to Orlando and didn't tell us?"

From the second: "What? Don't you realize a guy can change a lot in twelve years?"

The third said, "Do you know what you're doing?"

The fourth expressed this sentiment: "I thought you were smarter than that."

And one from Ted. "I'd like to see you in my office."

I stood and bumped into Jill, who'd entered my cubicle. "Did Maggie's blog post come out early this week? People have inundated me with personal emails this morning."

Jill nodded and kept her voice low. "She's asked for a response from you. Wants you to agree to an interview with her today or tomorrow for Wednesday's post."

I shook my head. "Ted wants to see me. I'll read her blog later." I hurried to Ted's office and took a seat in front of him.

He squinted at me. "So that guy you were with Friday evening is your fiancé?"

"He's asked but I haven't answered yet."

He sighed and relaxed his shoulders. "Are you leaving us?"

"I don't know. I'll tell you next Monday after I make my decision."

He steepled his hands on his desk and leaned toward me. "I'd hate to lose you." He lowered his eyes. "You're a great CAD tech." He rose from his desk and glanced at me. "Keep me posted."

Back at my desk, I pulled up Maggie's post.

"Our beloved Rebecca Hill, widow of Pastor Michael Hill, has been pursued by Benson Peterson of Orlando. Pastor Peterson admitted to wooing Becca in recent hours, to become his wife. Verified reports prove, however, Mr. Peterson has never been to Pleasant Springs prior to his visit this past weekend. Which leads me to believe he and Becca must be involved in an Internet relationship. Either that or a spur-of-the-moment romance. Becca said, 'Ben and I have known each other for sixteen years.' But my research clarifies they haven't seen each other for the past twelve. Has Becca been sneaking off to Florida? Or is something else going on and we will have to wait to find out what?

"I invite Becca to contact me and give us the complete story. I plan to share the facts here with my readers on Wednesday's post. Please help us, Becca, to figure out this situation. And if you find yourself in a condition needing prayer, my followers and I would love to pray for you."

"Oh, no she didn't." I jumped up, zipped to Jill's desk, and spit out my words. "Condition needing prayer?"

Jill stood and placed her hand on my arm. "Maybe she didn't mean it the way it sounds."

"We know exactly what she meant." I clenched my fists. "I've had enough of her meddling." After I took a deep breath, I said, "Will you call and ask her to meet us at Mama Lou's for lunch today? If I call her, it won't be pretty."

~

Before Jill and I walked to Mama Lou's, I shot Ben a text: **Maggie wasted no time. New blog post today. Pray. Having lunch together.** I included a link to the post.

Once inside the restaurant, we caught the server's attention and ordered the day's special—chicken and rice casserole—before we ambled toward Maggie's booth along the side windows. We knew Maggie well. She wasn't there for lunch. She only wanted a story.

Maggie frowned when she saw Jill with me. "Can't manage the fire alone?"

I nudged Jill. "She's my protective gear."

Jill and I sat next to one another in the booth opposite Maggie.

I peered at her. "Why did you need to make such a big deal out of this? Nobody's business but mine and Ben's."

"Because I report small town happenings. People love to read what I have to say."

"And what are you planning to say on Wednesday?"

"You tell me."

I looked at Jill. "Will you leave Maggie and me alone together for five minutes?"

Jill startled but moved out of her seat. "I'll be back in five." She headed toward the restrooms.

I narrowed my eyes at Maggie. "Why do you want to destroy me and my reputation?"

"The town finds it fascinating you've received a marriage proposal from someone you don't know well. They want to understand the details of why and how this all came to be."

I scanned the restaurant and spoke above a whisper. "Do you think the town would be interested to hear about things you've done in the past?"

She gasped and stiffened. "You wouldn't dare." Her face paled.

I paused. "No, I wouldn't. You don't want word to get out about what you shared with Michael and me in counseling, and I don't want people to make a big deal about my relationship with Ben." I reached for her hand. "Think about other people before you hit publish. How are their hurts and struggles different from yours?"

She moved her hand to her lap and spoke in a haughty tone. "It's out there. There's nothing I can do."

"Delete the post. And in the future, you can tell the truth. You jumped to conclusions without knowing all the facts." I sighed and planted my palms flat on the table. "If you need something else, tell your followers that I'm praying about how to answer Ben's marriage proposal and will have an answer for him by Sunday."

"And you'll give me the scoop before you announce it to the public?"

"As long as you agree to print the truth and not speculations."

Maggie jumped up, came over to my side of the table, and hugged my neck. "Only the truth. And thanks for keeping my past between us." She darted out the door.

Jill sat across from me. "What did you say to receive that kind of response?"

I leaned back and smiled. "If I told you, I'd have to kill you."

Nine

After our lunch, Jill and I walked back to the office and wrapped up our day without further questions from coworkers about my sanity.

On my way out of the office that afternoon, I received a text from Ben: **Sorry I made a mess of things yesterday and said too much. I'll make it up to you.**

And how did he expect to do that?

At home, while I was on the cell with my mom, my doorbell rang. "Wait a minute, someone's at the door." I opened to a delivery person who held a vase filled with red, pink, orange, and yellow gerbera daisies. I put the phone to my ear. "Mom, it's a bouquet of daisies. They're like the ones I carried in my wedding bouquet. Are they from you and dad?" My eyes filled with tears.

"No honey, call me back when you find out who sent them."

I took the vase from the driver's hands, thanked him, and closed the door. Only my parents, Jill, and Michael knew these daisies were my favorites. After I placed the vase on my kitchen table, I pulled out the card.

> "Becca, these flowers remind me of you—a rare beauty. I look forward to seeing you again this weekend. Ben."

My hand shook when I set the card on the table. I sent three texts.

To Mom: They're from Ben Peterson, a pastor Michael and I knew in Chattanooga who now lives in Orlando. We're kind of dating.

I know. I saw Maggie's blog post.

Oops.

To Jill: Ben sent me the most beautiful bouquet. Can you come over?

Emergency vet visit. Taking Babs to see Doc Winston.

Poor Babs.

To Ben: A thoughtful gift. How did you know?

A wedding photo Annie took of you. Assumed they were favorites.

I brought my hand to my chest. He knew how to woo. I smiled. I couldn't wait to learn what else he came up with.

~

On Tuesday, Jill filled me in on what happened to Babs—her dog swallowed a pebble. Doc said because of its size, the pebble should pass on its own and Babs would be fine.

That evening, Ben called and wanted to chat. He asked about my day and if I'd met with Maggie. I brought him up to date and reminded him to read her blog the following day.

Maggie's Wednesday post contained two sentences regarding Ben and me. "Becca Hill will update me on Sunday whether she will accept Ben Peterson's proposal of marriage. Watch for my special edition Sunday afternoon and be the first to know."

Ben called me at noon. "Who will hear first? Maggie or me?"

I chuckled. "You will, if I invite you to visit this weekend."

We chatted that evening, too, and Thursday. He spent his time getting to know me better by asking me questions and discussing the Bible. I found it sweet when he said he missed me. But that precious comment came moments before he asked if I wanted him to come to visit the following day. I grinned and told him, yes.

~

Friday, when I got off at noon, I drove to Mama Lou's Café to meet Risa for lunch. She lived alone and loved people. Her wisdom and understanding of the Bible amazed me, and she spent a significant amount of time mentoring younger women and praying for them.

After speaking to Grizzly outside, I stepped into the restaurant.

Risa greeted me at the door with a hug. "I'm happy to see you. I want to hear about your new beau." She hooked her elbow into mine. "We're back here in the corner away from the eavesdroppers."

I took a seat next to her at a square table, where I could see everyone who came into the café. "This is a fantastic table for chatting. Thank you for thinking of me."

She nodded. "You'll be comfortable here. After all the rigamarole Maggie caused you this week, we don't need wayward ears listening in on us."

"I trust you to keep whatever I say confidential, but I'm not at liberty to say much myself per Ben's request." I reviewed the specials board.

"Oh, my. I'm not sure I like the sounds of that."

"He's a private man and dealing with personal issues he wishes to keep quiet."

The server, who'd waited on us on prior visits, brought me a water and hot chocolate and Risa a cup of coffee. She asked about our day and took our orders.

After our waitress hurried away, Risa listed what she knew about Ben and said, "What else can you tell me about mister handsome?"

I mentioned his attributes and how he'd wooed me all week with flowers, phone calls, and texts.

"He sounds charming."

Risa's comment reminded me of what Annie told me years before. She charmed Ben through the way she teased and flirted with him. I needed to find the emails she sent me as a new bride. She taught me how to flirt with my husband.

While we ate, I told Risa how Michael and I first met Ben and his wife on a college campus and how he and Annie pursued and mentored Michael and me.

Risa reached over and touched my hand. "And now he's pursuing you again, dear."

"Yes, he is." I pondered that thought for a moment. "The first time was to lead us to Christ and God's love. This time, he's leading me to serve alongside him in ministry. My heart's desire since Michael died."

I filled her in on how Ben left Chattanooga to take a position at Hart Fellowship as their Young Adult Pastor a year after we went to seminary. I also shared that he later became their Missions Pastor and had a daughter in college.

Toward the end of our meal, Risa's phone pinged with a text. She stood and grabbed her lunch ticket. "I've got to skedaddle. I promised to sit with a sick friend while her husband goes to the grocery store." She patted my hand. "I'll be praying for you and Ben."

She shuffled to the counter to pay her tab before I thanked her.

I prayed all week on how to answer Ben on Sunday. Marrying him could be a fantastic opportunity for me to serve the Lord in full-time service. But his church was too large, and he wanted me to rush into this with little forethought. We would face challenging times if I fell in love with him and he didn't return those feelings. I'd placed him on a pedestal years before for the strong role he played in my becoming a Christian. Wouldn't take much for me to love him.

At home, after lunch with Risa, I booted up my computer. Michael scolded me for keeping emails forever, but I knew they might come in handy.

Annie sent me marriage tips from time to time during my marriage to Michael. She told me how she teased and flirted with Ben in different situations. Things that I might want to use with Michael. And I did.

I searched for Annie's name and found over fifty emails. I opened the oldest one first.

"Ben is often quiet and way too serious. To get him to relax with me, I sometimes act silly. This brings a smile to his face and leads to relaxing conversation."

In another, she wrote, "I love to tease and flirt to lighten the mood after Ben's had a stressful day at the church. I often sit across from him in the living room and gaze at him with a glint in my eyes. When he looks at me, I grin and tilt my head in a playful way until he calls me over to the couch next to him and lavishes me with his kisses." I sighed. That wouldn't happen with me for a while.

I read ten or more emails before I shut down my computer to prepare supper.

My heart filled with gratitude for the tips my friend sent me long ago and for Risa's prayers for me to make the right decision regarding marriage.

The course of my life would change forever, no matter what I decided.

Ten

Ben was due to arrive soon after 5:30 for supper. I prepared spaghetti and meatballs, salad, and garlic bread.

When he arrived at 5:45 p.m., I wanted to hug him but didn't think he'd approve. Instead, I took his jacket.

"Supper is ready." I placed his jacket on the back of my living room chair. "Italian night."

"Is that garlic I smell?" We entered the kitchen, and he picked up the flower vase that sat on my table. "Which color is your favorite?"

"The orange."

"You'd look pretty in orange."

I raised my eyebrows. "But not in the other colors?"

"You would be lovely in any color." He returned the vase to the center of my table.

"I asked you to woo me, not lie to me."

"You are a beautiful woman." He held my hand and peered into my eyes. "That's not a lie."

I thanked him and tried to calm my heart.

After supper, cleanup, and chatting over a cup of coffee, Ben built a fire, and we took our seats together on the sofa in the living room.

I pinched my bottom lip. "Are you still as sure about marrying me now as you were when you sent the letter?"

He nodded. "I'm convinced that you are to be my bride for as long as the Lord keeps us alive." He placed his arm across my shoulder. "How am I doing? Do I have the wooing down this week?"

My chest tightened. I jumped up and spun to face him. "You're doing an excellent job of pursuing and winning me over, but is it for real? Or a part of your plan to get me to agree to marry you? Now I'm more confused than I was last week."

He stood and put his hands on my shoulders. "Let me be honest with you. I'm not ready to love again because I can't give you my whole heart. But I'll get there if you'll give me time to heal. I need you, Becca. We can make this work. I'm sure we can."

I gazed into his eyes. My voice quivered. "Kiss me goodnight?"

He dropped his hands to his sides and took a step back. His tone hardened. "I told you I'm not ready to love again and now you want me to kiss you?"

I trudged to the chair, snatched his jacket, made my way to the front door, and faced him. "We have a problem. I can't decide until after we've kissed because I need to know if there's chemistry between us." I shoved the jacket toward his chest and released it.

He let it fall to the floor. "But that's not what this is about." He raked his hand through his hair. "You're not playing fair."

My body tensed. "I'm not playing at all. Are you?"

He shook his head and scowled. "I'll kiss you at the wedding."

My pulse skyrocketed, and I got in his face. "That won't work for me."

"It's got to. There's no other way. Annie and I didn't

kiss until we married." He glanced down. "She's the only woman I've ever kissed that way."

"What?" I opened my eyes wide and took a step backward. "The only woman you've kissed?" I scrunched my shoulders. "Who does that nowadays?"

He pushed his jacket to the side with his foot and took a step closer to me. "A kiss is intimate and for our special day. Are you okay with that?"

"I guess." I picked up his coat and handed it to him. "Can we leave for Chattanooga tomorrow morning at 9:00?"

Ben kissed my cheek. "Thank you. I'll be here."

~

On Saturday morning when I awoke, I found a text from Risa: **You're in my prayers. Read Psalm 37:4-5. I love you.**

I smiled, picked up my Bible, which laid on top of my dresser, and opened it. "Take delight in the Lord, and he will give you the desires of your heart. Commit your way to the Lord; trust in him and he will do this."

I read it aloud a second time. I hadn't voiced to Risa the turmoil between my mind and my heart, but she addressed it here. God would give me the desires of my heart. I could love Ben, and I'd trust that in time, he'd love me too.

Ben arrived at 8:55, stepped inside, and greeted me with another kiss on my cheek. "What do you have planned for us today?"

"A trip to Ooltewah to meet my parents."

"Parents? Today?"

I grinned. "Please tell me that you're not wearing your faded green T-shirt underneath your jacket."

He unzipped his coat and pulled it back to reveal the

teal shirt I'd picked out for him the Saturday before.

I wanted to touch it and him but realized that could be detrimental to my ego. "You look great." I turned away and grabbed my jacket and purse. I offered to drive, but Ben insisted I allow him the pleasure to drive his rental—a white Toyota Corolla.

Our trip to my parent's home took longer than our drive the week before. Ooltewah was located east of Chattanooga and one hour and twenty minutes from Pleasant Springs.

"What should I expect when I meet your parents?"

"An interrogation. But be thankful my brother, Nick, won't be there."

He sounded nervous. "What questions will they ask?"

"We'll find out together." I smirked. "They'll love you if they think you'll take good care of me. Focus on that—how you can provide for me and make me happy."

"So, they know I've asked you to marry me?"

"Mom read Maggie's blog post."

Ben groaned. "This won't be easy, will it?"

~

My parents are great, but I should have warned Ben that they weren't church people. My dad uses a lot of four-letter words.

He asked Ben in a crude way why the hurry to marry me, and when Ben stuttered, Dad laughed and patted Ben on the back. "I get it, son. Becca's mother and I look forward to having a grandbaby real soon."

I gasped. "No, Dad. I'm not expecting."

"Well, that's too bad, sugar. Hope it won't take long."

Dad then quizzed Ben to make sure he made enough

money to offer me a nice place to live. He made Ben promise to allow me to fly home whenever I wanted to visit.

After an hour and thirty minutes, we stood to leave. That was long enough to subject Ben to my parents.

My mom stood and walked us to the door. "Ben, do you love my baby girl?"

I didn't give Ben time to respond, and I spoke at a fast pace. "That's a crazy question. How many people do you know who get married when they don't love each other? I mean, on television or in a mail-order bride novel, but in real life? That stuff doesn't happen."

Ben grasped my arm and escorted me outside. I hollered back. "Bye. Love you both."

Ben opened my car door before he strode to the other side, and I climbed in. After he started the rental, he asked me where I wanted to go for lunch. I selected my favorite pizza place a few miles from my parents' home.

He pulled into the parking lot, turned off the ignition, and twisted toward me. "Thanks for rescuing me from your mom's question, but I could have said yes, because God calls us to love everyone."

"But that's not what she wanted to know, so you would have lied."

"I suppose." He cleared his throat. "By what we discussed with your parents, it sounds to me that you have agreed to my offer of marriage, or did I read too much into that visit?"

I stared out the windshield. "Do you think we will ever have an actual marriage?"

"What do you mean by actual?"

"One that's not an arrangement?"

He exhaled a deep sigh. "We discussed this last night. I'm not ready to share my heart. I want to, but I can't."

"Annie?"

"I can't betray her and loving you would do that. If I allow myself to fall in love with you, I'm afraid I'll forget her and I . . ."

I reached for his hand. "We'll get through this together. If you still want to move ahead, I'll marry you."

Eleven

Although I no longer believed that falling in love would betray Michael, I had experienced not wanting to forget him. As the years passed, memories faded too. That realization saddened me, and I understood what disturbed Ben. I needed to give him time and space and support him in his endeavor to begin a new chapter in his life with me. But could I do that without demanding my own way?

After lunch, we drove back to Pleasant Springs and took a walk along a paved trail at Turtle Creek Park located near my home. The temperature hovered in the upper thirties, and with the sunshine, my jacket kept me warm. When we neared the pond, seven ducks joined us for treats, which we didn't have. One male mallard waddled behind us on part of the path and quacked several times before he returned to the pond.

During our walk, Ben and I agreed it was time for me to visit him in Orlando, meet his daughter Riley, and accompany him to church. We decided on the following weekend.

He held my hand and led me to a bench in the park. "How does two weeks from now sound to you for our wedding?"

"Too soon. What about two months from now—the first weekend in April?"

"Let's compromise—first weekend in March."

I pulled up the calendar on my cell. "Four weeks?"

"The wedding can be small. Either here or in Orlando. You choose."

"I'll want my parents there and Jill. I'll invite Nick, too, but he may not make it. Others might want to attend, but it's unnecessary. All of them would love to travel to sunny Florida." I wrinkled my nose. "We can check out locations while I'm there. Your church will be too large."

"We have a small chapel that will be perfect. I'll check to find out if it's available the first Saturday in March."

We agreed on that plan and drove back to my place where I fixed sandwiches for supper. Or should I say, dinner. While we ate, Ben told me that in Florida that's what they call the evening meal. I'd need to remember that. I wouldn't want to embarrass him in front of his friends and coworkers.

After our sandwiches, we popped popcorn in the microwave and selected a movie to watch.

"Would you like something to drink?"

Ben opted for sweet tea, and I selected water.

During the movie, he bumped his near empty glass of tea, and it spilled on my end table. I stood and zipped to the kitchen for a towel. When I returned, I wiped the spill and decided it was a suitable time to act silly. I used the towel to pretend to wipe off Ben's arm, although the tea hadn't spilled on him.

He jumped up. "What are you doing now? I didn't get wet."

"I was only teasing."

"Well, stop." He sounded harsh. "I don't take to teasing well."

"I can see that." At least not from me. "And I don't take to your grumpiness well." I returned the towel to the kitchen and sat at my table. I didn't want to be near Ben. Annie was wrong about the silliness. Worthless emails. And Ben was wrong to think I'd be a good wife for him. I may have told him I'd marry him, but I had four weeks to change my mind. Didn't I?

Ben peered at me from the doorway and remained harsh. "What are you doing? I expected you to come right back."

I shrugged. "I needed alone time."

"I paused the movie." He took a seat next to me. His voice softened. "Are you okay?"

"Maybe you should leave now. Been a long day."

He stood. "I'll see myself out." He kissed my cheek. "I'll pick you up in the morning for church at 9:30. Okay?"

"Sure."

When he closed the front door, I returned to my living room and called Jill. I told her that I'd agreed to marry Ben, but every few minutes I regretted that decision. She tried to reassure me that everything would work out. I wasn't as optimistic. Did Ben have as many doubts as I had?

~

Ben sat at the desk in his motel room and shook his head. The night before, Becca wanted him to kiss her. He hated that she asked. He hurt her when he refused, but he wasn't ready to go there. Why didn't she understand? And her teasing? Why did she want to touch him? Reminded him of times with Annie and how much he missed her. Ben rose, walked to the window, and closed the curtains. And her parents? Not at all what he expected. He took a seat on the edge of the bed and bowed his head. Perhaps this was a bad idea. A mismatch. He groaned. But she agreed to marry him. That's what he wanted or what the Lord wanted for him. *Right, Lord?*

He spent twenty-five minutes on his knees before he turned in for the night.

~

Sunday morning, I wandered around my small home in a daze. I couldn't believe I'd agreed to marry a man who might never love me. What kind of life would that be? I sat on my sofa, opened the photos on my phone and stared at a picture of Michael.

"Why did you fall from that ladder? Did the gutters need cleaning at that moment?"

I lost my true love and planned to marry someone who wanted a companion because he was lonely, thought it would help him keep his job, and needed someone to take care of him. The poor guy couldn't even buy his own clothing without help.

The doorbell rang at 9:25. I jumped at the sound, picked up my coat and purse, and opened the door. My chest felt like a ten-pound weight rested on it. We greeted one another, and I stepped outside. Neither of us spoke on the short drive to the church.

After Ben pulled into the lot and parked, he said in a hesitant tone, "Are we going to announce our news this morning?"

"I told Maggie she'd get the scoop today."

He opened his door and came around to open mine. When I climbed out, he took my hand and caught my eye. "You look lovely this morning." He kissed my cheek. "Neither the comment nor the kiss was intended for anyone to see or hear except you. We're on rocky ground, but after a prayerful night, I still have faith this will work and that it's God's will for us."

I gazed back at him. "Thank you for sharing that. I didn't sleep well either." I took a deep breath. "I'm sure everything will be fine."

When inside the church, we slipped into a pew near the back. Ben placed his arm around my shoulder and pulled me toward him. But that was for show. He didn't want me to touch him, and I was sure he didn't want to touch me either. I remained stiff and kept three inches between us.

Twelve

Pastor Oldham strutted past us on his way to the platform, turned back, and greeted Ben like he was a long-lost cousin he hadn't seen in years. "Will you be in town again next weekend? I'd love to have you preach for us."

Ben stood and spoke in his melodious, pastor voice. "I'd love to preach for you sometime, but next week won't work. Becca will be in Florida with me. I plan to introduce her to my church family and the city of Orlando."

"Things must be serious then." Pastor Oldham laughed and patted Ben on the back.

Ben opened his mouth to speak, but I rose, grasped his elbow, and leaned toward his ear. "Maggie needs to hear first."

He told Pastor Oldham that he'd meet with him after service and arrange something for a later date.

We took our seats, and Ben lowered his voice. "Where is Maggie?"

I searched the sanctuary and caught her eye. She rushed toward us with one minute remaining before one of our deacons would step to the front for announcements.

"Sorry. Natalie Simmons had her first date last night since her divorce. I had to get the scoop." Maggie sat next to me and grabbed my arm. "Hurry. What's your decision?" She peered at Ben. "And where are you staying this weekend? Not at my bed-and-breakfast." She glared at me.

"I'm at the motel on Main Street. I like to mix things up a bit."

She pouted and jerked her head toward the front of the church. "Oh, no. Deacon Jones."

I faced Ben. "Do you want to tell her?"

He grinned. "She said, yes."

Maggie hugged me and hurried away. Straight to Pastor Oldham. From the back of the church, we heard her tell him our news. Maggie didn't need a microphone.

~

After service, Ben spent time with my pastor while people extended me their best wishes. I smiled at their sweet comments, but an ache wrapped around my heart. What had I agreed to?

When Ben joined me, we slipped outside and headed to the nearby town of Poplar Ridge to visit a barbeque place called Pete's. I gave him directions for the twenty-minute trek. "Go north on Main, turn left at the first stop sign onto Chicken Coop Road. Go three miles and turn right at Miller's Hog Farm onto Rattlesnake Road. We'll pass through Shady View, and six miles later, we'll turn into Pete's parking lot."

He chuckled. "You mean we don't have to turn onto Lizard Hollow Road?"

His joke wasn't funny. Clancy County didn't have a Lizard Hollow Road. I kept a straight face. "That's south of town. We're traveling north."

He widened his eyes. "There's really a Lizard Hollow?"

I ignored him.

The road between Shady View and Poplar Ridge was hilly and curvy with a posted speed limit of forty-five miles per hour. Ben stayed behind a car going forty miles per hour for five minutes.

Five minutes too long for me. "Just pass the guy."

"There's a double yellow line."

We drove around a curve. "Straight shot. Go."

"What's the hurry? Does Pete's close at noon?"

"Just do it. I'm hungry. No one patrols this road, and everyone passes here."

"I don't. So chill."

"That's just plain stupid." I crossed my arms.

We arrived at the restaurant and had a fifteen-minute wait.

Ben held my hand while we stood along the wall near the doorway. "Smells wonderful in here. This was a great idea. I love good barbeque."

I nodded.

He squeezed my hand and nudged my arm with his elbow. "Maggie sure got excited to hear our news."

I nodded again.

"Why am I getting the silent treatment? Because I wouldn't pass that car, or am I still being punished for last night?"

"I'm afraid whatever I say or do will be wrong. Better to keep quiet and not cause you problems."

"Whoa." He shook his head. "After we finish lunch, let's go to your place and talk in private. Okay?"

The host called our name, and we followed him to a two-person table near the windows. We took our seats and scanned the menus. I ordered the pulled pork with coleslaw, and Ben ordered the beef brisket with baked beans.

Ben tried to make small talk, but I didn't respond with much.

"This won't work if you can't talk to me." He opened his hand and reached across the table. "Please?"

I looked at my hands in my lap. "You don't need to trouble yourself with wooing me any longer. I've agreed to marry you. Let's try to be civil with one another."

He pulled back his hand, gaped at me, and slumped back in his chair. "Can you at least act like you enjoy being with me?"

"I'm not feeling it today."

The server brought our food to the table and scurried away. Ben and I ate in silence.

On our way back to Pleasant Springs and my bungalow, Ben clenched his jaw and mumbled something.

"What?"

"I said, after I drop you off, I'll go straight to the airport. I'd rather sit with strangers, than with someone I know who refuses to speak to me."

In a flippant tone, I said, "Fine with me."

Ben swerved into an apple orchard's driveway and parked. "I've had enough. What do you want?"

I couldn't tell him what I wanted because I needed him to fall in love with me. I shifted in my seat. "You can't kiss me, and I realize you don't want me to touch you, but I'm feeling unwanted right now." My stomach churned. "When you drop me off, will you at least hug me goodbye like I'm important to you?"

"You've been pushing me away all day because you

want a hug?" He raised his shoulders and lifted his palms. "I don't get it." Ben leaned closer. "You *are* important to me." He brushed his finger along my cheek. "Hold on." He jumped out of the car, dashed to my side, and offered his hand. When I stepped outside, he wrapped me in his arms. "I'm sorry I haven't made you feel valued. I'll work on that. Okay?"

I was where I needed to be. But I shouldn't have had to ask to be there.

~

Ben didn't drop me off like he'd said earlier. With another hour before he had to leave, we sat on my sofa and made plans for my trip to Orlando the following weekend.

"What did you mean when you told Pastor Oldham that you wanted me to meet your church family? I'll only meet a few of them, right?"

"Pastor Young will want me to introduce you to the congregation at all three services. It's a big deal, and everyone will want to see my bride."

"You'll introduce me to 15,000 people?" I wrung my hands together.

"You'll do fine. I'll be next to you, holding your hand. There's nothing to worry about."

"There's 15,000 things to worry about."

He chuckled. "Smile and nod to whatever I tell them." He nudged my elbow. "You can do that, can't you?"

I doubted I'd remember to breathe with of all those eyes staring at me.

Thirteen

Jill and I met in my living room Monday evening to work on our yarn projects for the children's home. We'd gotten behind with Ben coming into town on the weekends, and with the forecast of several inches of snow, more children needed hats, scarves, and mittens.

"We should do this every evening this week to catch up with the demand." Jill looked up from the chair where she worked on her knitting. "Are you available?"

I continued with a row of single crochet stitches from my seat on the sofa. "Except for Friday. I'm leaving for Orlando and won't be home until Sunday evening."

We agreed to meet, eat, and work on our yarn projects the next three nights.

"How's Babs?"

"She's fine. Everything came out okay."

I snickered. "And how's Doc Winston?"

She glared at me. "What's that supposed to mean?"

"A simple question." I smirked and batted my eyes. "Why are you sensitive about the *fine* doctor?"

"I made one little comment months ago and you won't let me forget it."

"One tiny comment about how good looking he is and how he's single, brilliant, charming, and funny." I lowered the scarf to my lap.

Jill stared at her knitting and bit her lip.

"Has he asked you out?"

She widened her eyes and dropped her mitten. "Of course not."

"Why not ask him?"

"Would you?"

"I've never met him." I shook my head. "You thought I should ask Ben out, so why not take your own advice?"

"Doc doesn't pay any attention to me. But he likes Babs a lot." She tilted her head. "You've said little about your weekend with Ben? Why?"

I sighed. "He told me what he needs in a wife, but he doesn't seem to pay attention to what I need. I shouldn't have to keep telling him. He's been married before and should understand how this works."

"But you said he came through with winning you over."

"He did. But because it wasn't heartfelt, it meant nothing. Only made me feel good at the time."

"How do you know it wasn't heartfelt? Although he's not ready to express his feelings for you because of Annie, it doesn't mean there are none." She rose from the chair and sat next to me on the couch. "Give him time to comprehend all that's going on inside of him. And remember, you've been dealing with your grief for five years, not two like him."

"You're right." I rubbed the middle of my forehead and closed my eyes.

"And don't allow yourself to fall in love with him. Keep your relationship friendly but not serious. If you do that, you won't hurt as much."

I puckered my lips and glanced at her with puppy dog eyes. "You're too late with that advice."

"What? You can't fall in love that fast."

"Tell my heart." I released a lengthy breath. "I'm in for a bumpy ride."

~

Ben received mixed messages on Tuesday when he announced to the church staff that he was engaged. Pastor Young congratulated him, as did others, but two of the female ministry assistants showed disappointment. They had both been trying to fix him up with a family member.

Keith joined Ben in his office after the meeting. "This seems sudden. Where did you meet her?"

Ben explained their relationship with discretion and assured Keith that he knew what he was doing. He also asked Keith to be his best man.

When Keith slipped out, Ben checked on the availability of the chapel for the first Saturday in March and found it reserved for another wedding. He booked the next day instead and sent Becca a text.

After he arrived home that evening, he called his daughter Riley. "I have someone I'd like you to meet this weekend. Can you come home for a visit?" He walked from the living room to the kitchen.

"Who is she?"

"A woman I've known for many years. In fact, you spent time with her and her husband when you were a little girl."

"She's married?"

Ben shook his head at his phone and told Riley that Becca's husband was a pastor and a friend who died five years earlier.

"Hold on a minute." Riley turned down her music. "Why didn't you tell me you were dating?"

"We've only been dating for two weeks. I wanted to make sure the relationship looked promising before I mentioned it to you."

She sounded unsure. "How serious is it?"

"Can you come home? We'll discuss this in person." He opened the refrigerator and stuck up his nose at what he saw.

"I have to work this weekend, and if I try to change my schedule this late, they might fire me."

"Then we'll come to you." He pulled out a package of moldy cheese from the fridge and closed the door. "I want you to meet her as soon as possible."

"Why? What's the hurry? Not like you're getting married this weekend." She laughed and snorted at the same time.

Ben bit his cheek. "Um." He tossed the cheese into the trash.

She became somber. "Dad? What have you done?"

"What's that supposed to mean?"

"Did the two of you elope after two weeks?"

"You know me better than that." He wiped perspiration from his brow.

"I'll skip my afternoon classes and be home for dinner Thursday."

"But she won't be here until Friday."

"That's okay. I don't want to meet *her,* anyway."

~

By Wednesday, I'd submitted a resignation letter to my boss. I hated to give up my job. My coworkers had become family. I also dropped off a wedding announcement to the local newspaper and arranged with my parents and Jill to attend my wedding. My brother, Dr. Nicolas Stewart, couldn't attend that weekend, which didn't surprise me but did annoy me. When he said he had a medical conference in New York, I cut him some slack.

Jill and I planned to shop for our dresses after my trip to visit Ben. We both looked forward to a shopping spree. My dad would give me away and Jill would be my maid of honor.

Maggie pleaded with me to send her an invitation, but I told her we planned to keep attendance small, and Jill could fill her in when she returned home.

I kept myself busy as much as possible at work, and at home I spent time on my children's home projects. I also read a handbook required in Florida before we could apply for a marriage license and completed a form we needed to take with us. At times, I wrestled with the crazy idea of marrying Ben. Then there were times a sweet peace came over me, and I believed I was in God's will. I preferred those times.

Ben sent me a text Thursday morning. **Not telling Riley marriage an arrangement.**

Why did he change his mind? She'd figure it out when she came for a visit.

I took Friday off and left for the airport at 6:45 a.m. After I got there, I did my best to relax and wait on my 9:45 flight.

My stomach growled. I shouldn't have skipped breakfast. I needed something to eat to hold me over, but my gut couldn't handle it.

Lord, are you sure I'm doing the right thing?

82

Fourteen

My heart skipped a beat as the plane prepared to land in Orlando. From my window, I saw palm trees and lakes everywhere. My first time in Paradise. We landed at 1:20 p.m.—ten minutes late. In the baggage area, my heart fluttered when Ben approached me. I didn't want to be attracted to him. I needed to remind myself that I was to be his companion and nothing more.

"How was your flight?" He kissed my cheek. Something that made this situation extra difficult.

"Uneventful." I gazed into his eyes and glanced away. I wanted to find a sparkle there. But none existed.

"How many bags do you have?"

"One. Black with an orange ribbon attached to the handle."

"That doesn't surprise me." Ben smiled. "Are you hungry? We can grab a bite on our way to get our marriage license."

"That would be great. I didn't have time during my layover in Atlanta to eat."

He grabbed my suitcase from the carousel, and we made our way to the parking garage. "How do you like our warmer temperature?"

"Nice." I fiddled with my purse strap. "How did

things go with Riley when she came home yesterday?"

"You'll find out when you see her later at the house." He nodded and grimaced. "She skipped classes to meet you and plans to head back first thing in the morning to get to work on time. We'll want a small lunch because she's fixing dinner for us."

We approached a dark blue Toyota Camry where Ben popped open the trunk and threw my luggage inside.

"How did she take the news?"

"Not well. She may ask you a hundred questions to determine if you're worthy of her dad."

"Did you end up telling her this is a bogus relationship?"

Ben slammed the trunk lid. "Keep your voice down." He grasped my elbow and escorted me to the passenger door, opened it, and slammed the door shut after I got inside. When he climbed behind the wheel, he pursed his lips and glared at me. "Bogus?" He shook his head. "Ours will be a real marriage." He started the car and backed out of the parking space.

I crossed my arms, stared ahead, and huffed. "Two weekends ago you said ours wouldn't be a real marriage. Have you changed your mind?"

"We'll apply for our license today and have an actual ceremony. That makes it a real marriage."

"Not to me. I expect you to at least treat me with respect, or I'll change my mind *before* the wedding."

He hit the brakes. "I do respect you."

"Slamming trunks and car doors say otherwise."

"What do you mean slamming doors?"

"Unbelievable." I lifted my palms. "Do you slam things on a regular basis?"

"I'm a calm and caring person." He tapped his

fingers on the steering wheel. "Most of the time."

I crossed my arms again. "I hope so."

He pulled out of the parking garage. "Looks like we both have a lot of praying to do before we enter the church Sunday morning."

~

Bogus? Lord, why did you give me this tiresome woman?

Ben found an empty fast-food drive-thru lane just north of the airport, pulled in, and ordered their lunch. They ate their sandwiches while he drove to the Orange County Courthouse. He gave Becca directions as they went, so she'd know how to get around the city, but she didn't respond.

Everything went well while applying for their marriage license considering they hadn't said much to one another since he'd picked her up from the airport. At least she hadn't brought up bogus relationships or fake marriages again.

With their license in hand, he drove south toward the airport and his house to a jewelry store in a strip mall to buy Becca a ring. "Do you think we can present ourselves to Riley as a couple who finds pleasure in one another's company?"

Becca still sounded upset. "I can if you can." She turned toward him. "Do you enjoy being with me?"

He cut her a look. "I wouldn't ask someone I disliked being with to be my wife."

"But do you like this Becca or the one you knew twelve years ago?"

"You're the same person you were then, and I enjoy spending time with you."

He pulled into the parking lot. "Let's look here for a

ring. If you don't find something today, we'll try another store tomorrow."

Becca found a ring she liked, but said it reminded her of the one Michael gave her. "I'd like to try another store before I decide."

"No problem." They left the store and drove toward Ben's house.

"We're near the airport again, right?"

He nodded. "From here it's about twelve minutes to my home in East Park and fifteen minutes to the church."

"That's convenient." I glanced out the windshield. "What have you told Riley about us?"

He sighed. "That God wants to pen a new chapter in my life that includes someone special to write it with me. I shared how we knew each other in the past, your experience as a pastor's wife, and how God led me in this."

"How long does she think we've been seeing each other?"

"I told her the truth—two weeks."

Becca opened her eyes wide. "How did she take that news?"

"Not well."

"And how would you take the news if she got engaged after dating a guy for two weeks?"

"Our situation is unique." He made a left at a traffic light. "We've known each other for many years."

"But not in recent years."

"She believes it will be an actual marriage and nothing unusual." Ben pulled into his subdivision.

"Don't you feel the least bit deceitful in this charade we're playing?"

He pulled into his driveway, pushed the remote to

open the garage door, and parked the car inside. He looked at Becca and spoke with frustration. "Why do you keep using words like 'bogus, deceit, and charade'?"

Her eyes glistened when she peered at him. "I'm feeling guilty. I'm not sure I can pull this off."

~

I reached for the door handle and paused. Ben was a pastor, and yet this arrangement didn't disturb him at all. Was I making a bigger deal out of the situation than I should?

At 5:45 p.m., we entered his Mediterranean style home through the laundry room and stepped into the kitchen, where Riley stirred a pot on the stove. What a beautiful young woman she'd become. She reminded me of her mother.

"Wow, that smells amazing." Ben hurried to his daughter's side and wrapped his arm around her shoulder. "Chicken tortilla soup?"

She grinned at Ben and eyed me. When he made the introductions, her features tightened, but she seemed polite. If she were a lot like Annie, I wouldn't expect anything less.

"I agree with your dad. Your soup smells fantastic." I scanned the room. "What can I do to help?"

The kitchen contained stainless steel appliances, with a glass-topped stove and a built-in microwave. A round table, which seated four, sat at the back of the room in front of two floor to ceiling windows and to the left of a patio door. Plenty of dark wood cabinets lined the walls, and a spacious granite countertop with flecks of black, white, teal, and rust provided plenty of food preparation space.

"Nothing. We'll be ready to eat in five minutes."

Ben grabbed my hand and led me through the dining room, past the sunken living room which laid across from the entryway, and to the guest bathroom on the left. He also pointed out that the room next to the bathroom was his office, which faced the front yard. "I'll give you a tour of the upstairs after dinner." He slipped back the way we came.

After I freshened up, I found Ben and Riley in the dining room, where Ben pulled out a chair for me before he sat to my right.

Riley took a seat across from us and sounded like the perfect hostess. "Tell me if I'm missing something you'd like to add to your soup."

Ben said the blessing, and we passed around tortillas, shredded cheese, sour cream, avocados, cilantro, and tortilla chips.

I took my first bite. "This is delicious. I'd love to have your recipe." I meant every word.

"One of Mom's specialties." Riley glanced at Ben, and he smiled. "If you don't mind, I'd like to fix this for Dad."

"Oh. Sure. No problem." I focused on my soup.

Ben reached over and grasped my hand where it rested on the table and squeezed. "Riley enjoys treating me with meals that held special meaning for us as a family. Tortilla soup was the first recipe she tried on her own when she was ten."

"Okay." I pulled my hand away from Ben's and took another bite of my soup. Had she fixed that recipe to exclude me from their private family moment?

Fifteen

After dinner, Riley loaded the dishwasher while Ben and I sat at the kitchen table and made plans for the following day. While we talked about shopping for a ring, touring the church, and visiting the chapel, I noticed Riley's eyes on us. When she finished with the dishes, we moved into the living room, a large room with a sofa, loveseat, coffee table, two chairs, and a television mounted on the wall.

Riley took a seat on the sofa to the left of the loveseat where Ben and I sat. "Dad said I met you when I was a little girl. Do you recall anything we did together that might help me remember you?" She crossed her legs at her ankles and folded her hands in her lap.

"My then fiancé, Michael, and I took you to the aquarium when you were six. Your mom and dad traveled to Knoxville for a wedding, and we babysat for the day." I twisted to my left to face Riley and mirrored her leg and hand placement.

"I don't remember. What else did we do?"

"A few weeks after Michael and I married, we went with you and your parents to Lake Winnepesaukah in Rossville, Georgia. We told you there that we planned to move away. You cried and begged me to stay."

Riley narrowed her eyes. "Are you the one who rode the swings that whirled round and round with me because they made Mom dizzy?"

I chuckled. "Round and round, again and again. We got in line at least five times."

Riley smiled, but it didn't appear sincere. She got up and left the room.

"Did I say something offensive?"

"I don't think so. She loved that day at Lake Winnie when you and Michael joined us." Ben stood. "Would you like to see the rest of the house?"

I followed him to his office. A modest wooden desk sat in the middle of the room with a laptop, pictures of Annie and Riley, and upon a closer look, a Bible opened to the Book of John. The room also included an office chair, a wooden filing cabinet, a bookshelf that overflowed with books, and a printer.

From the dining room, we climbed the stairs to the upper floor. I heard Riley across the hall and to the left in a room at the back of the house talking to herself. "That picture must be here somewhere." Her tone hardened. "But I'm sure she's not the lady I remember. We must have gone to Lake Winnie with someone else."

Ben turned to me. "Let me talk with her for a minute." He poked his head inside the room. "Are you okay?" He stepped inside and they spoke with muffled voices.

I waited in the hallway and busied myself by scanning photos on the wall of Ben and Annie's wedding, Annie pregnant with Riley, and family portraits taken over the years. I smiled at the photo taken during the time Michael and I attended the church where Ben and Annie served in Chattanooga. They'd given us a smaller copy.

I didn't hear Ben approach and jumped when he spoke my name. He took my hand and led me to the guest room at the front of the house—the room that was to become his. He whispered, "She'll come around. She's still surprised with the news."

"Why not fill her in? That was the original plan."

He kept his voice low. "I changed the plan. We'll talk about it later." When we reached the master suite, he cleared his throat. "And here is our room. Go on in and look around." He nudged me inside but didn't join me.

Roomy with a balcony at the back, a master bath and shower which faced the front of the house, and a king-sized bed. All I could fit into my bungalow was a full-size bed. Weird having such a large room and no one to share it with.

When I came out, Riley descended the stairs. Ben pulled me aside and lowered his voice. "The fewer people who know of our arrangement, the better. I want it to appear natural."

I peeked around Ben to see the stairway again. "And that didn't bother you at all when you said, 'our room'?"

He placed his hands on my upper arms and gazed into my eyes. "It will be our room one day. I wish you could accept this. I need you, Becca. Like I've said before, I'm not ready for a traditional marriage."

"Can you give me an idea of when you might be ready?"

He shook his head and spoke in a stern tone. "I can't."

I trailed behind him down the stairs. "Time for me to check into my hotel."

~

Ben ambled down the hallway to the kitchen, with Becca close behind.

Riley brewed a pot of coffee and stood next to the counter with her arms crossed. "If either of you would like dessert, I fixed a chocolate cake earlier today." She pointed to a cake on the kitchen table.

Ben glanced at Becca. "Would you like a slice before we go?"

She nodded and peered at Riley. "Looks wonderful."

Riley gathered plates and forks and put them on the kitchen table. Ben sat on Becca's right, and Riley took her place across from Becca on Ben's right.

Why was Becca difficult? What would happen after he introduced her to the church staff and congregation as his fiancée if she then called off the arrangement? That could further jeopardize his standing at the church and cause him humiliation. Should he consider a back-up plan?

Riley touched his hand. "Dad? Are you okay? You've only taken one bite of cake."

His eyes darted from Riley to Becca, who had both finished their dessert. He pushed his cake aside. "Let me run Becca to her hotel. I'll finish this when I return home." He rose and reached for Becca's hand.

She thanked Riley for dinner and followed Ben out to the garage. "Wait. Riley may not think much of me, but I'd like to ask her to be a bridesmaid for our wedding. Is that okay with you?"

He grinned. "Perfect."

They stepped back inside, where they found Riley with her back to them, putting dessert plates in the dishwasher and mumbling to herself. "How can he do this to me? I'll never call her mom. That's crazy. I won't do that even if Dad refuses to pay my college tuition."

Becca lifted her chin and pushed her shoulders back. "I don't expect to be your mom. But I would like to be your friend again."

Riley spun toward them and stared with widened eyes.

LUANN K. EDWARDS

Sixteen

Despite my hotel being just north of the airport, I got a good night's sleep. I stared out the hotel window at 9:30 a.m. waiting for Ben to arrive. I suggested the night before that he not pick me up for breakfast but spend time with Riley before she drove back to Jacksonville. Asking her to be a bridesmaid didn't go well. She wasted no time cutting me down and pouring out the tears—no doubt to get her dad to change his mind about me. She wasn't all that much like Annie, after all.

A knock on the door startled me from my musings. I grabbed my purse and hurried to answer it.

Ben appeared haggard, with dark circles under his eyes. "Ready for a full day starting with an engagement ring?"

"I am." I stepped into the hallway. "Did Riley get off okay this morning?"

"Not soon enough." We made our way outside. "I love that girl, but she wore me out last night and this morning. I didn't expect that kind of response from her." He opened my car door, lumbered to the driver's side, and climbed in. "She was pleased that you'd asked her to be in the wedding. She felt bad that she told you no without giving it any consideration."

I focused on my clasped hands in my lap. "She's hurting." She wasn't the only one.

"How are you doing? Are we still on for a wedding on March 4?"

"That's soon. Maybe that's what bothered her." Bothered me too.

His face held a blank expression. "Not a chance. I didn't give her the date." He started the car.

I clutched my chest. "What will she do when you tell her?"

"I'll send her a text after she gets back to her dorm."

"That's a terrible idea."

His eyes twinkled. A welcomed sight. He backed out of the parking spot and pulled onto the road. "I told her this morning. If you thought she was upset last night when we found her in the kitchen spouting off, you should have heard her with that bit of news." He shook his head, stopped at a traffic light, and sighed. "Will Jill be your maid of honor?"

I nodded. "I'll be happy to call Riley and ask her again if you think she plans to attend the wedding."

He shrugged. "I don't know. But I hope she does." The light changed to green, and we turned right. "That would be nice of you. Perhaps she'll rethink this." Ben took an entrance ramp to the right.

I glanced around me. "Were we on this road yesterday?"

"Yes. This is 528. You might drive this one often. We're going west to the Mall at Millenia. They have three jewelry stores, although I hope we won't need to visit all three. Should be there in twenty-five minutes."

Fifteen minutes later, Ben took the ramp for I-4 East, drove to Exit 78, and we pulled into the mall parking lot soon after.

Ben parked and faced me. "With this purchase and tomorrow's introduction at church, I need you to be sure you're ready to marry me."

I swallowed hard and bit the inside of my cheek. "I suppose."

"That's not sure enough." He brushed his finger across my chin. "What's holding you back?"

I averted my eyes from his. "The realization that you may never love me."

He spoke in a concerned tone. "I will honor and respect you from the beginning. Love will come. I'm sure of it."

I gazed at him. "How can you be certain?"

His eyes softened. "Love is trying to surface now. But I need more time."

Was he truthful? Or did he tell me what he assumed I needed to hear to go along with his scheme? "Then, I'm sure."

~

After searching for the perfect ring at our first stop and only taking two hours to decide, I selected a stunning solitaire diamond that would take a week to be sized. Ben planned to pick up the ring when ready and present it to me in Pleasant Springs.

After shopping, he took me to lunch at an Italian restaurant in the mall and then to the church to give me a tour. At the church, we parked in his normal parking space at the back of the building and entered a long hallway. The worship center sat to the right, but we made a left down another hallway which led to his office—the third door on the left. The desk inside held a gorgeous picture of Riley in what I presumed to be her prom dress and a crossed-eyed one of me with a butterfly on my nose.

I chuckled. "I can find you a better picture."

"This one is my favorite. I doubt you can find one cuter."

Pictures of adults and children from other countries lined the walls.

"Your mission trips?"

Ben nodded.

"Where are we going on this year's trips?"

"We'll have our first planning meeting within a month of our wedding with adult trips to Africa, Southeast Asia, and South America planned over the next year. We'll also offer two youth trips to Mexico this summer."

"Sounds exciting. I'm looking forward to those trips."

Ben introduced me to two staff members who were in their offices preparing for the following day's services. I also met his best friend, Pastor Keith, whose office was catty-corner from Ben's.

Keith seemed nice enough until Ben left me alone with him for a minute. Keith asked questions about my marriage and experience as a pastor's wife and asked if I knew what I was doing by marrying Ben. He smirked and told me that serving in a megachurch was much more demanding than in a small-town church. Something about him troubled me. I remained guarded and didn't say too much. When Ben returned, Keith changed back to his earlier, agreeable behavior.

Ben led me to the worship center through a side door the staff used, which was near the stage. He took my hand, and we made our way to the podium. "This is where we'll stand in the morning and address the crowd at all three services."

Five thousand people staring at me three different times the following day? I shuddered.

Ben wrapped his arm around my waist. "You're not going to faint, are you? You're pale and don't look well."

"I can't talk in front of that many people. You won't make me say anything, will you?"

"Just smile and act thrilled to be here with me."

He asked me for a miracle. "If I forget, nudge me."

From there, we returned to the office hallway, strolled to the end, and turned right into the next hallway. We passed the educational wing with classrooms on the right and the children's center on the left. The hallway continued to the chapel, also on the left, where we would hold our wedding ceremony. A perfect place for a small gathering of up to one hundred people. Pews lined both sides of the hardwood floor. Arched wooden beams hung overhead and windows behind the pulpit presented a lovely view of the church grounds, including six palm trees.

Ben told me that during church services people come to the chapel for prayer and on Sundays, after we married, we would pray for requests there during the third service. I anticipated that with pleasure. Praying for others was in my comfort zone. Speaking to a crowd? Not so much.

At 2:00 p.m., after Ben introduced me to the church's wedding coordinator, Charlotte Weston, we made our way out to the parking lot.

I checked my phone's weather app. The temperature had risen to seventy-eight degrees with plenty of sunshine. Twenty-five degrees warmer than back home.

"Can we spend time outdoors?"

"Sure. I'll take you to a park I think you'll like."

We drove south for a few minutes, paid a small fee, and drove into Moss Park, which was situated between two lakes—Lake Mary Jane and Lake Hart. Spanish moss hung from the numerous trees that lined the paved roadway. Ben parked the car, and we trudged through the sand along Lake Mary Jane. We observed white ibises and sandhill cranes. On the other side of us were unusual looking squirrels high above us in the trees. Ben told me that they were fox squirrels.

We took ten or more steps and stopped to read a sign. "Alligators here? Wild and dangerous?"

Ben covered his mouth. His eyes sparkled. "You're in Florida. There's over a million of them here." He held my hand. "Keep your eyes open. Not only for gators but water moccasins and rattlesnakes too. If you see them, leave them alone."

"But what if I come across a gator by accident?"

"They don't like people. You'll be safe."

"I'm ready to leave now." There was no way I wanted to encounter an alligator.

He led me to the paved roadway. "This is a place you can come to when you seek peace and beauty. I've been here many times and have only seen one gator. You'll be fine."

While we walked and chatted, I monitored the surrounding area. No gator was about to surprise me. When we returned to Ben's car, I gripped his arm. "With all those gators, how do you keep them out of your yard?"

Seventeen

Before Ben dropped me off at my hotel for the night, he tried to convince me that his yard was safe from gators. A wooden fence surrounded his backyard, and he'd never seen one in his or the neighbors' yards. Despite his reassurance, I'd spend a lot of time indoors or on the balcony.

On Sunday morning, I dressed in an emerald green, knee length A-line skirt and an ivory short-sleeved pullover sweater. Ben arrived at 8:00 a.m. and drove us to the church. He recapped what I should expect on my first Sunday at Hart Fellowship. The first service would begin at 9:00 and be the one we attended after our wedding. During the second service, he'd teach a class after my introduction to the congregation, and he'd take me to the airport after he introduced me in the third service. He opened my car door when we arrived at the church, took my hand, and led me inside to his office. On our way, I met other pastors who welcomed me with kindness.

We entered the worship center five minutes before 9:00 through the side door near the front and sat in the first row along the right side. I grasped Ben's hand in a death grip. I did not want to go on stage.

He released my hand, which caused me a moment of intense anxiety, and draped his arm across my shoulder. "I'm here for you." He pulled me closer. "Try to relax. They'll call us up after the song service."

I released a lengthy breath and enjoyed his embrace.

One pastor, whom I'd met earlier, entered the stage, welcomed the congregation, and prayed. We stood to sing, and I relaxed enough to join in. But they sang songs we had never sung in our church in Pleasant Springs. Two of the three were on my phone's favorites list, but I doubted our pianist would play or approve of them. She loved the old hymns.

After we sang, another man strode across the stage. Ben poked my arm. "He's Pastor Young. He'll present you to the congregation."

"We are excited for you to meet a special guest today." He motioned to Ben. "Pastor Peterson, come up and bring your friend."

When Ben and I rose from our chairs, I clung to his arm.

He whispered, "Breathe. Allow your love for the Lord to shine." He paused at the top of the stairs leading to the stage and gazed into my eyes. "Have I told you that you look amazing?"

I calmed with that soothing talk of his, and he led me to the podium.

Pastor Young handed a microphone to Ben. "Introduce us to this special lady." He shook my hand and stepped back.

Ben grinned and peered at the crowd. "As many of you know, these past two years have been difficult for me. Certain there would never be another woman to capture my heart, I didn't bother to consider otherwise.

But the Lord impressed upon me to contact this beautiful woman next to me and rekindle an appreciation we held for one another many years ago." He pulled his arm away from my hold, took my hand, and squeezed. "God knows best. I'm thankful I listened to Him." He faced me and cocked his head. "Rebecca Hill has agreed to be my wife, and I foresee a lifetime of serving the Lord together."

My heart soared. I experienced a moment of hopefulness. Something in his eye—a flicker of admiration or more.

The crowd stood, applauded, and cheered. I smiled and waved.

Ben handed the microphone back to Pastor Young, and we returned to our seats. Pastor shared with the congregation about Michael and my experience as a pastor's wife. He complimented Ben on his choice and congratulated us on our upcoming wedding, although he didn't share how soon that wedding would occur.

One service down—two to go.

~

The second service happened like the first. Easy. I could do this one more time with no problem. We left through the side door after my introduction and hurried down the hallway to the educational wing and to the classroom for Ben's study group. We received a standing ovation when we entered. We bolted to the front of the classroom, where I found a chair on the left and sat.

One class member called out after things quieted. "We'd like to get acquainted with your fiancée. May we ask her questions?"

Ben looked at me and raised his eyebrows. I could do this too. Not like this was a crowd of 100 or more. I nodded, and he motioned me to join him where he faced the class. "Tell them about yourself."

I grinned at the group of more than thirty men and women and relaxed at seeing their smiling faces. A mixed group of younger and older adults. "If you were in the first service, you heard my name is Rebecca Hill. As a pastor's wife for four years, I enjoyed working with my husband as we served the Lord in ministry. I'm excited to get to meet each of you and to serve alongside Ben."

"When's the wedding? Are we all invited?"

I eyed Ben, who stood to my left.

He took a step closer to the group. "We'll be keeping the wedding small. Becca's parents, Riley, and a few friends." He reached for my hand. "We'll marry three weeks from today."

A couple of ladies gasped, and I heard one say, "Oh, my."

"How did you meet?"

Ben motioned for me to answer.

"Ben and Annie reached out to my then boyfriend and me and shared with us about the Lord while we were in college. We attended the church where they served as associate pastors, and they mentored us. Annie and I became good friends, and Ben and Michael did too."

One woman brought her hand to her chest. "How sweet."

I nudged Ben in a playful way. "He can be."

The group laughed, and I returned to my chair.

Someone asked about Ben's parents, and he explained they were traveling out of the country and would not be able to attend the wedding.

After we answered the rest of their questions, Ben taught a lesson from 1 Corinthians 13. A lesson about love. He glanced at me several times as he spoke. Was it all a part of his plan to convince everyone that ours would be an actual marriage? Was the flicker in his eye during the first service also fake? I stared at my Bible and reread the passages. *Lord, help me to love him in this way. And may he learn to love me too.*

Eighteen

Ben dismissed class, and we made our way back to the worship center for the last service. We planted ourselves in the front row. Two introductions down and one to go. No big deal, until Pastor Young entered the stage.

My heart rate soared. Wasn't it supposed to be that other pastor?

Pastor Young glanced toward us and motioned for us to come on stage before he said anything. Ben took my hand and led me up the stairs.

The pastor skipped the opening prayer and told everyone that Ben had an important announcement to make. He pushed the microphone toward me. "Why don't you tell the congregation your name and why you are here with Ben today?"

My body trembled. I grasped for Ben's arm and clutched onto his elbow.

Ben took the microphone from Pastor Young's hand. "Rebecca did an excellent job answering questions in our class this morning, but I want to be the one to share this exciting news with you today." With a smile on his face, he shared the details. We exited the stage and dashed out into the hallway.

"I didn't know Pastor Young planned to bring us up first thing or ask you to talk." Ben embraced and released me. "Perhaps he wanted to help us get to the airport on time."

My heart pumped hard. I walked down the hallway to my right.

Ben grabbed my arm. "Wrong way." He pointed to a set of doors in the opposite direction. "We're parked outside of those."

I stared ahead and followed his lead. Outdoors, I stuttered. "I. Forgot. To smile." I held onto his arm. "Are you upset with me? I acted like a ninny."

He turned and faced me. "You looked radiant. No one thought you were a ninny."

I bit my lip and wrinkled my forehead. "Thanks for rescuing me."

We made it to the airport in time for me to catch my 2:30 flight.

Ben dropped me off at the departure curb for my airline, removed my luggage from the trunk, and hugged me. "I'll see you on Friday if your ring comes in before then. If not, I'll be there for sure the following weekend." He said other pastors complained about him taking too many Sundays off so it would be better for him to stay home the next weekend. He kissed the top of my head and returned to his car.

He didn't seem upset, but he must have been disappointed in me for not speaking when Pastor Young pushed the mic in my face. How often would I fail Ben? I shouldn't have agreed to marry him.

~

On Monday, Jill and I took our lunch break together and hurried to Mama Lou's. After we ordered, I filled her in on the details of my weekend away and included the gators and Riley.

"Sounds like things went well except for Riley." She took a sip of her sweet tea. "When are you going to call her and ask her again about being a bridesmaid?"

"Tonight, I guess."

The server brought our sandwiches to the table, and I said a quick prayer of thanks.

Jill's eyes twinkled. "I want to visit Moss Park while I'm there. We should have plenty of time those few days after your wedding to go gator watching."

"You can go by yourself." I chuckled. "No. I'll take you. You love an adventure."

We rushed through our meal, took a few leftovers to Grizzly who had wandered across the street, and zipped back to work.

That evening, I prayed while I sat at the kitchen table and called Riley. She answered on the third ring. After I greeted her, she said, "What do you want?"

"I wanted to check with you again. I'd love for you to be a part of our wedding. Will you reconsider?" I held my breath.

She paused for several seconds. "I'm not sure I'll be able to attend."

I exhaled and shook my head. "Your dad will be heartbroken if you're not there."

She hissed. "He didn't care about my broken heart when he announced your marriage. Why should I care?"

"Please don't allow your hurt to come between you and your dad. He loves you."

My phone slipped out of my hand and onto the table. I brought it back to my ear. "Riley?" She didn't respond. "Are you there?" I looked at my phone, assumed we'd been disconnected when I dropped it, and called her again. When she didn't answer, I called Ben.

He sounded cheerful. "I planned to call you."

"Why? What's up?"

"To say, hi, and ask about your day."

Sweet. "My day was okay until two minutes ago." I told him about my call to Riley.

"I'll call her later in the week to check in with her."

He asked me about work, Jill, and my family. He wanted to talk, which brought joy to my heart. Maybe this crazy arrangement could work.

~

Ben called me both Tuesday and Wednesday evenings—he said he wanted to hear my voice. I spent extra time in prayer thanking the Lord for Ben's attentiveness. I loved the changes in his wooing me. He acted sincere.

During his call on Wednesday, he told me the jeweler wouldn't have the ring sized until the following Monday, and he'd visit me the weekend after that. But on Thursday, he changed his mind. He wanted to come to Pleasant Springs to spend time together and said Pastor Young approved of his visits.

"I'd like to see you, too, but Jill and I plan to shop on Saturday for our dresses. I'm not sure how long that will take."

"We'll have Friday and Saturday evenings and part of Sunday. Sounds good to me."

When Ben arrived on Friday, we drove to Poplar Ridge and ate supper at Pete's. Afterward, we spent an hour back at my place before Ben left for the night. He lingered during our goodbye and gave me an extra hug on his way out the door.

On Saturday, Jill and I headed to Chattanooga at 9:00 a.m. We shopped at the better department stores to find the perfect dresses. Mine didn't need to be white or flashy—only a dressy dress. We were about to give up when we found two dresses at our fourth stop after we endured a salty taco lunch.

My dress, an orange chiffon, had ruffled cap sleeves and fell below my knees. Jill's was a similar pale blue dress with short sleeves. We looked fantastic.

We'd planned to visit Jill's sister, Lanie, while we were in town, but we ran out of time.

We purchased our dresses, bought new shoes, and left Chattanooga at 4:20 p.m. as two tired, but happy ladies.

Ben and I ate at Mama Lou's that evening. Lou was often in the kitchen, but she darted to our table to take our order. "Well, darlin', it's good to see you. I heard you had a new boyfriend." She stuck out her hand to Ben and introduced herself. "What can I get y'all tonight?" She winked at me. "Our special tonight is my famous meatloaf."

I opened my eyes wide and glanced at Ben. "I'm sure that's what my boyfriend wants."

Ben squinted. "As good as that sounds, I'm in the mood for a burger and fries."

"Sure thing." She turned to me. "The special?"

"Sounds great." I thanked her, and she scurried to the kitchen.

Ben kept his eyes focused on me and smirked.

"Believe me. After you taste her meatloaf, it will disappoint you that you didn't order it too."

"Never." Ben leaned forward and folded his hands on the table. "I called Riley today. She broke down and cried. Couldn't imagine I'd do this to her."

"Is she planning to attend?"

"She's too upset with me." He frowned and released a long breath.

"Is she angry about you remarrying or you not telling her you were dating?"

"Does it matter?"

"If she's angry about you getting remarried and thinks the way you do, then she may suppose you've forgotten or betrayed her mother. If that's the case, tell her the truth about our arrangement." I reached across the table for his hand. "But if she thinks the way Annie did, she may be upset because she was the last to know."

"How do you suggest I fix that?"

"Have a heart-to-heart talk, apologize again, and ask her to forgive you." I tilted my head. "If she's like Annie, she'll forgive."

Nineteen

Pastor Oldham preached a wonderful message on Sunday morning, and he announced Ben would speak the following weekend. People greeted us after the service and asked questions about our wedding. Maggie, of course, wanted the full scoop. I told her we could have lunch before her blog came out on Wednesday.

Back at my house, I cut up potatoes, put them into a casserole dish, and seasoned them with my favorite spice blend of salt, brown sugar, red pepper, garlic, and onion. I added smoked sausage and placed the dish in the oven.

Ben sat in my living room chair. He watched me while I set the table.

"We'll eat in forty minutes." I ambled toward him and took a seat on the sofa. "What are you thinking about?"

He shook his head. "I should grab a bite to eat on the road and head back to Chattanooga now." He rose from the chair and strode toward my front door.

I jumped up and followed him. "But why? I put lunch in the oven." I touched his arm. "Are you okay?"

He drew his eyebrows together. "I want to kiss you, but it's too soon." He wrapped me in a quick hug and released me. "Another two weeks. Then the first of many."

My knees weakened. After we said our goodbyes, I stood at my front window and watched Ben back out of the driveway. Warmth radiated throughout my body. A sign that he, too, was falling in love?

An hour later, Ben sent a text: **Sorry I bailed out on lunch.**

No problem. See you soon.

I called Jill, put my phone on speaker, and filled her in on what had happened. "In two weeks, Ben and I will be bound by our first kiss." I clapped my hands.

"I told you. He's a good guy. Give him time. A kiss is only the start."

"But it's likely now that this will become an actual marriage and not a dumb arrangement."

"As long as you don't push him or expect too much, too soon, you'll have a wonderful marriage."

I disconnected the call and twirled in anticipation— soon to be Mrs. Ben Peterson.

~

Ben landed at the Orlando International Airport at 9:55 p.m. He grabbed his suitcase and exited the plane. He couldn't go home until he worked off the tension that built up within him since he'd left Becca. On his way to the parking area, he muttered and chastised himself for his inability to keep his thoughts quiet. He hadn't expected to fall in love with Becca in three weeks. No. This wasn't love. Annie would always be his number one and forever in his heart.

After he climbed into his car and left the parking lot, he placed a call to Keith. "Hey, buddy. Can you get us two guest passes from your nephew to play racquetball tonight at the center?"

"Man, it's after 10:00. We're getting ready for bed. What's up with you?"

"Just got back from Pleasant Springs. I need a workout." Ben turned right onto 528.

"Sorry. No can do. You'll need to find another way to work off your stress." Keith chuckled. "Women can do that to you. Are you sure you want to get married again?"

Ben's thoughts drifted to holding Becca in his arms. "Things are good. I'll lift weights in my garage at home and be fine." He disconnected his call and drove the last few miles to his house. He'd be fine once he learned to keep his thoughts to himself.

~

Maggie and I met for lunch on Monday, and I gave her an update on our wedding. After I promised her pictures, she thanked me and went on her way.

Back in the office and throughout the week, I worked to get everything caught up and spent time with my replacement. My last day was Friday. I needed the following week to get ready for my move.

Ben and I spoke each evening. I told him that I prayed for him often and for the message he would preach on Sunday. He sounded more businesslike than usual, and when he spoke of our marriage, he again called it an arrangement. I needed to give him more time. He still struggled with his grief.

On Friday, I visited my parents for two hours before I headed back to Pleasant Springs to wait on Ben's visit.

He called me when I was halfway home. After our greetings, he said, "My plans have changed. I'll arrive tomorrow night and see you Sunday morning at church."

My stomach clenched. "Why?"

"I need to talk to Riley in person tomorrow. I'll drive to Jacksonville and fly to Chattanooga from there but won't get in until 10:00 p.m."

"Will you have my ring?" I focused on my empty ring finger.

"Got it."

"Okay. I'll pray all goes well and see you on Sunday."

I wasn't okay. He called to tell me he wasn't coming after he should have landed, and he said nothing about wanting to spend time with me like he had the week before. Was he having doubts?

Lord, I need confirmation from You that I'm doing the right thing. I need and want Ben's love. Tell me what I'm supposed to do.

~

Ben disconnected his call with Becca and groaned. "That was rude of me to call her last minute." He'd known all day he was going to visit Riley on Saturday. Why had he waited so long to notify Becca of the change? He paced through his living room and rationalized his actions. But in the end, he confirmed he'd been rude.

He strode into his office, sat at his desk, and pulled out his Bible to review the notes for Sunday's sermon. He'd selected prayer as his topic. While he reread the verses he'd chosen, he found a cross reference to 1 Peter 3:7. He read the verse, shook his head, pushed away from his desk, and made his way upstairs to move his clothing from the master closet to the guest room. He needed to get his mind off his sermon for a while. A sermon he no longer wanted to preach.

~

Sunday morning, I arrived five minutes before service and sat next to Jill. "Have you seen Ben?"

"I just got here." She nudged my arm. "Relax. Everything will work out." She faced the front of the church. "There he is now with Pastor Oldham."

The men took their seats at the front. Pastor Oldham began the service by welcoming the congregation. He invited everyone to stand, prayed for the service, and asked the song leader to come forward. After three hymns, our pastor returned to the podium, took an offering, and introduced Ben.

Ben smiled at me, and I melted. "Please open your Bibles to 1 Peter 3:7." He scanned the crowd and motioned for us to stand.

"I'll be reading from the New International Version." He looked at the text and paused for a few seconds. "Husbands, in the same way be considerate as you live with your wives and treat them with respect as the weaker partner and as heirs with you of the gracious gift of life, so that nothing will hinder your prayers."

He glanced my way. "The title of my message today is 'Hindered Prayers.'" He prayed and asked everyone to be seated.

"If you noticed, there are seven verses before the one I read that discuss the relationship of the wife in a marriage, but only one verse for husbands."

Several men looked at their wives and said, "Amen."

"That's not because wives need extra instruction. I suspect Peter understood husbands couldn't digest seven verses, so he gave our instructions in one."

The women chuckled.

"And I'm not here to discuss wives as the weaker partner. My Becca is a strong woman. I admire her spunk and spiritual strength."

Ben stepped away from the pulpit with his Bible in his hands and came down the steps to the level of the pews. "What I want to focus on today is that we men, as husbands, should care for and treat our wives with respect." He raised the Bible over his head. "That's what this book says. And not only our wives, but all the women in our lives. If they are believers, then they along with us will spend eternity with the Lord." Amens sounded throughout the church.

"I've struggled these past two weeks. Why couldn't I sense the Lord speaking to me. My prayers seemed to hit a wall. And then, I read this verse about hindered prayers. About treating others with respect, and I realized I hadn't been doing that well."

Ben reached out his hand and gazed at me. "Becca, honey, will you join me here at the front?"

I peered wide-eyed at Jill. Butterflies exploded in my gut. I stood and walked with weakened knees past eight rows of pews and took Ben's outstretched hand.

His eyes softened. "I've not given you the understanding and respect you deserve. When you arrived in Orlando two weeks ago, I told you what to do and what to say. I made fun of your concerns about alligators and other things and didn't consider your wants and needs." He placed his Bible between his upper arm and his body to hold it in place and took my other hand. "Please forgive me for what I've already mentioned and for my rudeness when I called you late Friday afternoon. I'll work hard at being the husband you deserve."

I spoke in a timid voice. "You're forgiven." He released my hands, and I returned to my seat amazed and delighted at the change in him.

Ben expanded on the theme of hindered prayers and finished his sermon. People approached me after the service ended, hugged my neck, and told me they would miss me. Ben received compliments on his sermon, handshakes, and congratulations.

We both drove to the Pizza Shack and ordered a quick lunch so Ben could make it to the airport on time for an earlier flight than usual. He told me that Riley seemed to be doing better with the wedding news, but she was still unhappy with him and confirmed she would not attend. She said she had to work and couldn't get off.

After lunch, we strolled to the parking lot hand in hand. Ben apologized for not arriving earlier in the weekend. "I'm disappointed we didn't get to spend much time together." He squeezed my hand when we neared his rental car, unlocked his doors, and climbed into the passenger side where he sat for a moment. When he came out, he held a small box in his right hand.

"I know this isn't the perfect place to give this to you, but I've got to get to the airport and want you to have this." He opened the box, slipped the ring onto my finger, embraced me, and kissed my cheek before he drove away.

His sermon and his apologies were the confirmation I needed to move forward and become his wife. *Thank you, Lord.*

Twenty

The following Saturday, Jill and I left for Orlando at 9:00 a.m. We loaded my Ford Taurus with boxes of clothing and personal items I couldn't leave behind. I stored my remaining things at either my parents' home or Jill's.

We stopped in McDonough, Georgia for lunch. After we ate our sandwiches, we rewarded ourselves with chocolate cake to celebrate our drive through Atlanta without any issues. We made another stop in Tifton, Georgia, to buy a café mocha for me and a chai tea latte for Jill. She envied me that I would have coffee shops available in Orlando that served these delectable treats. The closest specialty shop to Pleasant Springs was fifty miles away.

We arrived in Lake City, Florida, at 6:10 p.m. where we spent the night.

On Sunday morning, we checked out before 8:00, enjoyed a late breakfast in Wildwood, and pulled into Hart Fellowship with full tummies at 11:30 for a 1:30 ceremony. No rehearsal. No reception. Only the wedding with a small group of friends.

Mom and Dad flew down and rented a car. They

planned to spend four days on the Atlantic Coast after the wedding, and Jill and I arranged to hang out on the Gulf so we wouldn't run into them. How do you explain to your parents that your wedding wasn't really a wedding? Only a ceremony. Ben knew of our plans and was fine with them. He understood my time with Jill meant a lot to me.

We slipped inside the chapel foyer and found Charlotte Weston—the wedding coordinator Ben introduced me to two weeks earlier. She took us to the bridal room and said guests would be allowed into the chapel as soon as the prayer service ended around 1:15.

After we changed and redid our makeup, Jill pulled my hair into a loose bun, leaving wisps of hair hanging along each side of my face. Michael always told me how beautiful I looked with my hair styled that way. Would Ben think so too?

At 1:25, a knock sounded on our door. Charlotte entered with two small bouquets of white and orange gerbera daisies, handed them to us, and clutched her chest. "You ladies are gorgeous." She told us she'd counted twenty-seven people in attendance. Most of them were staff members—fellow pastor's and their spouses. She peered at me. "Your parents are here." She paused. "And Riley."

"Riley made it?" I grinned. "That's great."

"She did, and it thrilled Ben to see her." She chuckled. "He had tears in his eyes when she arrived. And he'll shed a few when he sees you. Annie fixed her hair that same way for special occasions."

"Annie?" I groaned and eyed Jill. "Take it out."

I reached up to pull out my bun, but Charlotte grabbed my arm. "No time. We're ready to begin." She cracked open the door, peeked out, and led us toward the entryway at the back of the chapel. I waved at my dad who stood on the opposite side of the doorway while he awaited his cue. We stayed out of sight until the pianist played, "Joyful, Joyful, We Adore Thee."

Charlotte signaled Jill who made her way to the front. When an upbeat rendition of the wedding march played, Charlotte motioned for my dad to join me, and we walked the aisle arm in arm. Everyone stood and turned to watch. I focused on Ben. His face glowed.

Riley stood in the front row. When I looked her way, her smile waned.

But when I reached Ben and gazed into his eyes, his smile grew. The music stopped, the guests sat, and the church's Teaching Pastor, Vince Davidson, spoke. My dad released my arm and gave me a quick peck on my cheek.

I tried to focus on the ceremony and what the pastor said, but my thoughts were on the promised kiss. The first of many.

We used traditional vows, exchanged rings, and came to my favorite part. "You may kiss your bride."

My stomach fluttered. I lifted my chin, wet my lips, and closed my eyes. Ben's breath tickled my nose. He kissed me to the right of my lips.

My eyes shot open. What was that? Not the kiss I'd longed to receive, nor the one Ben promised.

He pulled away and turned me to face the guests. With his head bent, he whispered. "Smile."

I doubted my fake smile would fool anyone.

Jill handed me my bouquet. The preacher announced, "Mr. and Mrs. Benson Peterson." My legs wobbled. I reached out to grab Jill and missed. Someone

broke my fall.
    I had married a liar.

Twenty-one

Ben swept me into his arms and carried me to the bridal room. He lowered me onto a sofa in a sitting position. "Are you okay? What happened?"

I stood, unsure if my legs would hold me, narrowed my eyes at Ben, and clenched my teeth. "Not. Now."

The only other person I saw was Jill. But Mom's gasp alerted me others heard my outburst. My dad rushed toward me. "What's goin' on here, sugar?"

I needed to say something fast, but truthful. Couldn't succumb to the same level of deceit as Ben. "My apologies to each of you. I expected something different to take place during the ceremony. When it didn't happen, my disappointment got the best of me. Everything will be fine." I faked another smile and touched my dad's arm. "I'm okay."

"Must have been some disappointment." My dad hugged me close and glared at Ben. "You bring her displeasure young man, and you'll answer to me."

Ben spoke in an agreeable tone. "Yes, Sir. You can count on me."

My dad released me and pointed his finger at Ben's face. "I better not hear otherwise." He glanced at my mom. "Let's leave these two alone to work through this."

He mumbled something about his shotgun on his way out the door.

Ben stepped closer. "I know what this is about. I can explain."

"Go. Away."

Jill raised her eyebrows. Did she realize what happened?

Ben looked at Jill. "The two of you need to join us in the foyer now. The staff has a gift they want to present before they leave. I'm sure they're waiting." He motioned me toward the door.

I stayed behind Ben across the room but didn't follow him out the door. Instead, I locked it behind him.

Jill crashed into my backside. "What's going on? What did Ben do or not do?"

"He didn't kiss me."

Jill scrunched her nose. "Yes, he did."

"Not a real one. He didn't kiss me on my lips. He promised me that." I sounded snotty. "The first of many, he said." I lowered my head and covered my face with my hands. "He lied to me. Everything he's done and said has been a lie."

"Oh, honey, what can I do?" Jill wrapped her arms around me. "Do you think everything will work out like you told your dad?"

I pulled away at the sound of a tap on the door.

Charlotte said, "We're all waiting for you. Hurry, people need to leave. We have something special to give you."

I peered at Jill. "Everything will be fine after you research how I can get an annulment in Florida. I have no plans or desire to be Ben's wife."

~

Cheers erupted when Jill and I entered the foyer.

Ben took my elbow and led me to a chair. He clutched an overstuffed envelope and kept his voice low. "What took you so long?"

"I needed time to freshen my makeup, but that didn't happen." I turned toward the group, apologized for my delay, and took my seat. The envelope appeared to be filled with cash. I didn't want to seem ungrateful.

Ben sat and grasped my limp hand. "Thank you all for attending today. We appreciate your being here and this gift from the church staff and their families."

He handed me the envelope and asked me to open it.

There was a card, cash, and three gift cards to various restaurants included. I opened the card and a folded piece of paper fell out onto my lap. The card read, "We wish you both the best and many happy years together. Enjoy your trip." Your trip? We hadn't planned a honeymoon. Wouldn't that be a hoot?

I handed the card and its contents to Ben, opened the sheet of paper, and widened my eyes. They paid for a honeymoon in the Florida Keys. Four nights starting the next day and returning home on Friday. I held back a sarcastic chuckle and handed the paper to Ben. "Y'all, that's the sweetest gift you could have given us." I nudged Ben's elbow. "Isn't that the best, honey?"

He eyed me and then the others. His voice rose an octave. "Unexpected, indeed." He thanked everyone.

Friends and family wished us well and said their goodbyes. I jumped up from my chair when my parents waved from the doorway. Couldn't let them get away without a hug. "Are you off to the coast?"

"We'll leave in the morning. You two have a lovely trip and we'll see you soon." Mom kissed my cheek.

Dad gave me one of his bear hugs. "You tell me if Ben doesn't treat you right. I'll set him straight."

"I can take care of myself."

Everyone else filed out the door except for Ben, Jill, and me.

Ben followed us into the bridal room to retrieve our belongings. "Jill, you're welcome to stay with us at the house. You can use Riley's room."

I grabbed my makeup bag and car keys from where I'd left them on a chair. "What happened to Riley? I didn't get to say hello or introduce her to Jill."

"She left early. Had to be back to study for a test tomorrow." He stared at me, expressionless. "She said to tell you that you looked beautiful, and she was glad she came."

I nodded. "Sorry I didn't talk with her." I spun toward Jill and then back to Ben. "Jill made plans to stay in a hotel. I'll drop things off at the house and stay with her tonight because we leave in the morning for the Gulf."

Ben flinched. "A change in plans. We have a trip to the Keys, remember?"

I stepped toward him. "You expect me to travel with you on an overnight trip? How will that work? The flyer information said we have a one-bedroom waterfront cottage."

"I'll call and ask if they can give us a two-bedroom."

"Great. You do that." I crossed my arms. "Because I'm not spending the night in the same room with you."

Jill grabbed my hand and pulled me into the corner of the room. "You need to work through this. You promised to marry him and now you have. Own it and do what's right."

I shook my head. How could my best friend turn on me like that? I fumed, gathered the rest of my things, and stormed out to my car with Jill and Ben on my heels. "Has everyone gone crazy or am I the biggest fool ever?" We stopped beside my car.

Jill spoke to Ben from behind me. "Take her home. I'll follow in her car so we can unload her stuff. Then I'll take the car to the hotel, and if it's okay with her, borrow it for the week. On Saturday, I can drop it off at your house before I fly home."

My body tensed. Jill spoke to Ben as if I were an unruly child and not her friend.

She touched my shoulder from behind and I flinched. "Does that sound okay with you? You and Ben need to work through this without me around."

I didn't dare speak. Ugliness boiled within me. I knew Jill thought her response to all that had happened was for my best. But I didn't agree.

Ben thanked Jill and linked his elbow in mine. "Please act happy. There are still people in their cars who may be watching us. We'll work this out." He led me to his Camry.

Until the annulment took place, which I would need to research myself, I would play his game. And beat him at it.

LUANN K. EDWARDS

Twenty-two

Ben carried the last of my boxes upstairs to the master bedroom while I sat in the living room and drank a cup of chamomile tea that he'd prepared for me.

He joined me on the sofa ten minutes later. "I planned to kiss you and wanted to—"

"Stop." I lifted my palm and stuck it in front of his face. "No more lies." I rose from the couch, headed up the stairs to my new, albeit temporary room, and changed into a pair of jean capris with a royal blue top.

I plopped onto the edge of the bed, crossed my arms, and remembered a proverb I'd heard several times growing up. "Fool me once, shame on you; fool me twice, shame on me." Ben would not fool me again.

The bed stood high off the floor. I slid off, unzipped my suitcase on top of the bed and ripped open my boxes that lined the floor. I sorted through my clothes and flipped some of them into piles on my bed and the rest I hurled into the dresser drawers and slammed the drawers shut. A five-day honeymoon with that man? What could I do to make him as miserable on this trip as he had me?

Into my suitcase, I threw in my shortest shorts, my two-piece swimsuit, and my low-cut orange top I wore to get Michael's attention when he'd been working too much.

I stomped my foot and snorted. Take that Mister Liar. My new hubby would soon find out what he was missing by not giving me a proper kiss.

My chest tightened, and my eyes grew large. What was I doing? A flood of guilt coursed through me. With shaky hands, I yanked everything out of my suitcase and in a hurry snatched my jeans, capris, modest tops, and my one-piece swimsuit from my bed.

I jumped at the sound of a knock. I closed my suitcase and dashed to the door.

Ben wore a black apron over his jeans and a bright yellow T-shirt. The man needed help. I told him no yellow. He listened about as well as a two-year-old. Taupe, jade, soft white, medium gray, but not yellow.

"I fixed dinner. Do you like shrimp, hushpuppies, and fries?"

I wanted to tell him that I wasn't hungry. But shrimp? "That sounds okay. I'll be down in a minute."

He nodded and strode to the stairs.

I closed the bedroom door and sighed. *Lord, what do you want me to do?*

~

After a quiet but delicious dinner, I helped with the dishes. "You did a fantastic job with our meal. I'll need to work hard to top that."

Ben placed leftovers in the refrigerator with his back to me. "There's always meatloaf."

Was he being funny or stating that if I left him, he'd do fine with the ladies from church, bringing him food again? I tossed the towel onto the counter and darted out of the kitchen toward the stairs.

"Wait. What did I do now?"

I spun to face him. "A couple's wedding day should be one of the happiest days of their lives. If today is one of the best days we'll share, then I'm not looking forward to any kind of a future with you."

Ben rushed to my side, faced me, and wrapped me in his arms. "I hurt you today, but that was not my intention. I do care about you."

Although I liked his hug too much, I wriggled free and shook my head. "I can't continue this charade." I bolted up the stairs to my room and slammed the door.

Ben called after me. The volume of his voice intensified when he repeated my name. He pounded on my door and jiggled the handle. "I have a key."

"Then use it." I took off my shoes and threw them at the door. "But I'm changing." I pulled out a pair of socks, took off the pair I wore, and put on the new—all while standing and hopping around to keep my balance. I might sin in other areas, but I wasn't about to sink to lying, which seemed easy for him.

"And what was that you said about respect three weeks ago? Something about slamming doors? Doesn't that apply to you too?"

I guess we acted a lot alike when we were frustrated with one another.

A few minutes later, my phone pinged with a text: **Pack for our trip. Stay open-minded. Pray. We can get through this. I need you.**

I lowered myself to the floor and leaned my back against the wall. **I'm packed.**

Need me. Of course. But would he ever want me?

~

Ben tossed and turned all night. How could he make this right? Somehow, he had to make Becca understand.

If she would listen to him, he'd explain how grief gripped him when he had planned to kiss her. His heart still ached for Annie—he'd never stop loving her. But he had to get a grip on his grief and focus on Becca. He promised her that in his sermon. He needed her in his life. But how could their arrangement work? Was it worth it to try?

Twenty-three

Mid-morning on Monday, we loaded Ben's car and made the six-hour trip to Marathon in the Florida Keys. I kept my nose in a book—a romance. Ben tried to talk to me five or six times, but I shushed him. The book's storyline had to be better than whatever he had to say. If I couldn't live my romance, I could find hope reading one.

Ben pulled into the resort at 5:10 p.m. and checked us in. The front of our cottage faced the ocean. Plenty of sand lay between our veranda and the sea. The view reminded me of a postcard. Perfect with an expanse of sparkling shades of sea green before me.

Ben took our luggage inside while I returned to the car for my sunhat. I walked back to the veranda and stared again at the beauty.

The door opened behind me. "Are you going to come inside and look around?"

I couldn't take my eyes off the ocean. "This place is beautiful. I've never seen anything as lovely as this."

He stepped onto the veranda and ambled close to my side. "I have. You."

I flinched and snapped at him. "Stop it. I doubt there's anyone here who knows you. No need to play games with me."

His shoulders sagged, and he turned to head back inside.

I squeezed my eyes shut. What was wrong with me? As a Christian, I shouldn't be hateful. But he lied to me and that hurt. And how did I respond? I ignored him since the wedding, spouted off more times than I could count, and wouldn't give him a chance to apologize or explain.

I slipped out of my shoes, climbed down the stairs, and trudged across the sand to a wooden lounge chair. When I sat, I hugged my knees to my chest. An annulment would be better for both of us. He didn't deserve my animosity.

~

Ben paced through the sitting area for the umpteenth time with his phone in hand and searched for a nearby pizza place. He doubted he'd get Becca out of the chair to go with him to get a bite to eat.

All that tension and anxiety over just one kiss. If he could go back to the wedding and do it over again, he'd kiss her like she wanted to be kissed. But Annie? Memories of her continued to slip away. He found it hard to remember the sound of her voice. He couldn't let her go.

But if he didn't, would he lose Becca? He watched her from the window. His heart ached that she didn't understand—she, of all people, should. Had Michael not meant as much to her as Annie had to him?

Becca rose from her chair and moseyed toward the cottage. Maybe now they could talk. But she only made it as far as the veranda before she sat in a wicker chair facing the ocean and shook her head.

~

Annulments were complicated. I found from my research that I could claim I was under duress when I agreed to marry Ben, but that wasn't true. Fraud was a better description. He lied to get me to marry him. We wouldn't be consummating our marriage, so I had that in my favor too.

Ben stepped out onto the veranda. "I ordered pizza thirty minutes ago, and it should be here in ten. Do you want to eat out here?"

I stood. "It's getting dark. I'll come inside."

The cottage included an efficiency kitchen with a table for two; a sitting area which held a chair, end table, sofa, and television; and the bedroom with a king bed. The bathroom was attached to the bedroom. Ben had put my suitcase on the bed and his in the sitting area.

I returned to the kitchen. "You should take the bed. I'll take the couch."

"I'll be fine on the sofa."

We both turned toward the door when we heard footsteps on the stairs to our veranda. Ben opened the door to the pizza delivery person, tipped him, and laid the pizza box on the table. We located plates in the cabinet, took our seats, and had a word of prayer. The pizza tasted good, but it didn't sit well on my stomach.

I ate one slice and placed my plate in the dishwasher. "Can we walk along the beach this evening?"

He sounded hopeful. "Together?"

I nodded and strolled to the window facing the water. "The sound of the waves hitting shore calms me. Might be a good thing."

Ben joined me at the window. "May I talk while we walk, or do you need total quiet?"

I peered into his eyes. "I don't know what I need."

His voice was tender. "Perhaps I can help you figure that out. If you'll let me."

We put the pizza leftovers in the refrigerator and went outside. A beautiful evening awaited us. We watched water birds while we meandered along the shore. Because I'd been nasty to Ben, I allowed him to hold my hand when he reached for it. Someone could be there who knew him. Not likely, but possible. I waited for him to speak to me with his soothing pastor's voice. But what he did next surprised me. He sang, "Amazing Grace." I'd forgotten Ben could sing well. God blessed him with a beautiful tenor voice.

He continued with verses two and three. How could I stay upset with a man singing about the grace of our Lord? In verse four, I joined him the best I could with the harmony. I'm not a singer, but we made sweet music together.

When we finished, he faced me and brushed the back of his finger down my cheek. "You looked amazing yesterday. Your dress. Your hair. Your smile. Until I ruined everything." His finger glided over my lips. "I wanted to kiss you. Planned to. But at the last moment, Annie invaded my thoughts, and I couldn't do it. Please forgive me."

My heart pounded in my ears. How could I forgive him? "You don't understand how much you hurt me. You broke a promise I counted on."

"I do understand and I'm sorry I failed you." He ran his hand down the side of my hair.

I turned my face toward the water. He shattered my trust. But holding a grudge and not forgiving him would hurt me more than him.

"You won't forgive me?"

I glanced at Ben. "I do forgive you, but I'm having a tough time trusting you."

He stared at my lips and moved closer.

I backed away and raised my palm—my tone harsher than it needed to be. "Don't. I doubt you're ready yet." I turned away, ran back to the cottage, and hurried inside.

If I allowed him to kiss me, it would be harder to prove fraud, wouldn't it?

Twenty-four

Ben stayed outside for longer than I expected, and I worried about him. I wanted to make sure he was okay but didn't want him to think I cared. But he must have realized that I'd fallen in love with him, and my struggles were because he didn't return my love. Would he ever?

I sat on the bed and opened another book.

A few minutes later, Ben came inside the cottage and stood outside the bedroom door. "I hope we can drive into Key West tomorrow and view the sights. Are you up for that?"

"Sure." I slipped from the bed and walked toward him. "What time do you want to leave?"

"After breakfast—by 9:00 will be good."

I slid past him to the kitchen for a bottle of water and spoke with my back to him. "If you need the bathroom during the night, come into the bedroom. I doubt you'll wake me."

He cleared his throat. "I'll be fine, but thanks."

I turned toward him. "You stopped twice during the six-hour trip here to use the restroom. Come in if you need to." I stepped closer and touched his arm. "Don't make yourself miserable."

He kissed my cheek and pulled me close.

I wiggled away. "I can't do this. Heartfelt wooing only." I stared into the kitchen. "We can play the part of a married couple in public, but not in private." I darted into the bedroom and found an extra lightweight blanket and pillows in the closet. He remained standing in the same place near the doorway with his eyes fixed on me. I zipped past him again and placed the linens on the sofa before I turned and faced him.

Ben released a heavy sigh. "That *was* heartfelt."

~

When I awoke the following morning at 6:00, I peeked into the sitting area and found Ben asleep on the sofa. He appeared uncomfortable with his feet hanging over the end of the couch. I dashed into the bathroom, plugged my phone into the charger, and took my shower. My goal was to be ready before Ben woke up. I threw on my clothes and opened the bedroom door, so he'd know it was safe to come in.

He stirred and opened his eyes. "Hey. You're up early. Love the wet head look."

I smiled—my first genuine one since the wedding. "I'm going to dry it now. The bathroom is all yours."

He rose from the couch, stretched, rubbed his neck, and gathered a set of clothes he'd laid out the night before. "I'll be out in fifteen minutes max, and we'll get breakfast." He strode past me groaning and rolling his shoulders.

I didn't think he used the bathroom during the night. The one-bedroom set-up was awkward. After I dried my hair, worship music boomed from the bathroom. I liked that about him. His choice of music matched mine.

My thoughts turned to Jill. I couldn't stay angry with

her. She did what she felt she had to do. I said a quick prayer for her trip and searched for my phone. I wanted to text her to apologize and find out how she was doing.

When I realized where I'd left my cell—in the bathroom—I checked my watch. Ben said fifteen minutes, it had been closer to twenty. I expected he'd be dressed.

I rapped on the bathroom door. No answer. His music was loud. I tried a second time. When he didn't respond, I tried the door and pushed it open.

"Yikes, Becca. What are you doing?" Ben stood in front of the mirror while shaving with a towel wrapped around his waist. He spun around and faced me.

Surprised by seeing him half-dressed, I giggled.

He sounded annoyed. "Out. Now." He pointed to the door.

I couldn't hide my grin. "May I get my phone?"

He unplugged my charger and tossed the phone onto the bed. "Get out of here."

I snatched my phone, bolted out to the kitchen table, and sent an apology text to Jill. I followed that one with another: **Having a good time?** I hit send and chuckled again.

Ben stormed out of the bedroom fully dressed and loomed over me. "What is wrong with you? Sunday, you acted like a spoiled brat, yesterday like a pouty child, and just now—weird."

I rose from my chair and glared at him. "Weird?"

He grabbed his wallet and keys that he'd left on the kitchen counter and stuck them in his pants' pockets. He spoke in a spiteful tone. "Let's go. I can't wait to discover what other qualities of yours surface today."

My chin quivered. I picked up my room key and

sunhat from where I'd left them on the kitchen table and ran out the door, straight to the shoreline.

"Becca." Ben called to me from the veranda. A minute later, I received his text: **I'm leaving without you. Be back after dark.**

Why bother to come back at all? I waded along the shore for fifteen minutes, unable to focus on its beauty. Spoiled brat? Weird? That was what he thought of me? I picked up a shell, used it to write Ben's name in the sand along the water's edge, and stomped on it until the waves carried his name out to sea.

When my stomach growled, I turned back and traipsed to the resort's restaurant for breakfast. The hostess seated me outside at a table for two. I ordered a blueberry muffin, yogurt parfait, and a bottle of water.

A few minutes later, a dark-haired, good-looking gentleman asked to join me at my table. Was his accent British or Australian? Not sure, but he drew me in with his charm and sparkling eyes. His conversation could get my mind off Ben for a while. I pointed to the seat across from me. "Of course."

When he sat, my chest tightened. I shouldn't have said yes. But I didn't want to be rude. Besides, Ben and I weren't *really* married. I'd enjoy morning conversation with the man and spend the rest of my day reading out on the veranda or lounging near the shore. But what if the man were trouble? I twisted a strand of hair around my finger. I should have gone with Ben. I wished I'd gone with Ben.

Twenty-five

The gentleman's name, per the business card he handed me, was Brayden Hale, an artist. He was in Florida promoting his artwork. In his romantic accent, he complimented me on my radiant hair, high cheekbones, long lashes, and full lips. He said my freckles added to my beauty. He pulled up one of his paintings on his phone and offered to paint my portrait like he had the young woman who modeled for him. A gifted artist, no doubt.

"I'm flattered, but I won't have time to sit for a portrait. My husband and I have plans for the week."

"Oh? Appeared as though he left upset this morning. Are you sure he's coming back?"

I raised my eyebrows. "He'll be back. He may return soon." He might have changed his mind and returned early. Right?

Mr. Hale flipped over his business card and scribbled something.

My stomach churned. He'd written, "Cottage Six."

"Come visit me if you get lonely while you wait." He rose, grinned at me, and sauntered off.

I changed my opinion of him. There wasn't anything appealing about the man. Nobody tried that kind of line on me back in Pleasant Springs. Why had I allowed him to hook me with his charm?

Alone in my room after breakfast and having spent time in prayer, I sent Jill another text: **Big fight. Ben left. Flirty stranger. Lurking outside?**

I gazed out my window at the ocean and longed to read outdoors, but I didn't want to run into Hale again.

Jill responded to my text: **Call Ben.**

Can't.

I'd experienced many emotions the past few weeks. Uncertainty, heartache, and anxiety. And three hours earlier, Ben attacked my character—who I was. A spoiled brat and weird? The latter cut deep.

My thoughts returned to Hale. What a ladies' man. My freckles added to my beauty? Gag. He outdid Ben's smooth talk, but in a flattering, deceptive sort of way. Women must fall at his feet. I couldn't allow myself to be one of them.

I spent the next twenty minutes with my Bible and thanked God for protecting me from Hale and his charm. But I felt trapped for being cooped up inside. I slipped out onto the veranda with my Bible where I could get back inside in a hurry if I spotted Hale coming my way. When I glanced to my left, four cottages down, Mister Charm waved.

I didn't respond. Instead, I acted as if I hadn't seen him. I relaxed back in my chair and took pleasure in the sound of the waves hitting shore. My ringtone for Jill played on my phone.

She sounded worried. "Are you okay?"

"I'm fine."

"Well, I called Ben. He's on his way back to make sure you're safe."

I huffed. "You didn't need to do that." I stood, went inside, and locked the door with the deadbolt. "He was angry with me this morning. And it wasn't my fault."

"What happened?"

I shared the story with her and how he'd called me names.

"You acted like a spoiled brat after the wedding, but I would never say you're weird."

"But I was sure he'd be dressed by then." I chuckled despite my hurt. "He was too cute—his expression— priceless." I sobered. "Until he turned on me and yelled."

"I have an assignment for you."

"Oh?" I paced through the sitting area.

"Read 1 Peter 3. Those verses that come before the one Ben preached on when he was in Pleasant Springs. Then read 1 Corinthians 13. The entire chapter."

I plopped onto the sofa. "I've read them before. Many times."

"But to bring harmony to you and Ben, you need to read *and do* them."

A beep alerted me to another caller. Jill said she had more to say on this topic and asked me to call her back after I read the verses.

The other caller was Ben. Concern edged his voice. "Becca, honey, are you okay?"

Why did he call me honey? I told him I was fine.

"What's going on? Are you inside the cottage?"

"Yes."

"What happened?"

I told him about the man who joined me for breakfast and how he wanted to paint my portrait. "Don't worry, Ben. I told him no."

"Has he bothered you since?"

"No." I told Ben how I'd gone out on the veranda for ten minutes and saw Hale waving at me from his cottage. "I'm staying put now." I reached for my Bible that I'd placed on the end table earlier and thumbed through it.

"On my way. Should be there in thirty minutes."

"I appreciate your concern, but I'm fine. I don't want to ruin your day any more than I already have."

"You need me, and I'll be there." His turn signal clicked. "Getting gas. See you soon." He said goodbye, but before I could disconnect, he insisted I close and lock the windows.

"But it's a beautiful day, and that's unnecessary."

"Please. For me. What would I do if something happened to you?"

I smiled and brought my hand to my chest. "I'll close them now."

"And Becca. You're not weird."

"Spoiled brat?"

He spoke in a teasing tone. "Perhaps a little?"

After I hung up, I laid my Bible on the kitchen table, locked the windows, and closed the blinds. No need to allow Hale to peek in at me.

I returned to the table and pondered the verses Jill suggested I read.

From 1 Peter 3, I gleaned that a wife's beauty should come from within—a gentle and quiet spirit. That didn't sound fun.

1 Corinthians 13 reminded me that love is patient and kind. Not easily angered end doesn't keep a record of wrongs. Always protects, trusts, hopes, and perseveres.

Gentle, kind, and patient. Didn't matter what Ben

did or didn't do. God called me to love him, if not as a husband in an actual marriage, then as a friend and fellow believer in Christ. Ben needed me to be that for him. But I wasn't sure I could.

I called Jill. "That was Ben on the phone. He's on his way to rescue me, but I'm fine."

"Good. I've been praying for you."

"What else did you want to tell me?" I rested my elbow on the table and placed my palm on my forehead.

"Did you read the verses?"

I told her yes and what stood out to me.

"Great. Ben needs you to be that woman. Instead of fighting him, give him what he needs—your support and encouragement. Be his helper."

"That's not as easy as it sounds." I lifted my head.

"If I can do it, you can."

I wrinkled my nose. "What are you talking about?"

"I'm flying home on Friday instead of Saturday to take a part-time job to help someone out on weekends."

I got up, wandered to the windows, and peered through the blinds. "Who?"

"Doc Winston. He needs help for a few months until his niece moves to town. His full-time assistant, Penny, is retiring. She'll continue to work until Emily arrives, but Penny wants to cut back on her hours. She's asked for Saturdays off."

I released the blind. "You saw the need and offered to fill it in hopes of a future with Doc?"

"You know me too well." She laughed. "Ben has a need, and you offered to fill his. I foresee by my working with Doc that we can get to know each other better. Maybe something will happen between us like you hope will happen between you and Ben."

"In the meantime, we'll support one another."

"Exactly. Are you in?"

"Yes, I'm in." A knock sounded at the door. "I've got to go. Ben's outside."

"Use the peep hole if you have one to make sure."

"I will. Love you."

We disconnected our call. I looked outside and gasped.

Twenty-six

Hale, with an impish grin, stood tall on my veranda. Instead of opening the door, I opened the window and spoke in a perky voice. "What's up?"

"Will you go for a walk with me along the beach? Too beautiful to be stuck inside."

I thanked him for the offer. "I'm waiting for my husband to get back. We have plans."

His words dripped like honey. "Cottage Six, beautiful, if you change your mind." He blew me a kiss.

I closed the window and blinds and shuddered. I wouldn't change my mind.

Within seconds, footsteps pounded on the stairs and Ben's voice blared. I reopened the blinds and cracked the window open.

Hale and Ben stood on the veranda facing one another. Ben's face glowed fire red. He pointed toward the beach. "I don't know what your game is, but you'll not be playing it with my wife. Get out of here."

Hale raised his palms, moseyed down the steps, and turned to face Ben. He grinned when he noticed me standing inside at the window. "Goodbye, lovely lady. Thanks for spending time with me today. I'll never forget you." He chuckled and sauntered toward his cottage.

Ben bolted down the three steps and stopped at the bottom. He widened his stance and glared after Hale while he walked away.

I unlocked the door, ventured outside, and spoke in a reassuring tone. "Everything's fine. Come inside."

Ben bounded up the steps and followed me into the cottage. The door slammed behind me.

I jerked at the sound and spun to face him.

He narrowed his eyes and raised his voice. "What did he mean by his last comment?"

I understood Ben's concern. I responded with calmness. "Nothing. He's a troublemaker and trying to get you riled up." I took a step toward him. "He invited himself to my table for breakfast. We were together for ten minutes at most." I reached out to touch Ben's arm. "Can we take a walk together along the beach and talk?"

Ben scowled and took a deep breath. "Not here. Let's drive to another beach. We'll get dinner while we're out."

We drove forty-five miles northeast past Coco Plum Beach, Curry Hammock State Park, and Long Key State Park before he pulled into Founder's Park in Islamorada. When I asked him why we didn't stop at any of those other places, he said he wanted to get farther away from my stalker.

The park's beach, which faced the Florida Bay, was small but charming. The palm trees swayed in the soft breeze that made its way across our path.

After ten minutes of a peaceful walk and wading along the shore near mangrove trees, Ben pointed to a canopy-covered picnic table, and we ambled toward it. I smiled as squirrels and lizards scurried nearby.

"You wanted to talk?" Ben sat facing the water and

patted the bench on his right.

I took a seat next to him and folded my hands on the table. "I want to be honest with you. Although I told you nothing happened when I was with that guy, that's not the whole truth."

Ben stiffened.

"I found him attractive and rationalized that there wouldn't be anything wrong with spending time together. But then it hit me. I made a big mistake. The best thing for me was to get away from him." I touched Ben's hand. "That's what I did. Avoided him. And prayed."

Ben grimaced and crossed his arms. "But how could you consider spending time with him was okay?"

I frowned and fiddled with my ring. "Because you and I aren't really married."

His face flushed, and he clenched his teeth. "But we are."

"Yes, we have a signed marriage license and had a ceremony, but we haven't. . . we haven't. Kissed."

His tone turned gentle. "I tried."

I watched the water birds dart along the shore, and the seagulls fly overhead and matched his gentle tone. "When you kiss me the first time, I want it to signify your pledge to me like you did Annie. A commitment toward an actual marriage and not an arrangement."

He held my hand. "What if I'm ready before you are?"

I gazed into his eyes and grinned. "I doubt that will happen." Couldn't he see that I was already in love with him?

~

On Wednesday morning, I again peeked out the

bedroom door and found Ben asleep on the sofa. I dashed into the shower and got ready for our day. Ben wanted to take me to Key West and show me places he thought I'd like.

When I opened the bedroom door, he sat up and groaned.

"Are you okay?"

He stood and stretched. "Body's stiff. Neck aches." He shook his head. "Other than that, I'm fine."

"Tonight, I'll take the couch."

He objected, but I told him I'd win this one.

Ben chuckled and rushed past me to the restroom. Five minutes later, he poked his head out. "Do you have your phone?"

I nodded and raised my brows. "But I may need tissues." I moved toward him.

He yanked three from the box and placed them into my hand. "I'm locking it today." He smirked and closed the door. When his music played, I had to strain my ear to hear it. He wasn't taking any chances.

After I tidied his blankets and pillow, I read my Bible and prayed. I committed to work on my relationship with my husband and focus on loving him the way he needed me to love him—with a quiet, gentle spirit.

We stopped for breakfast along the way and got into Key West at 10:05 a.m. Ben parked along the curb in front of a small shop. When we climbed out of the car, the weather welcomed us with a perfect temperature of seventy-eight degrees, sunshine, and a light breeze.

"I'll enjoy living in Florida. Except for the gators."

"You'll forget all about them." Ben came around to the passenger side and joined me on the sidewalk.

"Instead, you're likely to find Palmetto Bugs, spiders, and lizards."

"What are Palmetto Bugs?"

"Flying cockroaches."

"Ew." I glanced to my right. "Are we going inside the photography shop?"

He pointed to a sign on the next block. "The Butterfly and Nature Conservatory." He took my hand and led me toward the entrance.

I stopped and released his hand outside the door. "This is sweet of you to bring me here."

"You loved the exhibit in Chattanooga. Didn't you?"

"Yes." I smiled and looked across the street. "Do you expect to see anyone who knows you?"

"It's possible."

I peered into his eyes. "Is that why you wanted to hold my hand?"

Ben's face softened, and he lowered his voice. "I held your hand because I find pleasure being with you and look forward to getting to know you better."

"I suppose living together will accomplish that."

He reached for my hand again, and we entered the conservatory hand in hand. I couldn't hide my silly grin.

Thankful I'd brought my camera, I took photos of blue, red and black, and my favorite—orange butterflies. There were small birds and flamingos too. One hundred twenty-eight photos later, we wandered through the gift shop where I eyed a jewelry display and stared at a blue and orange butterfly necklace. I wanted to buy it but didn't need another piece of jewelry.

When we left the conservatory, we strolled down the street toward the ocean. We sat on a bench to watch and listen while children laughed and played along the edge of the water. We then ate at a South Beach café.

After lunch, I dragged Ben past a noisy rooster that roamed the street, and we entered a quaint shop that sold a variety of jewelry, candles, and home décor. Excitement filled my voice. "I love this shop." I slipped over to their jewelry display and found another butterfly necklace. So delicate.

Ben stood on my right. "May I purchase that for you?"

He was being sweet again. "Thank you, but I'm good." I turned toward the door. "Did you want to look around for anything else?"

"Maybe later. I'd like to pick something up for Riley, but not here."

We exited the shop and meandered along the sidewalk past stores and toward our car. From across the street, someone called Ben's name and waved. Ben grasped my hand as the man crossed the road and hurried toward us.

Twenty-seven

Ben introduced me to Matt Shipley, a former member of Hart Fellowship.

He squinted and shook his head. "Your wife?"

While Ben explained Annie's death, I wrapped my elbow around his and squeezed his upper arm. I experienced the anguish of telling someone about a tragic death. Believing your loved one had suffered fear or pain, if only for a moment, stirred the emotions. His voice remained steady until the end of his story when tears puddled his eyes. I rested my head on his shoulder and hoped it brought him comfort.

Matt spoke with kindness and compassion and prayed for Ben. After his prayer, Matt turned his attention to me. "You have been and will continue to be a gift from God for Ben. Your love combined with the Lord's is providing healing for Ben's broken heart." He shook our hands and hurried off to his car, which was parked across the street.

I stared after the man while he pulled out of his parking space. "He seemed nice." I released Ben's arm, and we continued our stroll toward his car. "Do you know him well?"

"He taught classes while he attended the church, and people flocked to him for prayer and encouragement. Speaks life into people's souls. Knows just what to say and do."

"Has he ever spoken life into you?"

"Yes. Just now." Ben stopped and grabbed my hand. "You are a gift from God."

I tilted my head. "Really?"

His eyes crinkled at the corners. "You are who I need, and I'm happy to be here with you."

He was happy with me? We seemed to be getting along better.

We took a few steps down the sidewalk and neared his car. I glanced at the photography shop on my left. "I'd like to go inside."

Ben said he wanted to check on something first, and he'd meet me inside in ten minutes.

I opened the door and waved. "Take your time. If the photos inside are as good as those in the window, I'll be here awhile."

Inside, I sent Jill a text: **I think Ben and I will make this work.**

~

Ben strode down the sidewalk and returned to the gift shop at the butterfly conservatory, where Becca had eyed the first necklace. The perfect gift to give her to confirm how he felt. She was who he needed in his life.

He asked an employee for help and admired the delicate piece of jewelry. What had Matt said? "Becca's love combined with the Lord's . . .?" Becca's love? She couldn't be falling in love with him yet. Could she? That wouldn't be good. To need her was one thing, but he wasn't ready to love her. He couldn't.

When the salesclerk asked him which necklace he was interested in, he hesitated. Would a piece of jewelry say more than he was ready to acknowledge? Their marriage needed to remain an arrangement for as long as possible. He would always love Annie.

He bought the necklace but planned to hide it until his feelings grew. If they grew.

~

On Thursday after breakfast, I wanted to spend time at the cottage on the beach. Of all the places we visited, this was my favorite. Sitting in a lounge chair under an umbrella with the sound of waves splashing along the shore and chatting with Ben. A perfect morning.

"We should go for a swim." Ben leapt from his chair.

I raised my eyebrows. "In the ocean?"

He nodded. "Let's change and jump in."

"Too cold for me. Temps are in the low seventies today. I can't imagine how cold the water must be."

"Then let's put on our shorts and wade along the shore." He grinned.

"You go inside and change. I've got my sunhat, and I'll roll up my pant legs and be fine."

Ben scanned the area. "Are you sure you'll be okay out here alone? I haven't seen the stalker today, but that doesn't mean he's not lurking nearby."

I batted my eyes at him and poured on the southern charm. "Are you playing the part of my protector today, Pastor Peterson?"

He wrinkled his brow. "I want to make sure you're safe." He turned and wandered to the cottage.

I closed my eyes and relished the breeze as it drifted across my face and the joy that bubbled in my heart. Ben and I had crossed over into a meaningful relationship.

"Hey, lovely lady." Hale relaxed in the chair vacated by Ben. "I thought he'd never leave."

I trembled at the sound of his voice. "Excuse me." I rose from my chair without making eye contact. "I left something in the cottage that I need." What I needed was Ben. I didn't want to put another wedge between us. To be seen with Hale would do that. I hurried to the cabin.

Ben stood over my suitcase that I left opened on the sofa where I'd slept the previous night. Disgust laced his voice. "What's this?" He pulled out my orange top and tossed it at me.

I looked at the shirt I'd caught, gazed at Ben, and stammered. "I didn't mean to bring it with me."

He took a step closer, yanked the top from my hands, and waved it in front of my face. His eyes hardened. "Is this what you wore when you lured Hale?"

"Lured Hale?" My heart pounded. I wanted to lash out but needed to keep my composure. "I wore something like I'm wearing now—jeans and a T-shirt." *Lord, please. Not again.* "I must have picked up the orange top with something else by accident when I packed."

"Is he still out there?" He pointed toward the door.

Biting my tongue and willing myself not to get angry, I said, "I came inside as soon as he sat. He just wants to cause trouble."

"I'm not sure I can believe you. You're pretty free with those batting eyes of yours, your hugs, and flirting." He flung my shirt on top of the rest of the clothes in my suitcase. "Pack your stuff. We're checking out."

"But we have another night."

"And I have things to take care of at home."

Was that the truth or did he want to get me away from Hale?

Twenty-eight

What had I done to make Ben consider I had a thing for Hale? I admitted my attraction when I first met the man, but also how wrong I'd been. Why had that put a wedge between Ben and me? I had hoped my honesty would build trust.

I checked the cottage one last time and wandered out to Ben's car with my suitcase. He threw my bag into the trunk.

"Are we stopping soon for lunch?" I opened the passenger door and climbed inside.

Ben lowered himself behind the steering wheel. "That depends on if I can lose your boyfriend. He watched us load the car."

I had enough. I clenched my teeth and twisted toward him. "He. Is. NOT. My. Boyfriend."

Ben backed out, pulled onto US-1, and headed north. "Then why did he watch us?"

"I don't know." I crossed my arms. "Or care."

"Did you give him your address or phone number?"

I shook my head. "Don't you get it? The only man I'm interested in spending time with is you."

"You admitted you were attracted to him."

"For two minutes. I made a mistake. The Lord's

forgiven me." My tone softened. "I hope you will too."

Ben looked out the rearview mirror. "Doesn't appear that he followed us. That's good. But that guy seems to emerge out of nowhere." He glanced at me. "We'll stop for lunch in an hour when we get to Key Largo."

I opened the book I'd brought. The trip home would be as lousy as the one on the way down.

After forty-five or more minutes, Ben smacked the steering wheel and grunted. "All Hale would have to do is spread rumors about being with you. Those rumors could kill my reputation at the church."

He was concerned about the church hearing about this? His concern wasn't for me and how something between Hale and me would affect him? I snapped my book closed and clutched my middle.

"I need to ask you again. What were you wearing the morning you met Hale?"

I widened my eyes and glared at Ben. "I told you. Jeans and a T-shirt."

Did he think I threw myself at the man? I gnawed on my lower lip. "I'm trying to be who God wants me to be and the wife you need, but you're making this more difficult than I expected."

Without another word, he pulled into the parking lot and around the side of a pink restaurant in Key Largo. Pink? I stuck up my nose and ventured inside. Four waitstaff greeted us as if they were happy to see us, and a petite hostess sat us in a booth along the windows. Our server chatted as though we were long-lost friends. The outside didn't impress me, but inside I found warmth and comfort—something I craved.

We both ordered a shrimp basket. When the server

dashed away, Ben picked up his phone, while I delighted in the decor. They'd painted the floor to look like the sea with a turtle swimming near our feet. Glass topped our table and covered old menus, recipes, and postcards. A painted blue sky and white puffy clouds covered the ceiling.

We ate in silence.

When we finished, Ben paid the bill and said he needed to use the restroom. I told him I'd wait for him outside near the car. I exited the restaurant and strolled across the parking lot to the passenger side while I read an email on my phone.

"Are you following me?"

I jumped at the sound of Hale's deep voice and spun to my right. "What are you doing here?" He wore a baseball cap and sunglasses.

"I stopped for lunch like you."

This had gone far enough. I gritted my teeth. "Stop following me. I'm not interested."

"I know you better than that." He smirked. "I'm on my way to Orlando for another art show. I noticed your license plates are Orange County. Visit me." He shoved another business card at me back-side up. He'd written, "Omni. Call for my room number."

I stepped back, raised my palms, and bumped against the car door. "No." His card fell to the ground.

Ben exited the restaurant and loped to my right. Hale jogged to my left and climbed into his vehicle.

When Ben arrived at my side, he picked up the card from the ground. His neck and cheeks reddened. He opened my door. "Get in."

Hale didn't help my case when he backed out near us, beeped, and waved while wearing a huge smile.

I did as Ben asked and got into the car. *Lord, make him believe me.*

Ben stared ahead and pulled out of the parking lot.

"He showed up out of nowhere." My voice wavered. "I didn't encourage him. I never have."

Ben lifted his hand and turned his palm toward me. "Stop. Not a word. I'm angry right now, and I don't want to say or do anything I'll regret."

I twisted toward the passenger window.

We made one stop along the way for gas and arrived home at 6:25 p.m. Ben pulled the suitcases from the trunk and carried them inside. "Help yourself to whatever you want in the fridge or pantry. I'll be in my room and plan to go to bed early."

I spoke in a soft tone. "Would you like me to fix you a sandwich or anything?"

"Not hungry." He picked up the suitcases. "I'll leave yours outside your bedroom door."

"Please talk to me." I followed him up the stairs. "Let me explain again everything that happened."

He stopped at the top of the stairway. "The best thing you can do right now is to leave me alone." He turned to his right and placed my luggage in front of my bedroom door and strode past me to his room on my left.

I spoke to his back. "What will you say to whoever finds out we came home early? We need the same story."

"I'll tell them I had personal business to take care of." His door clicked shut before I could say anything more.

~

Ben sat on the edge of his bed, brought both hands to his face, and cried out to the Lord. "Why did you give me this woman? She's a wild one." He gazed upward.

"What should I do with her?"

Love her.

He shook his head. "I'm not ready for that, Lord. Don't ask that of me."

Silence overtook him. He spent the rest of the evening in his room. He didn't want to take the chance of an encounter with Becca.

Twenty-nine

On Friday morning, I texted Jill, told her we came home a day early, and that I would be available to take her to the airport. She planned to be at the house by noon.

I traipsed down the stairs and into the kitchen for breakfast. No sign of Ben, and his car wasn't in the garage. After I prepared a bowl of cornflakes and milk, I stepped outside onto the covered back patio. Green grass that waved in the breeze met me, along with a cool sixty-five degrees. Back in Pleasant Springs, I would call that warm for this time of year. I found a small blanket on the back of a wicker chair, put it around my shoulders, and finished my cereal.

Back inside the kitchen, I tidied up and unloaded the dishwasher. To help me learn where everything belonged, I opened each cabinet and drawer. One held a calendar with dates marked for garbage pickup, house cleaners, and a landscape company. I canceled the cleaning service because I could take care of that. The person I spoke with told me they came every Friday to clean and expected to be at our house after lunch. I assured them I would take care of everything. Not wanting to run into an alligator, I left the landscaping to the professionals, who were also scheduled for that afternoon.

I completed a thorough cleaning of the kitchen and all three bathrooms before I took a reading break. After thirty-seven pages, the doorbell rang. Jill stood outside. We had little time before she needed to be at the airport. We hurried to a Chinese restaurant for lunch and chatted about her adventures in Florida and my flop of a honeymoon.

When I dropped her off at the airport, she said, "Are you still making plans for an annulment?"

"I doubt I'll need to. Ben may be talking to his lawyer now about a divorce."

~

Ben pulled into the garage and plodded into the kitchen. Becca was gone, but she left everything tidy. He hoped to feel better about their arrangement after he drove across town to his favorite park and went for a jog but doubted any relief would come soon.

He never expected her to be such a flirt, although he should have known. She flirted with him on their first Saturday together at the department store when she'd squeezed his upper arm. And the way she kept looking at her boss that night at the café? She couldn't keep her eyes off him. Ben was sure she attracted Hale with her playful eyes and enticing smile. But was she truthful when she said she hadn't worn the orange top when she met him? One look at that blouse, and Hale would have to be an idiot not to understand her intentions.

Ben found Becca to be a beautiful woman, but he realized the mistake he made to presume she'd be the perfect pastor's wife. Had the Lord really asked him to love her?

~

I returned home after dropping Jill off at the airport and found the landscaping company at work in the front yard. Inside, Ben sat at the desk in his office.

I stood just outside his opened door. "Did you have a good morning?"

He peered at me with dark, puffy eyes and nodded.

I stepped inside and approached his desk. "Have you had lunch? I'll be happy to fix you something."

"I'm fine." He rubbed the back of his neck. "Where are my cleaning people?"

"We don't need them any longer." I took a seat across from him and squirmed. "I called and told them that you'd remarried, and I'll take care of the house now."

"Shouldn't you have discussed that with me?"

He wanted to make cleaning an issue? "What if someone from your cleaning service attends your church? Wouldn't they question why your things were moved to the guest room?" I stood and placed my hands on my hips. "You said you needed me here to take care of things. To be your companion and assist you with everyday activities and such. My canceling the cleaning service shouldn't be a big deal."

I turned away and spoke in a defeated tone. "Forgive me." I darted out the door. I couldn't do anything right. If he'd listen, I would try again to explain what happened. I couldn't care less about Hale. Was this to be my new life? Always criticized? Always making amends—or at least trying?

Ben remained in his office for most of the afternoon, and I finished the cleaning and laundry. That brought added criticism later in the day. He didn't like the idea of me messing with his boxers, and he informed me that I didn't know how to fold socks.

I got a late start on my Swedish meatballs and noodles for dinner because I prayed longer than usual. When our meal was ready, Ben told me he had plans to meet Keith for dinner. He couldn't have told me that ahead of time? And what would he tell Keith about me? That I was a mistake?

Thirty

Saturday morning, I found Ben in the kitchen frying bacon. "That smells great. Do you have enough for me?"

"Sure." He removed the bacon from the skillet and placed it on a paper towel. "I'm fixing French toast too."

I set the table, and we took our seats next to one another. Ben prayed.

"I need to go to the church office for a few hours today, have lunch with one of our elders, and meet Keith for a game of racquetball this afternoon." He poured syrup and passed it to me.

"Is there anything I can do to help you?"

"Yes. Go shopping. Update your wardrobe with modest apparel. I remember nothing unusual about the outfit you wore to church when you visited, but people made comments."

"Comments?"

"Too short, too tight, things like that. I don't need people talking about you behind my back and causing me more trouble." He stared at his plate. "Get new casual clothes too. We should invite the staff over soon to thank them for their generosity. I don't want any of them criticizing your clothing selection, and I don't need you tempting me like . . ."

I tried to stifle my anger but lost. "Like what? Like I did Hale?"

He spoke in a calm tone. "I left you a credit card on the coffee table in the living room." Ben stood and carried his plate to the sink.

I glared at the side of his head. People had nothing better to do than to talk about what I wore to church? And my husband couldn't defend me because he still believed I lured that awful man Hale? My dresses weren't short or tight. Back in Pleasant Springs, no one ever said a word about my clothing being inappropriate. And folks there liked to gossip.

Ben faced me. "I'd appreciate it if you have something ready for me to eat when I get home around 4:30 today. I need to type my mission planning notes for the staff meeting scheduled for Monday morning."

Ben turned back to the sink, rinsed his dish, and put it in the dishwasher. After he dried his hands, he took a notepad he'd left on the counter and said goodbye.

I hurried to my room and got on my knees. *Lord, I can't do this. Not only does Ben not love me, but he hates me. I want to go home. If you want me here, please help me.* I got up from the floor and lumbered outside onto the balcony. *What do you want me to do?*

I sensed the Lord's answer. I scrambled to Ben's office with my laptop and found his mission planning notes in a folder on his desk. When I finished typing, I grabbed a quick sandwich and Ben's credit card. I'd shop and make sure my casual clothes wouldn't entice Ben, and I'd pick out a few new T-shirts for him. But there was nothing wrong with my Sunday church clothing. Nothing at all.

~

Ben arrived home at 4:25 p.m. and was pleased to find reheated Swedish meatballs waiting on him. He washed up and took his seat at the table. Becca was an excellent cook. He'd credit her that much. She appeared sloppy in her new baggy shirt when she brought bread and butter to the table, but she'd be attractive to him no matter what she wore. Perhaps he was harder on her than he needed to be, but with Keith telling him about the gossip surrounding Becca, Ben didn't know what else to do.

"I see you shopped today. What else did you do?"

"I hope you won't be upset when I tell you—"

Ben jumped from his chair. "You saw Hale?"

Becca winced and slumped her shoulders. "I have not and will not go anywhere near that man." She closed her eyes and bowed her head.

Ben returned to his chair and spoke in a soft tone. "Then why will I be upset with you?"

She lifted her face. Her eyes drooped. "I found your mission meeting notes in your office and typed them for you." She sat and looked at her hands. "I assumed your office wasn't off limits to me and that I haven't caused you further grief." She rose from her chair and carried her plate to the sink without eating.

Ben came up behind her. "I jumped to conclusions when I should have allowed you to speak." He thanked her for typing the notes. Something that would have taken him most of the evening. "Since my evening is free, would you like to take a walk with me at Moss Park?"

Becca spun and gazed into his eyes. "You want to spend time with me?"

"We need to get past your indis . . ." There was no need to mention it again. She knew she messed up and caused him anguish.

Becca closed her eyes again and turned her face away. "When will you have faith in me?" She shook her head and bolted up the stairs.

Ben leaned his back against the kitchen counter. Time to ease up on her and allow the Lord to mend their marriage. No matter how difficult their situation, God told Ben to love her. And he would do his best to honor the Lord.

~

I stepped inside my closet, grabbed my suitcase, and tossed it onto my bed. How much was I expected to endure? I tried. Didn't I? God couldn't want me to stay in a marriage where my husband refused to love or trust me.

A knock sounded at my door. "I want to believe you. Let's go for that walk and talk through this."

I stood motionless in front of my luggage. "Give me a minute." I closed my suitcase and returned it to my closet.

Ben waited outside my door. I crossed my arms and headed downstairs. He followed, and we drove to Moss Park. By 5:30 p.m. clouds had moved in, but the temperature was a pleasant seventy degrees, and we had one hour before sunset. We stayed on the pavement and didn't go near the lake.

I glanced at him while we walked side-by-side without holding hands. My heart hurt with the understanding we weren't yoked together in the simplest of ways. "You wanted to talk?"

He grimaced and rubbed his chin. "I can't help but

believe I made a mistake."

My knees weakened. "Do you want an annulment or divorce?"

Ben stopped and faced me. "What? No. That's not at all what I want." His chin quivered. "Do you?"

I shrugged and bit at my lip.

"I want this to work, and it will. God led me to you. He doesn't make mistakes."

"But you said, you did."

"I meant about you and Hale. I may have jumped to conclusions. Unfounded ones. Will you forgive me?"

He touched my cheek, and I liked it a lot. But I needed to guard my heart. Too soon to be optimistic about our relationship after him tormenting me about Hale. Was he sincere or manipulative? "Sure." I jerked away and broke into a jog.

He caught up to me and took my hand. "Your actions don't agree with your response. Talk to me."

I sat on a nearby bench, wrinkled my forehead, and narrowed my eyes. "For the past two days, you've made me feel like a failure. You convicted me of seducing Hale and implied I've tried it with you too. You've accused me of flaunting myself in front of your church and told me how to dress." I raised my shoulders and lifted my palms. "I forgive you, because God's forgiven me plenty, but that doesn't mean everything is good between us now."

He peered into my eyes. "What do you need from me? At this moment?"

"I need you to have faith in me. To . . ." I broke eye contact. I wanted him to love me like he loved Annie. But I needed to accept that may never happen. I shuddered.

He scooted closer to me and wrapped his arm around my shoulder. "I believe you, and if I ever misjudge you again, remind me of this moment. The moment I told you that I trust you, care about you, and want us to be together."

But could I trust him?

Thirty-one

Ben impressed me on our first Sunday morning as a married couple. He complimented me on my outfit, which was like the one I wore when I visited the church four weeks earlier—an A-line skirt and pullover short-sleeve sweater. Would anyone complain again? He spoke in a respectful manner throughout the morning and was attentive to my needs. A fantastic performance, but heartfelt?

Inside the church, Ben introduced me to many couples and families. I greeted each with a handshake, and they showered me with warmth and kindness.

Keith approached with his wife and followed Ben and me into the worship center. "And how are the newlyweds today?" He glanced at me. "Do you remember my wife, Ellie, from the wedding?"

I smiled and extended my hand. "Good to see you again. I hope we can become friends like these two are." I pointed at Ben and Keith.

"That would be nice." She spoke in a bubbly tone. "We should plan a get-together for the pastoral staff now that you're back from your honeymoon."

I nudged Ben's arm. "He mentioned the same thing."

Ben grinned. "Great idea. We'll have it at our place. Does Friday around 6:00 p.m. work for you two?"

He directed his question at Keith and Ellie.

Keith nodded. "With the time change this morning, it will still be daylight. You can cook something on that new grill of yours."

"I'll leave that to Becca. We'll check with the others and confirm with you early this week." Ben took my hand and led me to the front right section for the service.

During the second service, Ben taught a lesson in the educational wing and for the third, we prayed in the chapel for people with needs.

I enjoyed this time of prayer. To lift my voice to God on behalf of others had always held a special place in my heart.

One mom struggled with her adopted daughter. Her precious ten-year-old child harbored anger in her heart for a birth mother she may never meet. Anger she took out on her adoptive mom, whose deep love was seldom enough to help her child.

Love was supposed to be enough. I understood that, too, in my situation. I prayed it would be for this mom and made the same request after she walked away. May my love for Ben be enough.

After church, we ate lunch at a Japanese steak house and discussed our Friday night party. We planned to invite seventeen full- and part-time pastors and their spouses. Ben assured me they wouldn't all attend on such short notice. Thirty people in his living room and dining room would be tight.

I looked forward to planning, preparing the house and food, and playing hostess for the evening. I wished to make Ben proud of me. But could I pull that off?

~

Our week went well with no mention of Hale. Ben appeared relaxed and content. He spent time with me outside one evening while we chatted on the patio and inside later in the week when we watched a movie together.

Friday, I spent the morning making sure everything sparkled and the afternoon preparing two large casserole dishes filled with lasagna. Enough to feed the eighteen people who confirmed. We also planned to serve salad and garlic toast. Two couples volunteered to bring dessert, for which I was grateful. Although everything seemed in place and I felt well prepared, I experienced a tinge of nervousness. What if they didn't like me or thought I wasn't good enough to be Ben's wife?

I forgot to ask Ben if he'd confided in Keith. Did his best friend know that Ben's marriage was an arrangement?

Ben showered me with praise on how great the house looked when he came home early that afternoon to help me before guests arrived at 6:00 p.m. We sat at the kitchen table across from one another and sipped our coffee.

"Good Friday service is two weeks from today. Pastor Young asked the staff members if their spouses could read six or seven verses from the Easter story during the service. I told him that you will be happy to help."

My jaw dropped. "Why didn't you ask me first?"

Ben spoke in his melodious voice. "One service in the middle of the afternoon. Not that many people attend since most are at work. You'll do fine."

My hands shook. "Yes. I'll do fine because I won't

be there." I turned away from him.

He moved in front of me, laid his hand on my shoulder, and gave a gentle squeeze. "They keep the lights low during the reading except for a lamp shining on the Bible. You won't see anyone in the congregation."

I crossed my arms and pouted. "You don't understand what you're asking of me."

He took a seat next to me and reached for my hand. "Explain it to me. Why are you afraid?"

I pulled my hand away and looked down at my lap. "I was a straight-A student through my junior year of high school. I hadn't given a speech before and didn't want to. When I heard I would graduate in the top one percent of my class, I panicked." I took a deep breath and exhaled. "What if I were the valedictorian or salutatorian? They'd make me give a speech. I had to make sure that didn't happen. I made two B's my first semester of senior year."

"You did that on purpose?"

"I tried for three classes but ended with an A in one of them. I graduated third in my class, relieved I wouldn't have to speak. But then they told me to have something ready in case neither of the first two could make it." I bit my lip. "I prepared a brief speech but felt confident the other two students wouldn't pass on the opportunity. They were both on the debate team and loved an audience. One of them performed in all the school plays." I tugged at the hem of my top.

Ben scooted his chair closer and drew his eyebrows together. "Did you get called upon to speak?"

"The valedictorian got sick that morning and the salutatorian got caught in traffic—an accident blocked the main road into town, and she couldn't get to the school in time."

Concern edged Ben's voice. "What happened?"

"I stepped to the microphone, opened my mouth, and nothing came out." My throat tightened. "I forgot my notes at home. Since I couldn't remember my opening line, I said something lame, and students snickered and booed. I returned to my seat thankful I wouldn't have to face those people again." I dabbed at my eyes.

Ben leaned close. His lips brushed my cheek, and reassurance enveloped me. "This could be good for you and help you get over your fear. Just read—no ad lib or speech necessary. You can do this."

I focused on his eyes. "But what if something terrible happens?"

He took my hands and held them in a firm grip. "I'll rescue you."

"Only this once. Next time, ask me."

He pulled me into his arms and held me close. Worry lifted when I nuzzled my head into his neck.

Ben chuckled. "You smell like garlic. Were you planning to shower before our guests arrive?"

"Considering your comment, that might be a good idea." I squirmed out of his arms and headed toward the stairway. "Can you monitor the lasagna in the oven?"

He nodded. "And can you use that flowery scented shampoo you used in the Keys?"

I'm sure I blushed. I wasn't aware that he'd noticed my shampoo.

Thirty-two

With finishing touches made around the house, and to my hair and makeup, we were ready to greet our guests. Pastor Young and his wife, Liz, arrived first with Keith and Ellie Morgan.

I stood at Ben's side and welcomed each guest. I took the apple strudel from Ellie and peered back and forth between the two women. "The resemblance is amazing."

Ellie laughed. "Yes, but Mom isn't eight months pregnant."

I smiled and led our guests to the living room and offered them sweet tea or a soda while Ben remained near the front door. After serving their drinks, I returned to Ben's side. Over the next ten minutes, we greeted other pastors and their spouses including Pastor Vince and Worship Pastor, Lindsey Lewis, who brought an Italian cream cake that looked delicious.

Ben led everyone into the kitchen, where we had set up a buffet. Four guests ate there, eight in the dining room, and the rest in the living room at a folding table Ben borrowed from the church. Everyone enjoyed the meal amid conversation and laughter.

Several helped with cleanup, and we moved to the

living room at 7:30 for a time of group fellowship, or should I say, interrogate Becca time.

"Where did you grow up? Is your accent real? Is a toboggan a hat or a sled?"

And there were questions about how Ben and I met and where we visited while in Key West.

We opted to wait on dessert because we'd stuffed ourselves with lasagna. After a lull in conversation, I slipped into the kitchen to slice the apple strudel and Italian cream cake.

Ben followed. "Let me help."

"Sweet. But you have guests to tend to. I'm going to slice the strudel and cake and place them on dessert plates. When I have them all ready, I'll let you know, and everyone can come in here and select what they want."

"I'll start the coffee and head back to the living room."

"Great idea."

I worked at the counter near the sink that overlooked the side yard and filled over half of the plates by the time Ben finished the coffee and set out cups. Three minutes after he returned to our guests, I dropped a piece of strudel on the floor. I found an old towel to clean the sticky mess and took the towel to the laundry room. While I rinsed the towel in the utility sink, someone approached from behind. I thought it was Ben. When I peeked over my shoulder, Keith hovered nearby. Too close for me.

"Need any help?"

I side-stepped to the right, with my back to him, to allow extra space between us and to get closer to the door. "I'm good. Everything's ready."

He moved with me, placed his hand on my shoulder,

and spoke in a whisper near my ear. "Where would you like me to set the desserts? The table in the dining room?"

I shivered. What was he doing? I turned to face him and swallowed hard.

His smile grew wider, and his intense stare unnerved me.

I glanced toward the door to the kitchen and hoped Ben would return. "Step back."

"You don't mean that. I've known all evening you wanted to be alone with me."

Not again. First Hale, now Keith? "You're mistaken." I tossed the wet towel at his head.

He blocked the towel from hitting him, grabbed it, and stepped into the doorway to prevent my exit. "Feisty—my type of woman." He pointed through the kitchen to the back door that led to the patio. "I'll go out back. While everyone's eating their dessert, they won't miss us. Come outside where I'll be waiting for you." He stared at my lips. "We can talk about us."

My heart raced. I wanted to slap him, but I took two calming breaths and softened my voice. "Take the wet towel with you and wipe the patio table." I wanted him to think I would join him without committing to do so.

He smirked, strode through the kitchen, and exited through the back door. I counted to ten to calm myself, zipped over to the door, and locked it before I found Ben. How could I tell him that his best friend hit on me? I groaned. I couldn't. Our relationship wasn't strong enough for him to believe me.

Ben stood in the living room chatting with guests when I entered. He excused himself and strolled over to me. "Is everything ready?"

I tried to calm my shaking body. "Yes, but I'm not feeling well. I'm going upstairs. Tell everyone goodbye for me."

He cocked his head and shrugged. "All the planning and activity today?" He caressed my arm. "Get your rest."

I'd taken three steps up the stairs when the front doorbell rang. By the time I made it to the top, Keith said, "I got locked out when I went out back to see Ben's new grill."

Yeah. Right.

I closed my bedroom door behind me and climbed onto my bed. Why would Keith do such a thing? A pastor? Ben's best friend? I could only come up with one reason. Ben put him up to it to find out if I'd take the bait. Ben assumed I was a flirt and disloyal—a poor choice in a wife. Well, good. He found out that I'm not any of those things. But I found out that I couldn't trust Keith or Ben.

Thirty-three

Ben sat at the kitchen table Saturday morning with his coffee and checked the weather app on his phone. He glanced up when Becca padded into the kitchen. "Feeling better?"

She gazed around the room and mumbled her response, but he couldn't make it out.

"What?"

"Sure."

He stood and strode to the stove where she'd placed a skillet. "Are you okay?"

"Fine." She opened the refrigerator and pulled out eggs and bacon. "You want eggs or French toast?"

He twisted her toward him. "I want you to tell me what's bothering you? Sick? Upset?" He smiled. "Everything went well last night. Everyone had fun and raved about your lasagna." He lifted her chin. "They missed you when you left."

She didn't make eye contact and sounded grumpy. "Yeah, well. Can't be chipper and carefree every day." She jerked away from him and added bacon to the frying pan. "I have things to do like clean this kitchen and rearrange furniture in the living room."

"I'll help with that." He laid his hand on her

shoulder.

She flinched. Why would she do that? She often welcomed his touch.

Ben spoke in a gentle tone. "Did something happen last night that I don't know about?" He sighed. "Someone hurt your feelings?"

"I told you that I'm fine." She lowered a pie plate from the cabinet and cracked eggs for French toast. "I hope this is okay with you because it's what I want."

Ben retreated to the living room to give Becca space. She didn't appear to be ill and planned to eat a full breakfast. But she didn't want to talk about whatever bothered her. Someone must have said something she didn't like. Was that why she said she didn't feel well? She was fine when he made the coffee the night before. Who did she talk to after that?

~

Happy that Ben left me alone in the kitchen, I didn't want to see or talk to him. When I supposed things had gotten better between us, he turned on me again. Why did he tell Keith about Hale? No one's business except ours. And it was nothing. I hadn't heard anything further from the man and I was grateful.

I sent Ben a text: **Breakfast is ready**.

When he didn't respond, I trudged toward his office but found him in the living room resting on the sofa and told him it was time to eat.

He followed me into the kitchen, and we took our seats at the table across from one another.

I poured syrup on my French toast and took my first bite. My breakfast tasted terrible.

Ben cleared his throat.

"What?" I peered at him.

"We haven't prayed. May I ask the blessing?"

I folded my hands in my lap. "Sure."

Ben offered a prayer of thanksgiving for our meal and asked the Lord to help me with whatever bothered me. Like he didn't know.

When he finished, I rose from my chair, snatched my plate, and dumped the contents into the garbage disposal. After I loaded my dishes into the dishwasher, I turned to Ben, who watched me with wide eyes. "I'll be gone most of the day."

He stood, squished his eyebrows together, and ambled toward me. "Where are you going? I didn't know you made plans."

I raised my head high. "Not sure yet. Shopping, the park, a beach, Disney World?"

He placed his hands on my upper arms. "Please talk to me. What happened?"

I shook my head. He should be an actor. An award-winning performance. I ran from the kitchen to the stairs and stumbled on the third step. I picked myself up, climbed the remaining ones, and found solace in my room.

Until Ben rapped on my door. "I'd like to go with you."

He must have talked to Keith and learned I didn't take the bait. I guess that makes me worthy to spend time with him.

I opened the door and spoke in anger. "What if I go to the airport instead? Do you want to fly back to Pleasant Springs with me?"

He lifted his hands and took a step backward. "I'm certain now that I upset you. What did I do?"

"You and your best friend are quite the team. Who

came up with that crazy idea? You? Keith?"

Ben looked to his left and right. "I, uh, I don't know what you're talking about." He moved closer and reached out to touch me.

I backed away. Maybe Ben hadn't put Keith up to his shenanigans the night before.

Ben gazed into my eyes. "Whatever Keith did or said, it's because he's protective of me. Thinks you and I married too soon. He feels he needs to look out for my best interests."

I relaxed and released a long breath. Keith was not looking out for Ben's best interests, but Ben would never believe me if I told him what his best friend had done.

Ben reached out again to touch me. "So, what's your pleasure? Shopping, park, beach, Disney, or Pleasant Springs as long as we can get back for church tomorrow morning?"

I stared at my feet. "The beach will be great."

"Let's head out. You can tell me all about Keith and what he said that upset you."

Thirty-four

Before we left, I called Jill, but she didn't answer. I left a voicemail. "Checking in to find out how you're doing and to tell you about our party last night. Call when you get a chance."

Ben drove northeast. He told me I'd like Ponce Inlet, which was an hour and fifteen minutes away from our home. We'd walk along the beach, take in a panoramic view of the water from the tallest lighthouse in Florida, and eat lunch at a local seafood restaurant.

We'd driven thirty or more minutes when Ben said, "Do you want to talk about what's bothering you regarding Keith?"

"I'm good. I prayed before we left the house and let it go." He'd never believe me, and Keith wouldn't tell Ben anything about what happened. Better to forget it.

"But earlier you were upset with me too." He cut me a quick look. "I'm a good listener."

"Does he know about our arrangement?"

Ben jerked his head back. "No way. Other than you and me, only Jill knows."

"Did you mention anything personal from our honeymoon?"

He shook his head. "Personal? No. I told him about

our cottage and things we did in Key West. The same things we shared with everyone at the party last night."

"Nothing about Hale?"

Ben reached over and took my hand. "Time we let that go too." He squeezed my fingers. "Keith knows nothing about Hale."

"Then all is well." And bringing up what happened would raise questions in Ben's mind. What had I done to encourage Keith's advances? I didn't want to go there. I kept racking my brain trying to figure that out, and I did nothing. "Is he okay you won't be playing racquetball today?"

"I texted him. He's good."

When we arrived at the inlet, I slipped off my shoes and ran to the shore. The temperature hovered in the low seventies and a soft breeze blew across my face.

Ben called after me before I got to the water's edge. "This isn't a good place to wade."

I turned back and waved. "But that's what I love about the beach. I won't be long."

Ben hurried toward me. I spun around to the water, expecting it to be cooler than the Keys but screeched and jumped out when chilly water lapped against my ankles.

"I told you." He shook his head. "But in addition to the cold-water temperatures, this area is known for its shark attacks."

I pursed my lips. "Then why didn't you tell me that before we got here?" I kicked sand on his shoes.

He grinned and suggested we visit the lighthouse. "Are you ready for a climbing adventure?"

"How tall is it?"

"Not sure, but there's over two hundred steps. Are you up for it?"

I batted my hand in front of my face. "That's nothing. Remember the trip Michael and I took with you and Annie to Cloudland Canyon in North Georgia all those years ago?"

"All those steps? There must have been 10,000."

I chuckled and punched his arm. "More like 600." I stared out over the water while gentle waves caressed the shore. "We had a wonderful time. Beautiful scenery and waterfalls." I peered into his eyes. "Can we do it again sometime? When we're visiting friends and family in Tennessee?"

He touched my upper arm. "That's a great idea. We made wonderful memories that day."

"As I remember, you and Annie preached to us the entire time." I grabbed ahold of his arm to steady myself and slipped on my shoes.

"What? We didn't preach—we instructed the two of you on living out a godly marriage. You'd just gotten engaged."

"Your insights were invaluable. Michael and I followed your advice often during our marriage."

"Like what?"

"Praying together about everything. Putting the other person first. Sharing feelings with one another and showing Christ's love."

Ben wrinkled his nose. After he opened and closed his mouth, he gazed at me. "I'm not doing that, am I? We aren't praying together. I share little with you and put my needs high above yours." He pulled me into his embrace. "That will change." He released me, and his eyes crinkled at the corners.

I searched his face. "You're here with me now. Accompanied me to the beach. You put my needs before yours today. I feel blessed."

Ben took my hand. "Let's visit the lighthouse."

At the top, and after I caught my breath, I beheld a spectacular view. To the east, the ocean spread as far as I could see. Ben pointed to my right toward the marina and the restaurant where we'd eat lunch. We circled around to the west side of the lighthouse and looked across the intercoastal waterway, and to the north we spotted residential areas, restaurants, and a golf course. All breathtaking.

When we finished at the lighthouse, we walked across the road for lunch. Ben ordered the fried grouper, and I enjoyed the crab cakes. After we stuffed ourselves, we drove up I-95 to a large outlet mall where we window shopped, bought sunglasses, and devoured ice cream cones. We added memories that day. Personal memories of our own as newlyweds.

~

On Sunday morning at church, Keith's wife, Ellie, stood in the hallway, and we walked past her to get to the class Ben teaches during the second service. I was sure I'd caught her eye. I smiled and waved. She lifted her chin and turned her back on me. I glanced at Ben to see if he noticed, but he appeared oblivious to the scene.

Why would she treat me with disgust? She acted friendly at the party.

After the last service, Ben and I strolled out to our car.

He opened my door and said, "You and Ellie got along well at the party, so I invited her and Keith to join us for lunch. But they both acted odd and said they had other plans."

I told Ben what happened earlier with Ellie.

"I'll talk to Keith Tuesday. Perhaps he'll tell me what's going on with her."

And maybe Ben would learn what's going on with Keith and why he hit on me. I shuddered. I doubted Keith would ever confess to that.

Thirty-five

Ben arrived at the church on time Tuesday morning. His earlier jog readied him for the week's activities. He listened to his voicemail messages, read his email, and planned out his day. His thoughts fixated on Becca and the fulfilling weekend they'd shared, as well as their day spent together on Monday. He got her to reveal her heart's desires in ministry.

She blessed him when she shared how she looked forward to accompanying him on his upcoming mission trips. He'd scheduled informational classes and trainings and expected a rewarding return to the mission field after a two-year hiatus while his heart healed.

One item on his agenda was to find out what happened Friday night between Keith and Becca. She seemed to have let it go as she said, but Ben needed Keith to go easy on her and not upset her. They had enough problems without Keith's interference.

He picked up his phone and sent a text: **Are you available to talk?**

Headed your way.

Keith closed the door and sat across from Ben's desk. "Hey, man. What's up?"

Ben leaned back in his chair. "Everything okay with

you and Ellie?"

Keith chuckled and ran his hand through his hair. "Sure. Why do you ask?"

"According to Becca, Ellie acted upset Sunday at church."

Keith peered into the corner of Ben's office. "I didn't notice."

Ben nodded. "What happened Friday night between you and Becca? Did you give her a lecture on how she better not break my heart, or did you ask her loads of personal questions?"

"What?" He narrowed his eyes at Ben. "Is that what she said happened?"

Ben cocked his head to the left. "She said nothing except you upset her."

Keith stood and raised his hand. "Man, if I upset her, it's because I wouldn't play her game."

Ben rose from his chair. His heart pounded. "What game?"

"I didn't plan to tell you. You've been through enough." He looked behind him and moved closer to the desk. "I went into the kitchen to find out if I could help with desserts—you know, cut up the apple strudel we brought." He lowered his voice. "Becca made a pass at me. She rubbed my shoulders, whispered intimate things into my ear, and said she wanted us to spend time alone together."

Ben stepped back and clenched his fists at his sides. "Are you serious? Are you sure?" Ben shook his head. "You must have misunderstood her."

"Man, I wish I had. But I don't want to get near her again. Ellie's distraught. She wants nothing to do with your wife, and I can't blame her." He spun toward the door and rested his hand on the doorknob. "This is between you and me. No one else needs to know."

Ben returned to his chair and placed his head in his hands. *What now, Lord? Keith confirmed my wife is worse than I thought.*

~

I slipped out onto the back patio and gazed across the yard. My favorite tree stood twenty to twenty-five feet tall. Purple blooms graced our orchid tree. I sat on the wicker bench and thanked the Lord for a wonderful weekend with Ben. We connected, and I found satisfaction and encouragement in that.

The patio door opened behind me. I jerked and brought my hand to my chest. "You startled me. Is it lunchtime already?" I peeked at my watch: 11:15. Early for lunch. I took another glance at Ben.

His eyes bulged. "Get inside."

I leaped from the bench and stared at him with my mouth opened. "What's wrong? What happened?" My chin quivered. "Are you angry with me?"

"Now." He turned and marched into the kitchen.

I followed him and positioned myself across from him with the kitchen table between us.

Ben glared at me, placed both palms on the table, and bent toward me. "Did you assume he wouldn't tell me?"

I calmed my racing heart with two deep breaths and spoke in a soft tone. "Who are we talking about?"

He pretended to laugh. "Don't play games with me."

Keith wouldn't confess to hitting on me, so I didn't know what Ben meant. I straightened and backed toward the stove. "When you're calm, we'll talk." I darted through the kitchen and upstairs to my room. I locked the door and checked it twice.

In the middle of my recitation of Psalm 23, there was a loud knock. I jumped.

Ben jiggled the handle. Sounded as though he spoke through clenched teeth. "I'm as calm as I can be. Open. The. Door."

I placed my hand on the doorknob but didn't open it. "I can't do that right now. Tell me what the problem is."

"How could you humiliate me and my reputation as a pastor by inviting Keith to an intimate rendezvous?"

I yanked on the door. "Rats." I tried to unlock it but kicked it instead when my hands couldn't get it opened as fast as I wanted. Finally. I jerked it opened.

"A what?"

Ben fell against me, and the two of us stumbled. He caught me in his arms and asked if I was okay.

"Do you care?"

He released me and rubbed the back of his neck. "I'm disappointed in you, but I would never hurt you." He leaned against the doorframe. "But how could you do this to me? To us? Just when I trusted you again."

"I'm innocent. What you described never happened." I didn't expect him to believe me over Keith. But it broke my heart that I frustrated him again and that he accepted Keith's story of what happened instead of coming to my defense. I'm sure he would have defended Annie if someone had accused her of wrongdoing.

"So, you're saying Keith lied to me?"

"One of us has. You'll need to decide who."

"We had a problem with this on our honeymoon, didn't we?"

"I love you, Ben Peterson. I am not out to get you.

There's nothing more important to me right now than being the wife you need me to be." I sniffled and wiped my cheek. "A wife you'll describe one day in terms of love and admiration as you do Annie."

"You have an odd way of showing your love for me by throwing yourself at my best friend."

"I answer to God. He's called me to be your wife. I won't do anything to hurt or destroy you." I walked over to my dresser, snatched my purse, and zipped past him into the hallway. "It's time you ask God who your loyal friends are. You're believing the wrong one." I descended the stairs.

He hollered down the stairway. "Tell me your side of the story."

I turned at the bottom of the steps and looked up. "Why bother? You won't believe me."

Thirty-six

I climbed into my car and took off. I traveled south on 417, one of the few roads I remembered. I spotted signs stating North to Wildwood and South to Miami. I didn't know how far away Wildwood was but decided to drive until I was ready to stop. I hopped onto the Florida turnpike and drove north. I exited near Lake Apopka and found a fast-food place for lunch. While there, I checked my phone to locate a park I could visit in the area. Afterward, I used my GPS and drove farther north until I came to Trimble Park. I climbed out of my car and noticed a sign near the lake.

"NOTICE—Alligators and snakes are common in this area. They can be dangerous and should not be approached, frightened or fed. Please give them the respect they deserve. KEEP YOUR DISTANCE."

I peered back at my car. Did I need to be here? I took a deep breath, straightened my shoulders, and strolled a dirt path that led to a boardwalk on my left. Appeared to be my kind of trail. No tree roots or rocks to climb over. Easy. A good time to meditate on the Lord and ask for His help.

I prayed and walked. I admired the jungle-like atmosphere as the swampy area below the boardwalk turned green. Within moments, eighty-one degrees felt chilly. I checked behind me and in front of me on the trail and shivered. My heart rate shot up. Was someone watching me? I completed a full circle and scanned my surroundings. When I looked down, a pair of eyes in the green, plant-covered water stared at me.

A frog? Must have been a frog. I prayed, "Please be a frog."

I took a step closer to the railing and raised my hand to cover my mouth before my scream escaped. No frog had that long of a body. If I had made a sound, I could have frightened the huge gator. What would happen then? He must have been at least six feet long. My head told me to turn back and run as fast as I could, but my legs felt like mush.

What had Ben told me to do if I came across an alligator?

Without considering why I drove to the park and how upset Ben was with me, I texted him: **What should I do if I'm face-to-face with a gator?**

I backed away from the creature and kept my eyes on his. Thump. I screamed and turned. My ankle twisted and I lost my footing. An elderly couple grabbed my arms.

"Steady now. I've got you." The man chuckled. "What's got you spooked, young lady?"

"A huge gator." I pointed to the left. "Over there in the water."

The woman released me and lifted the camera from her neck. "Great. This setting makes a perfect picture."

The couple dashed over to the railing, and the woman snapped photos. "Oh, a baby. How sweet."

"A baby?" Were they crazy? I tried to get away, and

that couple got as close as possible.

"Only three feet long." The man waved me toward him. "Come, look."

I trembled and waved goodbye. Hopefully, that would be the last gator I encountered. Thankful my ankle didn't hurt, I bolted back to the parking lot where a white ibis and a great blue heron waded along the edge of the lake. After I calmed myself, I took a few pictures of the birds. When I glanced farther out into the water, two gators swam toward the shore. That was not the park for me.

I climbed into my car, peeked at my phone, and read Ben's text: Are you okay?

Fine. A couple came to my rescue.

Where are you?

Trimble Park.

Mount Dora? You're an hour away.

Leaving now.

Working late. Home by 7:00. I'll grab something to eat.

I put Ben's home address into my GPS to find my way back, thankful I wouldn't have to see him until later that evening.

Jill called on my drive home and apologized for not getting back with me sooner. I told her about my meeting with the gator and asked her about her part-time job with Doc Winston. She giggled like a schoolgirl when she talked about him. She still had faith that the plan might work for her to get to know him better.

I shared about the party, what Keith had done, and what he told Ben.

"Ben knew the truth and stuck up for you, didn't he?"

"I haven't told him what happened. We're talking

best friends." I exited the turnpike. "But I didn't expect Keith to fabricate a lie."

"You should have told Ben as soon as possible."

"You don't get it." I huffed. "If you told me that Ben made a pass at you, even if he told me that you flirted with him, I'd accept what you said. You're my bestie. I can depend upon you to tell me the truth."

"He needs to hear your side of what happened and then let him decide. Your silence may be mistaken for guilt."

"I'll think about it." I drove into a grocery store parking lot. "We'll talk later. I've got to go."

We disconnected our call. Would telling Ben the truth change anything?

~

Ben pulled into the garage and bowed his head. He needed guidance and wisdom. How could their marriage work? He couldn't trust Becca. He considered putting a tracking device on her car, but he shouldn't have to do that. She pursued Keith in their own home. How could he track that?

"Lord, what do you want me to do? Should I send her back to Pleasant Springs?"

Love her.

"Not again. I doubt that's possible, and not only because of Annie. Help me."

Ben strode through the back door and entered the kitchen. He stopped and checked the day's mail that Becca left for him on the counter. When he got upstairs, he paused at her door to check on her outing at Trimble Park.

She sang a worship song. No music—only Becca's voice as she lifted praises to God. Heartfelt praises full of love and adoration. He shook his head. How could that be after what she did?

Love her.

He moseyed down the hallway and went into his room.

Thirty-seven

When I entered the kitchen Wednesday morning, Ben's hand rested on the doorknob leading to the laundry room. "Heading out early this morning?"

He nodded. "I made your coffee."

I thanked him and asked if he'd be home for dinner.

"Not sure." He opened the door and turned back. "I wrote your verse numbers to read for the Good Friday service and left them on the table. Everyone will read from John 19. You'll be the third reader. Four others will read after you. If you read your verses each day for practice, they should be a breeze to read on Good Friday."

My throat tightened. I didn't want to read in front of anyone but arguing wouldn't have been in my best interest considering the strain on our relationship.

I pulled a bowl out of the cabinet and filled it with bran flakes. After adding sliced banana and milk, I sat at the table, prayed, and forced down my cereal. Ben hadn't bothered to ask me about the alligator encounter. He might have wished. . . that wasn't fair. I doubt he'd wish harm upon me. But would he care if I packed my bags and went home?

I picked up the notecard. Verses seventeen to

twenty-two from the English Standard Version. I opened my Bible app and read aloud my six verses. Didn't seem difficult. And they would dim the lights. I could do this with God's help.

Returning to my room, I opened my New International Version of the Bible and reread Psalm 59:16, a verse I'd read the evening before. "But I will sing of your strength, in the morning I will sing of your love; for you are my fortress, my refuge in times of trouble." Time to sing again.

~

I read my verses for the Good Friday service twice each day over the next week and felt confident I knew them well enough.

But those days were hard. No reprieve from Ben. We spoke to one another as little as possible. He'd missed several meals, so I stopped cooking. I pulled out my suitcase to pack my belongings twice and called Jill to tell her that I'd had enough. But when she asked me if God had released me from my commitment to love and honor my husband, I had to say no.

On Thursday, the day before the Good Friday service, I planned to prepare a new recipe—one that Annie had told me Ben loved. I sent him a text after I finished my lunch: **Home for dinner? I'd like to try something new.**

Expect me at 6:00.

Breakthrough? I hoped so.

~

Ben shut down his computer. He should have contacted Becca and told her that he wouldn't be home for dinner. Even if she didn't respect him, he should at least care enough to keep her abreast of his plans. He sent her a text: Leaving now. I'll grab something to eat.

Whatever. Leftover Chicken a la King in the fridge.

Becca had prepared one of his favorite meals while he putzed around the office for no reason. No reason except he didn't want to be with her or talk to her after what she'd done.

He strode down the hallway and stuck his head into Keith's office, who had also worked late. Keith chatted on his phone with his back to Ben. He didn't interrupt, but when he turned to leave, Keith said, "You're sure it looks real?"

Ben shook his head. What was Keith up to? Buying Ellie a fake piece of jewelry but wanted her to assume it was the real thing? Sounded like Keith.

~

On Friday morning, I found Ben sitting at the kitchen table with a cup of coffee after his jog. "You're still here? I've seen little of you for the past week. Glad to see you're still alive."

"About that." He peered at me, expressionless. "I should have been more thoughtful. I'll be home on time tonight. Perhaps earlier than normal with this being Good Friday."

I poured myself a cup of coffee and sat across from him. "We should talk to one another. The silence is getting to me."

"Great. Tell me your side of what happened with Keith."

I bowed my head. "You won't believe me."

"Try me."

"He's your best friend." I lifted my head. "I understand why you're loyal to him."

"But all you've told me is that you didn't do what

he's accused you of doing. So, what happened?"

About halfway through my story, Ben jumped out of his chair and glared at me.

"That's ridiculous. Keith would never do that."

I rose and narrowed my eyes. "But I would?" I headed toward the stairs and whirled back around. "Three weeks ago, you said if you ever misjudged me, remind you of the moment you said you trusted me, cared about me, and wanted us to be together." I took two deep breaths to calm my racing heart. "This is your reminder." I retreated to my room. I needed to prepare for the Good Friday service at noon.

After I cried out again to the Lord about our situation, I read my verses three times. I fixed my hair and makeup and ventured downstairs to the kitchen at 10:30. I popped a slice of bread into the toaster and poured a glass of orange juice. When I stepped outside on the patio with my toast and jelly in hand, something to the right side of the yard caught my eye. Something long, dark, bumpy, and . . . I screeched and dropped my food.

A gator? In our yard?

My phone pinged in my pocket. A text from Ben: Don't forget service. Be here by 11:30. Begins at noon. Ends at 1:00 p.m.

I peeked at my watch: 10:40. I needed to leave in thirty-five minutes. But what about that gator? I scrambled to pick up the toast I'd dropped. Food might entice him—I didn't want him on my patio. I darted inside and snatched a handful of paper towels. When I came back outside, the gator hadn't moved. I hoped he was dead. I made sure the area was clean, sped inside, and locked the back door. Time to call Ben.

He answered on the fifth ring. "You can't back out on me now."

"What kind of greeting is that?"

"I'm getting to know you. You'll find a way to get out of reading at this service."

I hesitated to tell him about the alligator, because he'd assume I made it up so I couldn't get to the church on time. But I forged ahead. "What happens if someone spots a gator in their yard? Who do they call to get rid of it?"

"There's a gator in our yard?"

"Out back. He's huge. Sunning himself."

"Are you making this up?"

"Hold on. He hasn't moved." *Please, Lord, don't let him move while I'm out there.* "I'll go back out on the patio and take his picture." My hands shook when I unlocked the back door and stepped outside. "They're slow movers, aren't they?" My phone slipped from my clammy hands. I caught it before it hit the pavement. I snapped a picture, hurried back inside, and texted it to Ben.

"He is big. But how did he get in the backyard? That's impossible."

I sounded frantic. "Who do I call?"

"The Nuisance Alligator Hotline. Give me a minute, I'll find the number."

He gave me the number and told me to give them our address and tell them where in the yard they could find the gator. "And get here on time. The trapper will take care of everything there."

I made the call and answered ridiculous questions: "How large is the gator?" Why was that even important?

"Do you feel threatened by the gator?"

"Of course, I feel threatened. There's an alligator in my yard."

They said they'd be out within two hours and would take care of him.

I zipped upstairs, changed into a cream-colored short sleeve top with a cranberry midi-length skirt, and drove to the church with two minutes to spare. Ben met me in the hallway near the offices.

I jabbered for a couple of minutes.

He placed his hand on my arm. "Take a deep breath and exhale."

I did as he said.

"We have a last-minute change. Keith informed me that everyone will read from the New International Version."

I whimpered and opened my eyes wide.

"Another deep breath. You'll do fine." He led me down the hallway to a room behind the stage where other staff spouses gathered and said he'd save me a seat in the worship center. I'd met four of the spouses at our party. Three welcomed me, two stood off to the side reading their verses aloud, and Ellie ignored me. I understood why. I took a seat on a sofa and reviewed the updated version from my Bible app.

Pastor Vince entered the room and greeted us. "The worship team will start the service. When they've sung three songs, we'll move into the scripture reading. After the second, fourth, and sixth readings, there will be a solo, and after the others, Pastor Young will speak. I'll direct everyone onto the stage. Questions?"

We exited the room and waited behind a stage curtain for our turn. During the third worship song, Pastor Vince approached me. "Two minutes and you're up."

"Oh, no. I'm not first. I'm third."

"Not according to my sheet. You're down for verses one through eleven. Let's go." He led me to the stage curtain.

Eleven verses instead of six? The first person instead of the third? How did this get mixed up? I sent Ben a quick text to let him know of the change and peeked through the curtain. The lights dimmed. I took a deep breath but couldn't move. Pastor Vince nudged me through the curtain and out onto the stage where a lamp shone on the Bible opened to John 19.

I shuffled to the microphone. My mouth went dry, and I swallowed hard. "Then Pilate took Jesus and had him flogged. The soldiers twisted . . ." The lights in the worship center lit up. People. Lots of people. I glanced at the Bible. "Together a, um . . ." My knees shook more than when I'd come face-to-face with the gator at the park earlier in the week. *Please, don't let me faint.*

A warm arm enveloped my shoulder. Ben whispered into the microphone, his eyes locking onto mine. "Did you forget your glasses this morning?" He smiled—a warm, endearing smile. "Let me help you." He finished the rest of my reading and led me off the stage to a chair in the hallway. He asked me to wait for him and rushed away. Ben rescued me like he promised.

Within minutes, my phone vibrated. The caller identified himself as Jason Eberhardt, the trapper from the alligator hotline. "Ma'am, I left your gator on the back patio."

"What?" I jumped up. "I don't want that beast on my patio."

"Ma'am. I don't carry rubber toys off the premises.

Next time, make sure it's alive before you call us. You may have kept me from an actual threat." He hung up.

A rubber toy? Who would do that? Who would leave a rubber alligator in our yard? Ben? Did he think this was funny?

My legs wobbled. I needed to get home. If Ben planted the gator in our yard, I didn't want to cause a scene at the church when I confronted him about it. I plodded outside to my car. What a day. Could it get any worse?

Thirty-eight

A rubber alligator lay on the back patio. I wouldn't touch it. I'm sure Ben thought this was funny. Get me upset and hope I'll leave? He could tell everyone that I hated Orlando and left him for Pleasant Springs.

I plopped onto a kitchen chair and rested my head on the table. "Why is this happening, Lord? Give me strength. Tell me how to fix my marriage."

Love him.

"I do love him, and told him I did, but it didn't faze him." I stood and opened the refrigerator.

Nothing appealed to me. "Forget it. I'm not hungry." I trudged up the stairs to my room and leaned against the balcony's railing.

Lord, show me what I need to do so Ben will recognize my genuine love and commitment to him.

~

Ben returned to the Good Friday service for ten minutes and left again to check on Becca. Where had she gone? He sneered and shook his head. She couldn't wait for ten minutes? Why didn't she stay put like he asked her to? They'd never be able to salvage their marriage. She was more than he could manage. He went back into the worship center.

When the service ended, he searched for Keith and Vince. Ben needed to find out how the order of service got messed up. Becca needed to get over her fear of speaking in front of people if she wanted to serve alongside him. But she may have been fine had there not been changes to the service. Keith collaborated with Vince on the program. They'd know what happened.

When he didn't find Keith or Vince in the worship center, Ben headed down the hallway that led to the offices. He poked his head into Keith's office while Keith and his wife talked. After their greetings, Ben said, "Why all the mix-ups today?"

Keith jerked his head back. "What do you mean?"

"You told me that Becca had verses seventeen through twenty-two. Then, two minutes before the readings began, she was told she had the first eleven."

Ellie looked at Keith. "Seventeen to twenty-two were my verses."

Keith pulled out his phone. "Oh, man. I texted Ellie her verses two weeks ago right before I gave you Becca's." Keith's eyes grew wide. "Since they were on my mind, I must have given you the wrong ones."

Logical explanation. Ben nodded. "What happened with the lights? Why did they come on when they did?"

Keith shrugged. "No idea. Talk to the tech crew about that."

"Thanks, buddy." Ben strode across the hall and into his office.

He debated whether he should call Becca to check on her, but decided he'd see her soon enough when he got home.

~

Thirty minutes later, at 1:30 p.m., I returned to the

kitchen for a bite to eat. I pulled out leftovers, warmed them in the microwave, and sat for a pleasant lunch. After three bites, the garage door moaned. Time to face Ben. He offered me grace at church, but I was sure it wouldn't last long. I must have embarrassed him when I messed up my reading. And if he's the one who left the gator in the yard, I wouldn't return the offer of grace anytime soon.

The door to the laundry room opened, and there stood Riley with a young man behind her.

I jumped from my chair. "Oh, my. Is your dad expecting you?"

Riley stuck up her nose. "Not the greeting I expected. Are we interrupting something?"

I raised my palms and apologized. "This is such a surprise. Your dad will be thrilled." They walked toward me, and I eyed Riley's friend. "I'm happy to see you and to meet your friend."

Riley grinned and latched her elbow around the boy's arm. "This is my fiancé, Jeremy White."

My mouth fell open. There would be no peace in the house that evening. "Fiancé?"

I shook his hand and welcomed him. I didn't believe he was the type of young man Ben wanted for his daughter. A cute kid, but with a grimy appearance. Greasy, long hair. Unkept beard. Sloppy dresser. And in need of a shower. Where had Riley found this guy? "How long have the two of you been dating?"

Riley bit at her lower lip. "We know each other from classes and projects we've worked on together, but we've only dated for two weeks."

I crossed my arms. "Oh? Well, I'm sure your dad will want to meet your fiancé."

Riley gazed at Jeremy with stars dancing in her eyes. "Why don't you get our luggage and I'll show you to your room."

Panic edged my voice. "Luggage? How long are you planning to stay?"

Riley frowned and spoke in a harsh tone. "If you don't mind, we planned to stay for the full weekend to celebrate Easter together." She glanced at Jeremy and then back at me. "Unless you don't want us here."

"No, no, no. Of course, I want you here. It's been a crazy day and—"

"Wow. Look at that." Jeremy strode to the back door and stared out to the patio. "A huge rubber alligator."

Riley peered at me. "What's that doing here?" She stepped closer. "Almost looks real."

"Your dad tried to pull a joke on me. Worked, except it wasn't funny."

She shook her head. "Not dad. He's never pulled a practical joke on anyone. Sounds like something his friend, Keith, would do."

I covered my mouth with my hand and let it drop. "Keith Morgan?"

"He's known for doing stuff like that. Gets away with it most of the time too."

Jeremy ambled toward the door to the garage. "I'll get our bags, Sweetie."

"Thank you, My Love."

"Wait." They couldn't go upstairs. "Why don't the two of you run to the grocery store and pick up a few things. Your dad would love for you to make your chicken tortilla soup while you're here, but I don't have those ingredients." I hurried to the kitchen drawer where we kept cash for emergencies, and this was a big one.

"Here's $40.00. Buy what you need."

They agreed and left through the garage. Thirty minutes, maybe forty-five—that's all the time I had to get all Ben's belongings into the master bedroom.

After I stripped the bed in the guest room, I removed all clothes from the closet and threw them into a heap on my bed. I emptied all the drawers and scanned the room to make sure I got everything. Next, I gathered all Ben's personal items from the hall bathroom and carried them into the master bath.

I placed fresh sheets on Ben's bed for Jeremy and fluffed the pillows. After a quick clean-up in the bathroom, I ran back to my room and hung a few articles of Ben's clothing in the master closet until the doorbell rang.

I pulled my bedroom door closed and bolted downstairs. Riley and Jeremy stood on the doorstep with three bags of groceries. I exhaled a long breath and moved aside.

"If you can take the grocery bags from Jeremy, he'll get our suitcases now."

Jeremy handed me his bags, and I carried them into the kitchen.

Riley pulled me aside. "Why are you all sweaty? It's not hot in here."

"I've been busy tidying the house for guests."

"So, you consider me your guest?" Her tone turned snooty. "Sorry. I'm family and was here first."

"I didn't mean it that way. You're more family than I am."

I emptied the grocery bags and put the cold foods in the refrigerator.

Riley stocked the shelves with the non-perishables.

"When's Dad planning to be home?"
    "I'll text him and ask."
    "Don't tell him I'm here. I want to surprise him."
    No doubt she'd accomplish that.

Thirty-nine

The aroma of simmering tortilla soup reminded my stomach that I'd only eaten a few bites for breakfast and lunch. I needed to get out of the kitchen and finish putting away Ben's clothes. What would he say when he found out that he had no bedroom tonight? What would he do when he realized Riley expected him to spend the night in the master bedroom with me? He should have told her the truth when he had the opportunity. What a mess. I rubbed my arms, climbed the stairs, and locked my door behind me.

There were empty drawers in the dresser, and I placed several of Ben's items inside. I expected it would take fifteen minutes to clear all Ben's belongings from my bed.

A rap on my bedroom door startled me.

"Can I see you for a minute?"

I opened the door a crack to Riley. She held a pair of running shoes.

"Why were Dad's shoes in the guest room under the bed?"

"He left them there?" I faked a smile.

"That's odd to me. But here." She plopped them into my hands and walked toward her room.

That was close. I released a long breath. Five minutes later, there was another knock.

"And this? Why was Dad's toothbrush in the hall bathroom?"

"Why do you assume that's your dad's? Couldn't we have had another guest leave it in there?"

"Dad has this quirky habit of leaving his toothbrush on the windowsill behind the curtain. It's his." She handed it to me. "You should know that by now."

"I guess I'm not all that observant." I tried to close my door, but Riley stuck her foot inside. "Your dad should be here soon. May I help you set the table?" I turned to peek at the clock on my dresser.

Riley nudged my door open. "What's this? First Dad's shoes in the guest room, then his toothbrush in the bathroom, and now his clothes on hangers all over the bed? Something's not right here." She stroked her chin. "Why was he using the guest bedroom and bathroom?" She brought her fingers to her parted lips and gasped. "Are the two of you fighting?"

I exhaled another long breath. "Fighting? Yes, we do that often." That was better than admitting to our arrangement, wasn't it? And it was true.

She drew her eyebrows together. "What do you fight about?"

This was a terrific opportunity to speak truth about relationships to the young woman before me who was engaged after two weeks of dating.

"Everything." I took her by the elbow and led her to my bed. We found a cleared spot and sat. "We should have dated longer. Even though we knew each other from years before, we didn't take into consideration how our previous marriages and circumstances in life had changed us. We expected the other person to be someone they were not, and we're both struggling to think the best about one another. When we lose trust, it's hard to gain it back."

"How can you not trust my dad?"

"It's more that he doesn't have faith in me."

"Why?" She widened her eyes. "Did you do something?"

I told Riley about our honeymoon and Hale. She patted my leg while I told her about Keith and how Ben believed his friend and not me.

Riley hugged me. "I believe you."

I peered at her and questioned why.

"As much as I want to dislike you, I know you love Dad."

I tilted my head to the right. "How do you know that?"

"From observing the two of you together."

I wrinkled my forehead. "You've seen my love for him?"

She nodded. "Last month when we first met—the way you looked at him when you talked about spending the day together and the glow on your face at the wedding. You want what's best for him like tortilla soup and cleaning out the guest room so everything will appear normal. That all points to love, right?"

I smiled. "I guess it does."

She scrunched her nose. "Besides, I'm uncomfortable around Keith."

"Why?"

She shrugged. "His personality. Don't care for the guy. Never have. I'd describe him as sneaky." She hesitated and bit her lip.

"What else?"

"I don't want to be accused of gossiping, but a friend of mine said Keith flirted with her about the time we graduated from high school. She's not always truthful, so it may not have happened."

"Have you shared this with your dad?"

She shook her head. "I probably should have told him then. He might not believe me now."

The garage door clanged. Riley and I climbed off the bed and darted into the hallway. She yelled for Jeremy. He came out of the guest room and followed us down the stairs.

I turned to Riley and her fiancé. "Wait in the living room. Let me welcome him home first. We had a rough morning. I hope to ease some tension before he sees you."

"He won't recognize Jeremy's car, so no telling him who's here."

I gave her a thumbs up and waited for Ben at the laundry room door.

"Who's here?"

"Before you see our visitors, I wanted to say how sorry I am for messing up my verses today. I let you down, and I hate that."

"No worries." He glanced out the back door to the patio. "What is that?"

"A rubber toy."

"You called the hotline for a toy alligator?"

I nodded. "Trapper Jason confirmed and chewed me out."

Ben covered his mouth with his hand, but despite his best efforts, he still chuckled.

"Maybe it's a tiny bit funny now." I pinched my

thumb and index finger together and raised them to my chin. "But whoever did this is a jerk."

"Perhaps." He took another look. "Too big for the neighbor boy to drop over the fence."

"Someone planted it in our yard for me to find. Did you tell anyone at the church about my experience at Trimble Park?"

"Only Doris. She came into my office while you and I texted back and forth."

One of the ministry assistants wouldn't have left me a gator. But who did she tell?

A noise down the hallway reminded me of our guests. "Follow me."

Forty

Ben stopped short of entering the living room when he saw Riley with a huge grin on her face and a young man on her arm. He glanced at Becca and back at Riley. "What are you doing here?" He narrowed his eyes at Jeremy. "And who are you?"

Riley pouted and balled her fists. "You don't act any happier to see me than Becca did."

Ben cleared his throat and strode toward his daughter. "Sorry, honey. I'm surprised you're here." He wrapped her in his arms. "I'm glad to have you home." He stepped back and stared at Jeremy.

"Dad, this is Jeremy White. My fiancé." She flashed her left hand in front of Ben's face. A small diamond encircled her ring finger.

Ben's veins popped out on his neck. "Your what?"

Jeremy thrust his hand out to Ben. His grin bloomed into a chuckle. "Great to meet you, Sir. I'm looking forward to marrying the love of my life."

Ben's chest tightened. He coughed and lumbered to the loveseat, sat, and stood again. He walked toward the doorway, turned around, lifted his palms, and stared at Riley. "What were you thinking? Engaged? Are you out of your mind?" He coughed again, took a seat on the loveseat, patted the cushion next to him for Becca, and waited for the younger couple to sit on the sofa.

Becca faced Riley. "Please get your dad a glass of water."

Riley jumped up and hurried to the kitchen. Jeremy followed on her heels.

Becca scooted closer to Ben and took his hand. "You're all clammy." She leaned near his ear and whispered. "Things aren't as bad as they seem." She rubbed his arm. "Everything's fine."

"This can't be happening." He smacked his knee. "Why didn't you text me and tell me they were here?"

Her shoulders sagged. "Riley asked me not to because she wanted to surprise you."

"She succeeded. And that guy she's with? No way will he marry my daughter." Ben ran his hand over his face. "Have they been upstairs? Are they planning to stay?"

Becca cringed. "I got everything of yours moved into the master, but—"

"Here, Dad. I hope you're okay." Riley handed Ben a glass of water. She and Jeremy returned to their seats.

Ben sipped at his drink and calmed his breathing. "Jeremy, welcome to our home. I'd like to know how the two of you met and how long you've been dating."

Ben listened and took everything in. When Riley said they'd only dated for two weeks, Ben leaped from the loveseat. "Two weeks? Are you crazy? And now you're engaged?"

Riley stood to match Ben's stance and pointed her finger at him. "How long did you and Becca date, daddy dear?"

"Um." Ben glanced at Becca. "Not long. But we

knew each other for years."

"And how's that working for you?" She cut Becca a look. "Jeremy and I have known each other for almost two years. That qualifies us as much as it does you and her."

Ben sat next to Becca and grabbed her hand. "The two of us are doing great."

Becca opened her eyes wide. "No. We are not."

Ben flinched. He leaned away from her and lifted his eyebrows. "We have an occasional squabble, but we—"

"Dad. Stop. Becca told me about your struggles and why you sleep in the guestroom. I know all about that guy in the Keys and Pastor Keith."

Riley looked at Becca. "Sorry. I'm sure you wanted to tell him. I didn't mean to blurt it out."

Ben shook his head and glared at Becca. "You shared our personal situation with my daughter? Why would you do that?"

Becca rose from her seat with her head held high and turned to Riley. "Will you and Jeremy set the table? I'd like five minutes with your dad." Becca led Ben to the entryway and rushed inside his office.

He closed the door behind him. "Well?"

She told him all that took place after his daughter arrived and how she'd missed his shoes and toothbrush, which raised questions for Riley. "When she asked if the two of us fight, that was easier to explain than our marriage arrangement. If anyone shares that information, it needs to be you."

He softened his tone. "You did all that after an encounter with a gator and a fiasco service at church, so everything would appear normal to my daughter?" His eyes glistened. "You've had a rough day, haven't you?"

"For me, yes, a difficult day. But when I consider what our Lord and Savior endured, what we remember on Good Friday, today was nothing."

Forty-one

Ben insisted they not discuss their marriage struggles until after dinner. Jeremy didn't need to be included in any further family discussions. If Ben told Riley the truth, perhaps she'd reconsider her engagement. He placed his fork and knife on his dinner plate. What was she thinking?

He couldn't blame Becca for admitting to marriage problems themselves. There were plenty. But he was curious as to what Becca told Riley about Keith. His best friend would not have hit on Becca. She must have misunderstood his intentions. Or perhaps Keith misinterpreted hers.

Ben knew Becca had a distressing day. He needed to let up on her so they could work on saving whatever marriage they had left. *God, help us.*

Becca and Riley cleared the dishes and loaded the dishwasher while Ben and Jeremy remained at the kitchen table.

Ben cleared his throat. "Which classes have you and Riley taken together?"

"We met in English Composition during first semester last year and critiqued each other's assignments. That's how we got to know each other." He rubbed his shaggy beard. "Second semester, we took College Algebra together. Last semester we took biology and worked as lab partners, and now we're in the same computer science class."

"Are you a business major too?"

"Yes, Sir. But accounting not marketing."

At least the boy had manners.

Ben stood, strode over to Riley, and lowered his voice while she added soap to the dishwasher. "Could we talk in private?"

"Do you mean without Becca and Jeremy or without Jeremy?"

"Jeremy. Becca should join us."

Riley pursed her lips, closed the dishwasher, and joined Jeremy at the table.

Ben remained close to the sink where Becca washed up the pots and pans, but he watched Riley and Jeremy.

"I'd like to go see that movie we talked about yesterday." She winked and touched his hand. "Why don't you go upstairs and get ready. I'll talk to Dad and Becca while you're gone."

"Sure thing, Sweetie." Jeremy jumped up and dashed toward the stairs.

When Becca finished drying the pots and pans, Ben led her and Riley to the living room.

Riley took a seat in a chair. "You hate Jeremy, don't you?"

Ben sat on the far end of the sofa near Riley's chair and Becca sat next to him. "Hate? No. But he's not who I expected you to bring home." He pressed his fist against his mouth.

She smirked. "He's a wonderful person."

"Let's change the subject." Ben rubbed his hands

down his pant legs. "I haven't been honest with you. It's true that Becca and I have been struggling." He glanced at Becca, and she nodded.

"Wait, Dad. I need to say something." When she had Ben's attention, she said, "As you know, Becca told me about Keith and how he hit on her and that his story is the opposite of hers. You should believe Becca—not Keith."

Ben shook his head. "Why? You don't like Becca."

"Like her? She's great, and Mom would approve because you all were friends for a long time." She leaned toward Ben and took his hand in hers. "I didn't like that you got engaged after only dating someone for two weeks and for not telling me sooner you were serious enough to ask her to marry you."

"And now you're doing the same?"

Riley smiled at Becca and looked back at Ben. "Becca loves you and that's what Mom would want. She wouldn't want you fighting over what Keith did or didn't do. But if you ask me—he's guilty."

Riley shared how she wasn't comfortable around Keith. Something about him made her uneasy. She also mentioned her friend's allegations.

"Why didn't you tell me this before?"

"Mom had been gone for about six months when I graduated from high school. Keith hung around here often then and was your moral support. I didn't want to come between you two." She squeezed Ben's hand. "I love you, Dad. I planned to leave soon for college, and you needed friends."

"That was a tough time for both of us." Ben returned a squeeze.

Riley gazed at him. "And that gator in the backyard?

That's got to be Keith." She stood. Her gaze fell upon Jeremy who'd made his way into the living room.

Gone was his grimy appearance. He'd pulled his clean hair back into a ponytail and wore a pair of dress khakis with a red, short-sleeved shirt. He appeared decent enough to be Riley's fiancé.

Riley met Jeremy at the doorway, where she interlocked her elbow in his. "Dad, Becca, I'd like you to meet my good friend, Jeremy." She released his arm, pulled off her ring, and stuck it in her pants pocket. "We're not engaged or dating."

Ben shot out of his seat. "A charade? Why?"

Becca hurried over to Riley, hugged her, and peered at Ben. "Isn't it obvious after what she said about us dating only two weeks and not telling her before our engagement?"

Forty-two

Riley frowned when she came out of the upstairs bathroom. "Where are you going with those?"

I strolled past her in the hallway with my arms filled with sheets, a pillow, and a light-weight blanket. "I'm taking them to the living room. Your dad is sleeping on the sofa tonight."

"But after what I told him about Keith and how much you love Dad, you two should have made up."

"Things aren't that simple." I lowered my chin onto the pillow to keep it from slipping out of my arms. "Let me get these downstairs and find your dad. He can better explain our situation."

"Jeremy's waiting for me. We need to leave now to make it to the movie on time. Dad can explain tomorrow."

Riley cut in front of me and whizzed down the stairs. I followed close behind. Jeremy and Ben who'd been chatting at the dining room table, ended their conversation, and stood. She grabbed Jeremy's hand and faced her dad. She told Ben that whatever he wanted to explain about why he'd be sleeping on the sofa would have to wait because she and Jeremy had plans. "Let's go."

Before they closed the door behind them, Jeremy said, "Your dad's chill."

Ben chuckled a moment until he glanced at me and scowled. "Why did you have to bring those down now? If she hadn't seen them, she may have assumed things were back to normal, and we'd patched things up."

"With that look on your face, that wouldn't be the truth now, would it?" I shoved my armload into his chest. "Good night."

I'd had a horrible, exhausting day. Since he planned to tell Riley the truth, what was the big deal about taking down his bedding? I should have left the task to him. I stomped up the steps.

Ben called my name. "Can we talk?"

My hand rested on my bedroom doorknob. A room I longed to share with my husband one day. I took a deep breath and ambled to the railing at the top of the stairs.

Ben waited at the bottom with his eyes on me. He climbed halfway up, and I met him in the middle where he wrapped his arms around me and told me he was sorry.

I remained stiff in his arms and pouted. "Talking sounds good." I pulled back, made my way to the living room, and sat in a chair.

Ben took a seat on the couch, opened his palms, and shrugged. "You don't want to sit next to me?"

If he only understood how much I wanted to sit with him, be with him, and love him. But after the past few weeks, I couldn't put myself out there again and be made to feel insignificant and untrustworthy. I stared at him with a straight face. "What do you want to talk about?"

He leaned back on the sofa and remained silent. A minute later, he stood. "Let's hold off this conversation until later. I'm not sure what to think. You don't act all that interested in working this out."

I jumped up. "Me? Ben, I love you. I've wanted to work this out from the beginning."

"You keep saying love—and Riley said that you love me. I've given you no reason to care about me like that." He gawked at me. "And the way I've treated you, doubted you? There's no way you can love me like you loved Michael, or the way Annie and I loved each other."

I shook my head. "What do I have to do to prove to you that I'm sincere?" I scanned the room and focused on a planter filled with succulents that sat on the coffee table. What more could I do or say? "I'm going upstairs now. See you in the morning."

I zipped to my room and closed the door. After I called Jill and shared the day's happenings and frustrations with her, I prayed. *Lord, what will prove to Ben that I love him?*

Speak.

What? That wouldn't work. Every time we talked, we argued. *Speak about what, Lord?*

~

Ben sat up and rubbed his neck. Reminded him of four weeks earlier on their fake honeymoon. How had his great idea erupted into such a weird mess? He needed to come clean and let Riley in on his and Becca's secret. But he needed to find a time when Jeremy wasn't nearby.

Jeremy was a bright kid. Ben liked him. Too bad the engagement was a charade. Jeremy would make a good son-in-law. But Jeremy and Riley weren't ready for marriage, like he and Becca weren't ready.

Ben ventured into the kitchen where the scent of bacon made his stomach growl. Becca stood barefooted at the stove. "Smells good in here."

Becca didn't turn around or speak.

She looked cute—no beautiful—in her navy capris and navy and white, polka dot top. Her wavy, strawberry blonde hair flowed over her shoulders. He yearned to walk up behind her and wrap her in another hug, but would she push him away again? He deserved it. To doubt her and believe Keith?

Did Keith know more about what happened at the Good Friday service than he let on? And what about the gator? It looked real. Was that what Ben overheard while Keith was on the phone? And if Keith were behind those, he could have lied about Becca too. Ben grimaced and cocked his head from side to side. But why?

Ben remembered the day after the party when Becca accused him and Keith of scheming against her. She wanted to know which one of them came up with such a crazy idea. The idea of Keith hitting on her? That didn't make sense.

He pulled plates out of the cabinet. "Have you talked to Riley this morning? Are they joining us for breakfast?"

Becca stepped aside and pointed to the skillet. "I hope so. I doubt the two of us can eat all this bacon?"

Ben moved next to her and put his hand on her back. "We can manage." He gazed into her eyes.

She flinched and spoke in a bossy tone. "Watch the bacon." She turned to the refrigerator and pulled out the egg carton. "I'll scramble the eggs."

Becca was still upset with him. He had to change that, or he might lose her. He realized he wanted her to be a major part of his life. But Annie?

Riley believed her mom would approve of Becca

being his wife. But was it too soon? What if he loved Becca, and he lost her too?

Ben pulled the bacon from the skillet and switched off the burner. "We need to talk."

"About what?" Riley wandered over to her dad with Jeremy close behind.

"Nothing. I was talking to Becca."

Becca eyed him and mouthed, "Nothing?"

"But I need to talk with you, too, in private as soon as we finish breakfast." He placed both hands on Riley's shoulders. "You shared the truth with us last night. Now I need to share the truth with you."

When the eggs were ready, they all took their seats and made small talk while they ate. When finished, Ben asked Jeremy if he could help Becca with the dishes and asked Riley to follow him into his office.

Ben glanced at Becca. He wanted to include her when he told Riley the truth, but he didn't want to be rude to Jeremy by not including him again. Becca seemed to understand. She nodded and shooed him away with her hand.

He could fall in love with that woman. But was he ready?

244

Forty-three

Jeremy and I chatted for ten minutes about school, church, and his future. After we cleaned the kitchen, he excused himself to take a thirty-minute walk around the neighborhood.

I followed him to the foyer and heard Riley's raised voice coming from Ben's office but couldn't make out what she said. Not wanting to eavesdrop, I closed the front door behind Jeremy and returned upstairs to read my Bible and pray for her and Ben.

Fifteen minutes later, there was a knock on my door. Riley pushed her way inside. "This must be terrible for you. I thought it was a quarrel, and you'd be back together soon. But it's a permanent arrangement."

"Permanent? Is that what your dad said?"

"Sounded like that's what he meant." She brushed her finger across her eyelid. "I wasn't wrong, was I? You're in love with him?"

How did I answer her? He implied this was a permanent arrangement. Where would that leave me?

I turned away from her, padded to the window, and stared at the flowering trees in the backyard.

The door clicked shut. "I see it when you look at him and the way you listen to his every word."

When I glanced back, Riley had made herself comfortable on the foot of my bed. "I do love him."

Riley slid off and moved toward me. "I'll tell Jeremy that we need to leave now. You and Dad need to be alone and work through this. Having us here only complicates things for you both."

I touched her arm. "That's sweet but unnecessary. Please stay. Jeremy is excited to go to church with you. When we talked earlier, it sounded like he doesn't attend."

"If he said he wants to go, then we'll stay. He wasn't thrilled when I first told him that we'd attend church."

Riley told me that she and Jeremy planned earlier to spend the day at one of the amusement parks nearby. Jeremy had a thing for killer whales. "We'll leave and that will give the two of you time to talk." She headed toward the door. She spun on her heel and faced me again. "I forgot something." She reached into her back pants pocket and pulled out an index card. "Here's the recipe for chicken tortilla soup. Now you can fix it for Dad. He'll like that."

"Are you sure you don't want me to save it for you to make when you're here?"

She averted her eyes. "That was selfish of me. Even when I knew you were the woman in the photo I tried to find, I still couldn't accept you. Dad upset me by not telling me sooner that he was dating." She shook her head and brushed her foot along the floor.

"Can you forgive him?"

"Sure." She grinned, gave me an awkward hug, and left my room.

Not sure how it happened, but I'd made a new friend.

Thirty minutes later, Ben rapped on my door. "The kids left for the day. Would you like to do something together?"

I opened the door to find my husband in a pair of navy shorts and a white polo shirt with a mixed bouquet in his hands. "What's that?"

"A peace offering. The shop didn't have any of your favorite daisies. Will these work?"

"Lovely." What were these supposed to fix? I took them from his hands and descended the stairs. "I'll find a vase."

Ben trailed behind me. "We can go to another beach. Spend time barefoot in the sand and have lunch at a restaurant on the water."

I pulled a vase from a kitchen cabinet and filled it with water. "I have laundry to do. Besides, don't you need to study and plan for your class tomorrow?"

"All finished. I need to add final changes to my notes for our missions meeting on Wednesday night but still have four days."

I turned to face him. "This is the informational meeting for those interested in taking a trip this year, right?" I placed the flowers in the vase and set them on the kitchen table.

He nodded and spoke with uncertainty. "Are you still planning to attend?"

"Yes. I have a heart for missions." Did he not want me to attend?

"Great. I'm looking forward to you being a part of the team."

Flowers and formality. Nothing changed. Just a part of the team.

I moseyed past him toward the sink.

"So, do you want to go to the beach? I think you'd like Cocoa."

I stopped but didn't turn to face him. "Sure. If that's what you want to do."

He stood behind me and ran his fingers through my hair. "If it's a chore to spend time with me, we can stay here and find something to do on our own." He turned me toward him. "But I'd like to spend time with you. To walk and talk. To work on our relationship."

"Our relationship?"

He rested his forehead on mine. "Yes. You're slipping away. I don't want to lose you."

"I'm not planning to leave you if that's what you mean." I stepped back and gazed into his eyes. "That's not what God wants from me."

"How can you be sure?"

I exhaled a lengthy breath. "One year after Michael's death, I began to ask the Lord to bring a man into my life who was like Michael. Someone with whom I could join in serving the Lord in ministry." I bit my lower lip. "Who could be more like Michael than you? You poured yourself into him, mentored, encouraged, and prayed for him to be a godly man. He followed after God in your footsteps." I touched his cheek. "*You* are the answer to my prayers."

He furrowed his brows. "When did you realize that? You told me to stop contacting you when I texted you the first time."

I stared down at my feet. "I guess I knew when I received your odd request in the mail. But I didn't want it to be true because of fear. Fear to leave all I knew and loved to move here and serve in a huge church when I wanted to stay in a small one."

Ben lifted my chin. "I'm thankful that I'm the answer to your prayers."

He wrapped me in his arms, and I hugged him back. This is what I'd wanted for weeks. I didn't need the beach.

LUANN K. EDWARDS

Forty-four

Ben enjoyed walking along the beach with Becca and holding her hand. Dark clouds hung in the distance, but joy lit his heart. Relief washed over him when Becca told him she had no plans to leave. He thanked the Lord for that blessing. Together, he hoped to figure out what was going on with Keith.

Becca stopped near a group of water birds pecking for tidbits along the shore. "Let's sit here in the sand."

They sat and faced the ocean where rough waves beat against the shore.

Ben squeezed her hand. "I'm still having trouble believing that Keith would hit on you." He shook his head. "My best friend."

She tried to jerk her hand away.

Ben held onto it and brought it to his chest. "I believe you. But perhaps you misread him."

"And Riley's friend?"

They talked about Riley's friend and how she wasn't reliable. She often stretched the truth.

"If you had been in the laundry room when Keith and I were alone and saw and heard him, you would have hurled him out the door."

"But why would he do that? To you, of all people?"

Becca yanked her hand away from Ben's, pulled her knees to her chest, and wrapped her arms around them.

Ben peered at Becca. "I mean, you're beautiful and sweet, but you're also my wife."

She stretched out her legs on the sand. "What else has he done in recent weeks that seems out of character for him?"

They talked about the gator, and Ben sent Doris a text: **Did you tell anyone about Becca's encounter with a gator at the park?**

They also discussed the Good Friday service and how it was possible that Keith was behind all that went wrong including changing the Bible translation at the last minute. Ben sent Doris a second text to see if she knew anything about that change.

Becca asked if Keith was the person who relayed the comments about her inappropriate clothing.

"That and other things." Ben's gut tightened. "What's that fool up to?"

"I suppose he doesn't like me or wants me to go back to Pleasant Springs. Maybe he thinks your friendship is in jeopardy with me here."

"That's crazy. He's not like that."

Becca gazed at the ocean. "More dark clouds are closing in on us."

"But this time the two of us will stand firm and get through them." Ben stood and reached for Becca's hand to help her up. "Time to pray for God's wisdom in this situation and seek Him together."

~

My heart soared. Ben's new outlook made my day look brighter than it had for weeks. When we climbed inside his car, he took my hands and prayed for our marriage, our upcoming mission trips, and for guidance in this situation with Keith. He asked me to pray too. We prayed together and asked the Lord to lead us and work through us to find the truth.

Ben drove to a burger place along the water. Because they were busy, we had to sit in the back of the dining area farthest from the shore. We took our seats at a table for four in the corner across from one another. After we placed our order, I soaked up his attention. If Riley hadn't told me earlier that Ben implied to her that our arrangement was permanent, I might have suspected he was wooing me again.

"How did Riley take the news this morning?" I drank a sip of water.

He ran his hand through his hair. "She lectured me. Something about I called her out on her charade, but I pulled the same thing on her."

"She got that right."

"At first, she sounded relieved, but then she got onto me for hurting you." He reached across the table and grasped my hand. "I never intended for our arrangement to cause you pain."

The server hurried past us carrying a tray of desserts that looked delicious. "I realize that."

Ben whispered my name.

When I faced him, he cocked his head.

"You are more important to me now than ever. I'm thankful the Lord brought you back into my life. I hope you believe that." He nodded and released my hand.

I didn't want to read too much into what he said. "Do you suppose our relationship will change soon?"

He leaned back in his chair. "Change how?"

"Riley implied you said the way things are now

between us are permanent."

He scooted to the edge of his seat. "I don't want that. Do you?"

I closed my eyes and rubbed my forehead. When I looked at him again, I said, "I've always wanted a real marriage with you. Haven't I made that clear?"

He reached for my hand again. "I'm happy to know that hasn't changed. I'm getting closer to wanting the same thing."

"When?" I lifted my chin.

He glanced to his left and right and shrugged. "Soon?"

I slumped my shoulders and used sarcasm. "Great." I folded my hands in my lap.

Ben picked up his utensils wrapped in a cloth napkin and stared at them. "Wrong answer?"

I sighed. "Whenever you're ready. I understand about Annie." I reached across the table and touched the utensils in his hand. "You're not the only person to experience these feelings of yours. I still love and miss Michael too. I always will. But he's not here, and my heart is big enough to love you both."

Ben lowered his eyes and sat expressionless for the next few minutes until our server brought our food. We prayed, but before I could ask him if he was okay, patrons cried out and moved tables away from the open-air windows. Rainwater poured onto their tables and chairs. Several people got drenched.

I scooted next to Ben and made room for an older couple to join us. I envied their relationship as I watched them share intimate smiles with one another. Would that ever be Ben and me?

Forty-five

Easter Sunday arrived. Riley and Jeremy were the first to get ready. They had fresh baked cinnamon rolls and coffee waiting for us, and I cleaned the kitchen afterward. The kids wanted to take Jeremy's car so they could come back to the house after the first service and fix lunch for us. I loved the idea.

I pulled Riley aside before she darted out the door. "Jeremy's a sweetheart, and he dotes on you. Why aren't you dating?"

"What does that mean—dotes?"

"He pampers you. He adores you."

Her face and neck turned red. "But he doesn't have a relationship with the Lord."

"I guess we'll need to pray about that." I chuckled.

She poked my arm and slipped out.

Ben stepped out of the downstairs bathroom. "Ready, beautiful lady?"

"Me?" I pointed at myself. "You look handsome today. But why the tie?"

"I wanted to dress up for Easter."

I straightened the knot on his tie. "Nice."

"Do you remember where I got this?"

"Should I?"

"You and Michael gave it to me one Christmas years ago. I stuck it away in a box and that's where I left it. I found it in the office closet with this card inside." He handed me the card and asked me to read it aloud.

"Ben, we will forever be indebted to you and Annie for your kindness and generosity. The love you've shown us and the time you've spent with us have been important in our walk with the Lord. We love you both and wish you the best Christmas ever. Michael and Becca."

I handed him the card. "Still true today. We owe you and Annie a lot. What if no one else had taken the time to share about Christ and how we could experience a personal relationship with Him in our lives?" I kissed his cheek. "Thank you. I love and appreciate you more today and in a different way than all those years ago."

Ben kissed the top of my head. "We should leave now so we're not late for service."

We arrived on time and rushed down the hall. People stared at us and whispered to one another.

I looked at Ben. "Is my dress bunched up, or did I sit on something dirty?"

He checked my outfit. "You look great."

"People are staring and making me uncomfortable. I suppose it's because I messed up at Friday's service." How long would it take for people to forget that?

He smiled and opened the side door to the sanctuary for me. "Everything worked out."

We took our regular seats in the front right section and enjoyed the service. From the worshipful singing to the powerful message of God's truth. Christ our Lord and risen Savior—our eternal hope.

Ben chatted with people after service. Most of the congregation filed out the main doors, which gave me an unobstructed view of Riley and Jeremy, who stood in the center section about halfway back. They were deep in a discussion. Jeremy sat and Riley plopped next to him, bouncing her head up and down.

I ambled over to say hello. "Everything okay?"

Riley grinned. "Great."

Jeremy crossed his arms. "I loved the service. But I felt like I missed something, or I needed more info." He rubbed his beard. "I asked if we could stay for the next service too."

"You realize it's the same service?"

"I need to listen to the message again." He patted his chest.

"Sounds good." I glanced at Riley, who held her palms together. I gave her a thumbs up and hurried to meet up with Ben, who waited for me at the side door.

"I hope you meant it when you said you liked Jeremy. There may be an engagement soon."

He grimaced. "Riley told me that Jeremy's relationship with the Lord was nonexistent."

"Today might be the day." I waggled my eyebrows. "He asked to stay and sit through the next service."

Ben widened his eyes. "Let's ask the class to pray."

"Lovely lady." My heart sank. Not him again. How did he find me at church? Brayden Hale strode toward us.

Ben pushed me aside and positioned himself in front of me. "What do you want?"

Hale hesitated, looked past Ben to me, then back at Ben. "I owe you both an apology."

I moved to Ben's right side and grabbed ahold of his

elbow.

Hale's eyes darted from mine to Ben's. "I acted like a jerk down in the Keys and don't know what possessed me to follow you from the resort. I want you to know that your wife honored you in every way." He peered at me. "I'm sorry I made you uncomfortable and caused problems between the two of you."

"Thank you for your apology." I squeezed Ben's elbow. "We both appreciate your honesty."

Ben reached out his hand. "Yes. Thank you."

Hale shook Ben's hand. "I'm glad I found this church to attend this morning. An employee at the hotel suggested it when I asked about a church for Easter service. He said he attends here." Hale smiled, said goodbye, and exited through the main worship center doors.

Ben exhaled a deep breath. "I never expected that to happen."

I faced him but didn't speak. If Ben still held any doubt about what took place between Hale and me, Hale's confession cleared that up.

Ben placed his hands on my upper arms. "I was wrong to doubt you. I'm sorry." He brushed his finger along my cheek.

I nodded. "We'd better get to class."

We hurried down the hallway to our classroom.

When we arrived, people stopped their conversations except for a few whispers. Ben strode to the front, and I took my seat at the end of the first row as usual.

Ben shared about Jeremy and asked the class to pray. "What other prayer requests do we have?"

After a few requests, Ben prayed and asked the Lord

to bless our time together and that hearts would be open to God's Word.

After he said "Amen" he focused on the class. The whispers continued. "Who would like to tell me what's going on this morning?"

An immediate hush spread across the room.

"Is this about Becca's reading of scripture during Friday's service?"

I turned and glanced around the room. People shook their heads. A lady behind me said, "That wasn't a big deal. I'd get stage fright, too, if I had to read in front of thousands of people."

I sank into my chair. Ben hadn't fooled them with his glasses' comment.

His face blanched. "Then what is this about?" He searched the room. "Someone, speak up."

A gentleman in the back jumped up. "Pastor, I don't listen to gossip. And I've seen the way your wife looks at you. I don't believe these stories. But some folks here accept anything they're told. Time for a lesson on Romans 1:28-29." He returned to his seat.

Gossip? I peered at Ben. My heart pounded and heat rose on my neck. What had Keith done?

Ben called the class to order and motioned to me. "Please join me up front."

What was he doing? I stood. My knees weakened as they had on Friday when the lights shone during my reading. I trudged to his side.

Ben wrapped his arm around my shoulder and turned me to face the group. His eyes beamed at me. "I've heard the rumors too." He scanned the class. "That's all they are. Becca is not guilty of whatever you heard she did and no matter who told you." He squeezed my shoulder and motioned me back to my chair. "Are there any other comments or questions before we begin our Easter lesson?"

No one responded. Ben taught a well-planned lesson that added depth to the morning sermon. At the end of his lesson, he asked the gentleman in the back row to read Romans 1:28-29 aloud to the class.

Forty-six

Ben mumbled while he and Becca walked to their car in the church parking lot. "Why would Keith slander you? He told me that he'd keep this between the two of us. No one else needed to find out what happened that day. I can't believe he'd do that."

Becca wrapped her arm around Ben's elbow. "The truth will come out."

Ben agreed. "I'm glad we took time to pray together before we had to pray for others in the chapel during third service. Animosity reared up inside of me. I wanted to find Keith and knock his teeth out."

Becca frowned. "I'm glad we prayed too. A pastor punching another pastor in the mouth would cause additional gossip for sure."

Ben opened Becca's door, strode to the driver's side, and climbed in. He turned toward her. "For the past twelve days, I've fought uncertainty about what happened between you and Keith. I'm ashamed of myself for doubting you."

She nodded and rubbed his arm. "What are you going to do? You won't really knock out your best friend's teeth, will you?"

Ben chuckled. "I need your help with my next steps.

We need to pray for wisdom. If Keith were anyone else, I'd talk to Pastor Young. But because Keith is John's son-in-law, I doubt that is wise. But taking the information to the Church Board may not be the best either."

"Do you suppose Pastor Young has heard Keith's version of the story?"

"If he hasn't, today's the day. He'll wait to call me into his office on Tuesday, which gives us plenty of time to pray."

~

We arrived home and found Riley and Jeremy with an opened Bible at the kitchen table.

I breathed in the savory aroma of chicken roasting in the oven. "Do I smell garlic and onions too?"

"Yes. Stuffed inside the chicken along with lemon and thyme. Makes it tender and juicy." Riley grinned. "Garlic mashed potatoes are ready to mash, but we got sidetracked with the Bible."

Ben eased over to the table. "A good reason to interrupt our lunch plans. Anything I can help with?"

Jeremy jumped up and reached out to shake Ben's hand. "Sir, thank you for welcoming me into your home. Today is the best day of my life." He gazed at Riley. "The first day of my new life living for the Lord."

Ben pulled his hand away and stretched out his fingers. "That's great, son." He hugged Jeremy. "Welcome to the family. God's family."

Jeremy winked at Riley.

What would the future bring for those two?

We enjoyed a fantastic lunch and conversation. Ben sat on Jeremy's left and tried to redirect his zeal and recommended Jeremy slow down and pray for God's leading. Ben cautioned him to not call each of his family members as he wanted to do to share his good news. He suggested Jeremy visit in person, let them witness the change in his life, and wait until they ask him about those changes.

Jeremy wrinkled his forehead. "But they need to learn about God's love and forgiveness."

I leaned toward him. "But be prepared. When you first tell them, they may not accept it. My parents thought I was crazy. When I first told them, they discussed committing me to a mental health institution."

Jeremy's shoulders slumped. "Do they believe now?"

I shook my head. "I'm still praying for them. But I had two friends from college and my brother who saw a change in me, asked me lots of questions, and then committed their lives to Christ."

Ben reached over to Jeremy and patted him on the shoulder. "Let your family observe the change. But if you feel God leading you to tell them everything you've experienced, then do so. Allow Him to guide you."

After we finished our meal and cleaned the kitchen, we said goodbye to Riley and Jeremy.

On his way out the door, Jeremy said, "I hope you don't mind if I come back with Riley on her next visit." He stopped and whispered in my ear. "I plan to spend more time with her."

~

On Tuesday morning, Ben arrived at the church with a knot in his gut. The day could be tough, but he knew God was with him.

Doris followed him into his office and greeted him. "Pastor Young asked me to tell you that he wants to meet with you first thing. He's in his office now."

"What's this about?"

"I can only speculate on that." She glanced behind her at the opened door and back at Ben. "You've heard the rumors?"

"That's all they are."

"I know you, and although I don't know Becca well, I've witnessed your interactions. I shouldn't say this, but if the rumors started with the other party involved or his wife, they hold no weight with me."

"Thank you, Doris." Ben smiled. "Did you get my texts about the Bible translation and the gator?"

She clutched her chest. "I forgot to text you back. Yes. Keith changed to the New International Version a week before the Good Friday service, and he knew about the gator. I went to see him after I'd been in your office, and he asked what I was chuckling about. I told him about Becca at the park. Did that cause further problems?"

"Everything will work out." He thanked her. "I better get to Pastor Young's office."

Ben stepped out into the hallway and lumbered toward John's open door. He pulled his shoulders back and straightened.

John looked up from his desk and greeted Ben. "Close the door and take a seat."

Ben did as instructed and played ignorant. "If this is about Becca not reading her verses, she feels terrible about that. Last-minute changes to the Bible translation, the verses they asked her to read, and the lights—"

John raised his palm. "Nothing to do with that." He rested back in his chair. "How's your marriage working out? Is Becca unhappy here in Orlando?"

"She's fine here." Ben crossed his ankle over his knee. "Although, she misses her family and best friend."

"And your marriage?"

"We've had our struggles. With both of us married before, we understood there would be a time of adjustment."

John furrowed his brow and narrowed his eyes. "You must know why I called you into my office." He cleared this throat. "What would cause her to chase after Keith?"

Ben lowered his leg and bent toward John. "You're assuming the gossipers are sharing truth."

John stared back. "I believe my daughter."

Ben eased back in his chair. *Lord, help me.* "I believe my wife. She tells a different story."

"Then I'd like her to tell it." He focused on his computer screen. "Ask her to be here at 1:00. I'll be here waiting for her."

Forty-seven

Ben texted me at 8:10 a.m. and asked me to meet him at 11:45 for lunch at a Tex-Mex restaurant near the church. His morning must have been tough with the rumors spreading, but I loved that he wanted to keep me abreast of what happened and spend time with me. I prayed and prepared myself for whatever news he might share. I wanted to be an encouragement to him. But when he didn't update me further, I grew curious and sent a text: Have you seen Keith?

Took the day off.

He must have known that Ben would learn about the rumors. Was Keith afraid Ben might knock his teeth out? I chuckled. Ben could get upset. I witnessed that. But it would shock me if he hit someone.

I changed into a short-sleeved, black knit top with a black and white flower-patterned skirt and drove to the restaurant.

Ben met me outside. He cleared his throat and bit his lip.

"What's wrong?"

He led me by the hand. "We'll talk after we sit."

The host led us to a booth along the windows.

Ben sat next to me, which was odd.

He wiped his palm on his pant leg and reached for my hand.

"Did you hear anything about the rumors this morning?"

He spoke in hushed tones. "Got called into the boss's office."

"What did he say?"

Ben released my hand and picked up the menu. "Let's order and then we'll talk." He attempted a smile that lasted two seconds.

Ben didn't need added stress in his life. Neither did I. What would happen to him? A reprimand because of his wife's supposed misbehavior. Not fair.

After we ordered our food, I scooted closer and rubbed his arm. I wanted to comfort him and make sure I could hear whatever he wanted to tell me.

He kissed my cheek. "I'm a blessed man." He chatted about his missions meeting the next evening and that he needed to prepare for next Sunday's lesson, but he avoided telling me about his conversation with Pastor Young.

Within several minutes, the server placed Ben's enchiladas and my quesadilla on the table and asked if we needed anything else before she hurried off.

We prayed and chatted further while we ate. He asked if I'd spoken to my family or Jill.

"When are you going to tell me about your conversation with Pastor Young?"

"Not much to tell." Ben told me their meeting was short. Pastor Young asked about our marriage and if I was happy in Orlando. "When he asked about the party, I told him that I believed your story of what happened that night." Ben wrapped his arm across my back.

"You did?" I rested my head on his shoulder. "Thank you."

Ben cleared his throat but said nothing.

"What?" I peered at him. "What don't you want to tell me?"

He swallowed and spoke in a whisper. "He wants to see you in his office to tell your side of what happened at the party."

I released a heavy sigh. "Makes sense." I shifted on the bench. "Tomorrow?"

Ben peeked at his watch. "In ten minutes. We need to leave now."

"And you waited until now to tell me?" I huffed. "No wonder you were sweet to me."

"I told you, I'm getting to know you well." He fiddled with a button on his golf shirt. "I wanted you to enjoy your lunch. If I'd told you when you arrived, you wouldn't have been able to eat."

He scooted out of the booth, and I followed him to the door.

"I'll meet you there." I got into my car and drove the five minutes to the church. Ben and I walked inside together and turned down the hallway.

Ben stopped me outside of his office and kept his voice low. "Pastor Young said I can be there with you."

I strutted into Ben's office. He entered behind me and closed the door.

I spoke in an annoyed tone. "Is that supposed to make me feel better? And were all the nice things you said to me while we were at lunch a ploy to build me up before I met with Pastor Young? Or were other staff members in the restaurant, and you wanted to perform for them?"

Ben placed his hands on my upper arms and gazed into my eyes. "Everything that happened there was genuine." He cocked his head. "I tried to put you at ease because you get nervous. But it was heartfelt." He brought his hand to his chest. "I care about you."

I stared out his office door window and down the hallway. "I'll go alone. Is his office the one on the end to the right?"

"Yes. I'll be praying for you."

I plodded down the hallway and stopped outside of Pastor Young's door.

"Come in and have a seat." He pointed to a lady wearing a royal blue dress. "This is Doris Clark. She'll take notes on our conversation." I relaxed. I'd only heard wonderful things about Doris from Ben. Of course, for several weeks only good things were said about Keith too.

Forty-eight

Ben paced across his office and prayed. *Lord, open John's heart to hear truth. Help Becca recount what happened and in no way embellish the facts. Give her assurance that You are with her.*

He sat at his desk and woke up his computer. His wallpaper popped onto the screen. He stared at a wedding photo taken of Becca and him during their vows. For better, for worse . . . to love and to cherish.

Ben looked back through his pictures and found his former background—one with Annie, Riley, and him. A favorite.

He wanted to honor his vows to Becca, but he struggled to let go of his true love, Annie. He propped his elbow on his desk and rested his hand on his forehead. *Lord, I need assurance too. Show me when it's time for me to commit to loving and cherishing again.*

~

My mouth went dry. Pastor Young asked me to tell him what happened the night of the party. How Keith came to be in the laundry room alone with me and what took place while he was there.

"May I have a drink of water?"

Doris jumped up and opened a small refrigerator in

the corner of the office. "Here you are. I should have offered you one when you came in."

I thanked her and took a sip. "Ben and I went into the kitchen to prepare the desserts. When things were underway, he slipped out to attend to our guests." I continued the story of how I'd made a mess on the floor and why I went into the laundry room. I told him that Keith snuck behind me and the discussion and actions that followed. My story ended by reminding Pastor Young how Keith rang the front doorbell to get back inside because he got locked out when he'd stepped outdoors.

"That's much different from Keith's story."

"I'm sure it is."

He wiped his brow, thanked me for coming in, and asked me to send Ben to his office.

After I thanked him, too, I said, "I love Ben. I wouldn't do anything to jeopardize his standing with the church or our marriage. But I also understand Keith's relationship with you and why it's important for you to believe him. I'm praying for you to make the right decision as you follow the Lord's leading."

I smiled at Doris on my way out the door and hurried to Ben's office. His forehead rested on his hand. "Are you okay?"

He glanced up, stood, and darted to the front of his desk. "Yes. Are you?"

I nodded. "Pastor Young wants to see you in his office. I'm going home."

Ben hugged me. "I'll be home early. See you soon." He released me, and we walked into the hallway. After I watched him walk down the hall, I dashed to my car and drove home to rest.

~

John sat alone in his office when Ben entered and closed the door. "If Becca lied, she's a tremendous actress. But I'm stuck in the middle on this one." John brought his elbows to the top of his desk and steepled his fingers. "This situation isn't our only concern."

Ben sat in a chair across from John's desk. "What do you mean?"

"We've received complaints about how you're running the missions program. How you're treating the parishioners and ministry assistants. Seems that every week there's added information that makes me believe you need time off."

"May we talk about each of those, so I understand?"

John took a sheet of paper from a folder on his desk and placed it in front of him. "Some of the people who support us with their finances, so we can take mission trips, have concerns about you and the way you're overseeing the funds."

"What?"

"There's a handful of people who have been on trips with you in the past who say you've been short with them. They no longer want to travel with you. One of the ministry assistants threatened to quit unless we make sure she won't have to work with you again."

Ben shook his head. "Things are better. After Annie died, I had bad days, but I've prayed about that daily and the Lord is helping me."

John leaned in. "I'm sure you've tried. And it thrilled us to learn you were getting married again. But you're not yourself yet."

Ben peered at him. "What now?"

"I'm putting you on administrative paid leave until

the Board and I can discuss all that's happened. We meet on Friday. They may want Becca to share her side of the story again, so you can let her know."

"What about my missions planning meeting tomorrow night?"

John moistened his lips. "I've asked Keith to lead the meeting because he led three of the trips since Annie's passing."

Ben stood. "So, I get sent home and Keith gets missions?"

John rose and widened his stance. "You get sent home to work on your marriage and make sure nothing like this happens again."

"Which means, you've prosecuted Becca," Ben pointed to himself, "and blame me for what's happened?"

John extended his palms at chest level. "Don't make this more difficult than it is. If this allegation were the only obstacle, I could keep you here. But it's not. The list of criticisms about you keeps mounting."

Ben stiffened. "Who are these people?" His chest tightened. "I need names."

"The information will remain confidential." John softened his tone. "The Board will check into the complaints and sort this out."

"When can I expect to return to my duties?" Ben took a step closer to John's desk. Would he have a position to come back to?

John returned to his seat. "I'll contact you as soon as I learn something."

Ben turned, walked to the door, and reached for the doorknob.

John kept his tone soft. "Becca's account of what

happened is convincing, but I don't know what to make of the other accusations." He sighed. "Pray for the Board and me to make the right decisions on this. I've considered you as one of the best on our team. This is a tough place for me to be."

Ben slipped through the door, headed to his office for his belongings, and strode to his car.

276

Forty-nine

Poor Ben. We skipped dinner Tuesday evening and instead prayed together. After he poured out his heart while we sat on the back patio, he went for a jog to help relieve his stress. He spent the rest of the evening in his room.

What hurt him most was the mishandling of funds. He'd strived to be above reproach and walk in integrity. He believed he'd been less grouchy and racked his brain as to which assistant hated to work with him. In Ben's opinion, Doris was the best assistant on the team, and he hoped it wasn't her.

Before going to bed Tuesday evening, I called Jill to fill her in. She prayed that truth would prevail and reminded me that God would direct the outcome.

Jill said she had news to share too.

"About Doc Winston?"

"Nothing new there." She sighed. "But my sister might return to Pleasant Springs soon."

"After all these years? Why? Are your parents, okay?"

Jill chuckled. "They're fine. The funny thing is when Mom told me that Lanie may move home, I asked the same question."

"Will be good for you to have her home and for me to get to know her better."

She agreed and we disconnected our call.

When Ben came to breakfast Wednesday morning, he wore the same clothes he'd jogged in the evening before. Bags hung under his dark eyes. His hair, which he kept neat, stuck up and out all over his head.

I poured him a cup of coffee. "Did you get much sleep?"

He shook his head.

I offered to go for a jog with him, something I despised.

He declined and plopped into his chair.

"Bacon and eggs, French toast, or pancakes?"

"Nothing."

My heart ached. How much of what happened was because of me? All of it? Did he resent me? *Lord, help him. Help me to help him.*

I shuffled to the refrigerator for a carton of orange juice and poured myself a glass.

Ben mumbled. "Toast and orange juice."

I tried to sound chipper. "Coming right up." I popped two slices of bread into the toaster and poured a second glass of orange juice. When I placed the juice on the table for Ben, he pulled me onto his lap and wrapped his arms around me.

We'd been married for one month. I longed for this kind of intimacy and affection, but the closeness turned my stomach. He hadn't showered or brushed his teeth. I tried to relax in his embrace because he needed reassurance, but I was grateful when the toast popped up.

"Let me butter the toast and I'll be right back." I jumped up and glanced back at him. He slumped his shoulders and lowered his head.

I hurried to the toaster, buttered our bread, grabbed the jelly, and brought everything to the table. After I prayed a quick prayer of thanksgiving, I stood behind Ben and rubbed his neck, back, and shoulders while he ate.

He eased into my touch, reached his hand to cover mine where it rested on his shoulder, and thanked me. "I appreciate your concern and being here for me." He rose from his chair and pulled me close again. "I'm going to get my shower. Perhaps we can do something special today to celebrate our monthiversary."

He remembered? Did he feel obligated to do something special with me?

Ben trudged out of the kitchen, turned back, and returned to my side. "Just want you to know that as lousy as I feel right now, I'm not upset with you. We'll get through this together."

~

After he showered and dressed, Ben picked his dirty clothes off the bathroom floor and plugged his nose. He carried them into his room and dropped them into the hamper he kept in his closet. He considered spraying them with a disinfectant and decided to never sleep in his clothes again. They reeked.

When he didn't find Becca downstairs, he went into his office and closed the door. He sat, placed his phone face down on his desk, and groaned. Was he out-of-line when he pulled Becca onto his lap earlier? He behaved toward her the way he would have with Annie.

Ben bowed his head. *Lord, this turmoil about betraying Annie and now with what's going on with Keith is messing with my mind and heart. I know you want me to love Becca, and I believe I do, but I want to be certain of her loyalty and love before I fully commit. Before I can love her like I did Annie.*

He also prayed for the missions meeting that would take place that evening and called out names from the list of over 200 people who'd registered to attend. He loved his teams and the changes that took place in their lives after being on a trip sharing Christ's love. These trips were his favorite thing to do, and it hurt to realize that mission trips may no longer happen for him at Hart Fellowship.

After his prayer, he flipped over his phone and read a text from Pastor Oldham, the pastor at Becca's old church in Pleasant Springs. **Are you available to preach two weeks from Sunday?**

That would thrill Becca. And it would be good for him, too, during this time of uncertainty.

He texted his response: **I think we can work that out. Let me check with Becca.**

Pastor Oldham texted him back: **Call me when you have a few minutes, and I'll fill you in.**

~

When I left my room at 9:30 a.m., after my prayer time, Ben's bedroom and bathroom doors were open. I moseyed down the stairs to check on him. I ambled to his office door and raised my hand to knock. He called out the names of several people. I recognized a few from church. He prayed for them and the upcoming mission trips.

I pulled myself away from his door and busied myself around the house while I waited for him.

He appeared ten minutes before noon. "Ready to grab lunch?"

"You seem to be feeling better?" I grinned.

"I'm practicing what I preach. Jesus said in Luke 6:27-28 to love your enemies, do good to them, bless, and pray for them. I prayed for Keith and everyone on the list who signed up for tonight's meeting. I turned it over to God and realized He's in control of this situation. Not me, John Young, or the Board. Only God."

"You are a wise man." After Keith's lies, and the possibility of Ben being pulled from the mission trips and losing his position, he was faithful to pray and ask God to bless Keith. Something Michael would have done too. "I'm proud to have you as my husband and to serve alongside you."

He reached his arms out to me and I welcomed them. "Do I smell better now?"

I nodded. "Would you like a ham and cheese sandwich?"

He pulled back and peered into my eyes. "I know of a steakhouse that I think you'll like. We have our monthiversary to celebrate."

"Am I dressed for it?"

Ben assured me that my capris and flowery top would be fine for the lunch crowd. We had plenty of time to chat on the drive because the restaurant was thirty minutes west of our home toward Disney World.

The host led us to a table for two along the back wall. Ben ordered steak, and I selected the salmon salad, which tasted delicious. But when I tried a bite of his filet, I pouted. "Now I wish I'd ordered steak."

"We'll come back soon, and you can order whatever you want."

I marveled at the peace that shone on Ben's face. He smiled often, his eyes sparkled, and his entire demeanor had brightened since that morning.

We opted not to order dessert and strolled to the car hand in hand. He opened my door before opening his own, and he climbed inside.

On our way home, he pointed to his cell. "Would you find Riley in my texts and ask her how Jeremy is doing?"

"Sure. I wondered about that, too, when I prayed for them this morning."

I removed the phone from the car mount, opened his texting list to find a recent one from Riley, and noticed one from my former pastor. "You've been texting Pastor Oldham?"

"Ah. Yes."

"Why? Anything I should know about?"

"Send Riley the text, and I'll tell you why he contacted me."

I sent off the text to Riley and returned Ben's cell to the car phone holder.

He told me that he was asked to preach in Pleasant Springs two weeks from Sunday.

I clapped my hands together. "And you said, yes, right?"

"Well, I wanted to ask you first, but I guess I have your answer."

I reached for his phone again. "Would you like me to text him for you?"

Ben pushed my hand away. "I'll take care of it when we get home."

"Why didn't you tell me this sooner?"

"I hoped to wait until we were alone. I envisioned you embracing me in a bear hug."

What was going on with him? He looked forward to my hugs?

Fifty

Later Wednesday afternoon, while Ben and I stood and chatted in the living room, I asked him if he'd heard from Riley. She'd responded with news that Jeremy spent all his free time reading the Bible. He had many questions, and Riley wanted to bring him home the following weekend for Ben to answer them.

"What do you think about them visiting again this weekend?"

"That's fine. I won't have to move your stuff out of your room again, will I?"

He wrinkled his nose. "Riley may have told Jeremy, so there's no reason to do so." Ben chuckled. "We'll let Jeremy sleep on the sofa."

I bit my lip.

"What's wrong?"

"I've prayed about something and sense it's what the Lord wants me to do."

Ben raised his brow.

"I want to attend tonight's mission meeting."

He stiffened and spoke in a firm tone. "No." He shook his head. "You can't go."

"But why?" I placed my hands on my hips. "I'm signed up to attend. They asked you to stay home, not me."

"I can't let you do that. They won't want you there."

I plopped onto the sofa and crossed my arms.

Ben sat on my left, rested his elbow on his knee, and covered his forehead with his hand. "My response may have been too harsh."

I stared straight ahead. "You think?"

He let out a heavy sigh and brushed his finger across my cheek. "If you believe the Lord is prompting you to go, then go. I'll not stand in the way of something God may want to accomplish through you. We're in this together."

I blinked four or five times. "Really?"

"I trust your judgement."

He trusted me? When did that happen?

After we ate a small dinner, I changed my clothes and left for the church with Ben's blessing.

When I arrived, I parked near the door closest to the educational wing where the meeting would take place and hurried inside. I made my way to the children's worship center, where men, women, and youth gathered to learn about the upcoming short-term mission trips. I'd prayed all the way there but hesitated when I approached the opened door. A voice in my head said, "You're not welcome here. Go home."

I lifted my head, threw my shoulders back, and marched forward through the door near the back of the room. God had given me a mission. I didn't understand what He had for me to do, but He wanted me inside.

I slipped into the back row to be as inconspicuous as possible and clutched my Bible to my chest. The muscles in my neck twitched, and my hands shook. I pasted on a smile and watched Keith, near the front of the room, talking to Pastor Vince. Keith turned and stepped out the door closest to him.

I had escaped his notice. *Thank you, Lord.*

The room filled with youth and their parents along with other adults.

Pastor Vince moved to the podium. "Pastor Morgan had to step out for a few minutes and asked me to open in prayer."

The gentleman from our class who'd said he didn't listen to gossip jumped up. "Where's Pastor Peterson?"

Speak.

Now, Lord? I stiffened. I couldn't budge. *No way. There are too many people. High School graduation all over again.*

Isaiah 41:10 echoed in my ears. "So do not fear, for I am with you."

My heart raced. I rose from my chair, glanced toward the back door, and drifted to the front of the room. "I'd like to answer that question."

Whispers and "Oh's" sounded around me.

Pastor Vince darted his eyes toward the door that Keith had exited and spoke into my ear. "Are you sure about this, Becca?"

I whispered, "Yes," and laid my Bible on the lectern. With my hand over my heart, I exhaled a calming breath and looked around the room. How much should I say? I focused on the gentleman.

"Pastor Young placed Ben on administrative leave because of the rumors surrounding me and accusations against him." I mentioned he'd been accused of being rude to parishioners and short-tempered to ministry assistants.

The gentleman tsked. "Lies. Ben Peterson is one of

the kindest men I know." He returned to his seat. Amens sounded.

Someone near the back said, "Are you here to clear your name?"

I shook my head. "Although the allegations against me are untrue, I'd like to ask you to pray for my husband."

More whispers but many of those in attendance offered genuine smiles and positive nods.

"Unless you've loved and lost someone dear to you, you cannot comprehend how grief can come upon you at any moment." I paused. Michael gripped my thoughts. "Memories return on special occasions, at the mention of their name, hearing a word that carried special meaning, or the mention of a favorite place. Often upon hearing, seeing, or even smelling these triggers, they may bring happiness to our hearts or disturb us in ways we can't understand. We may become grouchy or short with those closest to us."

Pastor Vince stood to my right. He kept glancing toward the door and tapping his foot.

"What I'm trying to say is that Ben loves each one of you. He's prayed for everyone who registered for this meeting. A meeting he wanted to attend and lead."

I read five verses about love from 1 Corinthians 13 and scanned the room. "If you feel Ben has wronged you, please forgive him. He suffered a significant loss in losing Annie. A woman I, too, loved and admired. Ben's a good man. I believe he's doing better and hope my love for him helps him to conquer his grief. If I can't love him enough, God can and does."

Pastor Vince grabbed my arm and spoke into my ear. "Thank you. We'll pray for Ben." He shoved me forward and muttered. "I'll escort you out. Keith is down the hallway. If he sees you—"

"What's she doing here?" Keith rushed toward me. His face reddened. "Go home." He pointed to the door. "You're not welcome here."

I searched the group for affirmation. Mouths hung open. Several people stood and frowned at Keith.

Didn't appear Keith noticed them. "I told you to leave. You will not be joining the mission trips. We don't need your kind along." He looked at the group. "Her story is a big, fat lie. She flirted with me—not the other way around."

Pastor Vince took my arm again and escorted me out the back door.

Outside the meeting room, he apologized. "I knew there'd be a scene if Keith came back inside and saw you." Pastor Vince shook his head. "I think the Board will sort all this out on Friday. Might be best if you stay away until then."

I darted down the hallway and out to my car without looking back. I wanted to get as far away from Keith as possible.

Fifty-one

Ben returned to his desk to pray for Becca and those who'd signed up to attend the meeting. He hoped they wouldn't shun her. The garage door moaned open, and Ben rose from his chair. Had Becca changed her mind and not attended? He met her in the kitchen. "Home early. Everything okay?"

She shook her head. Tears filled her eyes. "They asked me to leave."

He stepped closer and touched her shoulder. "Keith?"

"And Pastor Vince."

Ben offered to fix a cup of chamomile tea and asked her to sit and tell him what happened.

"I can't talk about it. Maybe tomorrow. I'm going to bed." She padded toward the stairway and turned back to Ben. "I'm sorry if I made things worse." Becca hurried up the stairs.

Ben took a seat at the kitchen table. She couldn't have made things worse for attending a church-wide meeting. Why would Becca think she had?

An hour later, Ben's phone buzzed with a text from Doris: Wow! That girl loves you. You should have seen her. Call me.

Ben cocked his head at his phone, wrinkled his brow, and called Doris.

"Ben, you won't believe this. She spoke to the entire group. Walked to the front and took over. Pastor Vince didn't know what to do. She even read scripture. You'd think she's been doing this her entire life."

Ben stroked his forehead. "Are you talking about Becca?"

"Yes. And more people attended than we expected." Doris chuckled. "She had something to say, and she said it. She wanted everyone to know what a wonderful man you are and how much she loves you."

Ben stood and paced across the kitchen. "What else did she say?"

"Pastor Young asked me to record everything because he couldn't be there. I'll send you a copy of Becca's part tomorrow when I figure out how to do it." She laughed and then got serious. "Oh, and Keith was ugly. No other word for the way he reacted when he came into the room and saw Becca at the front sharing her prayer request."

"Prayer request?"

"Yes, for the man she loves. So sweet."

"Send me the recording when you can."

~

Soon after Ben's jog and shower the following day, Doris came through with her promise: **Audio of Becca's prayer request attached. Her love and loyalty for you speak volumes.**

Love and loyalty? Ben edwonloaded the recording and pushed play. Eight minutes later, the audio stopped, and he descended the stairs to find Becca.

She sat at the kitchen table with her back to him and

stared out the window.

Ben greeted her, and she turned to face him. He poured them both a cup of coffee and took a seat next to her on her left. "You're an amazing woman."

She shook her head. "Nowhere near amazing." She frowned and rubbed her finger back and forth across the table in front of her. "I made things worse for you."

Ben smiled, took her hand, and brought it to his lips. "Let's leave what happened in the Lord's hands." He placed his phone in the middle of the table. "Doris sent me an audio copy of your prayer request from last night's meeting."

Becca's right hand covered her mouth.

Ben pulled her hand away. "Do you realize how many people were there in that room when you gave your speech?"

"Prayer request—not a speech." She narrowed her eyes. "Maybe 100 people."

He gave her the total count. "And one prayer request doesn't take seven and a half minutes to share."

"That's ridiculous."

He reached over to his phone and hit play. "Listen for yourself."

~

I spoke for more than seven minutes? In front of over 200 people? Ben called it a miracle.

He stood, pulled me out of my chair, locked me in a hug, and told me how proud he was of me for conquering my fear. "I'll expect to share the podium with you the next time I bring the message at church. *If* I'm allowed to stay and bring a message."

"I don't think sharing the podium will be necessary."

Ben pulled back and peered into my eyes. "Let's celebrate tomorrow night."

"If they don't clear our names from the allegations, there won't be anything to celebrate."

"I want to celebrate you." He ran his fingers through my hair. "You took a bold stand last night. That's worth celebrating."

Oh, my heart. His eyes lowered to my lips. The moment I prayed for, hoped for, and waited for.

He took a step back. "There are preparations to make and errands I need to run to pull this celebration off." He strode toward the door to the laundry room. "If I can't finish before lunch, I'll call and tell you."

"What? Are you planning a party?"

"A party of two. You and me." He pointed at me with both index fingers, slid sideways through the door, and out into the garage.

What? Had he lost his mind? We were in crisis mode, and he danced out the door. I plopped onto a kitchen chair and grinned. He was rather cute. I sighed. But when would I get a real kiss?

~

Ben chided himself. He almost lost it in there. The urge to kiss Becca was strong. A good time to distance himself from her. He needed to make several stops in preparation to celebrate Becca the following evening.

He traveled north on 417, stopped to buy wrapping paper, and visited multiple florists near Waterford Lakes Town Center to purchase as many orange gerbera daisies as he could find. While he drove, he planned how to tell Becca the rest of the news from Pastor Oldham.

Fifty-two

My phone rang while I brushed my teeth on Friday morning. Why was Ben calling me? I rinsed my mouth and tried to click the answer button but missed his call. I sent him a text: What's up?

Breakfast is served.

Sweet. Be right down. He did plan to celebrate me.

Downstairs in the dining room, he had set the table with ham and cheese omelets, whole grain toast, coffee, and orange juice. He lit two red candles that he'd placed in the center of the table.

"All this for me?"

He smiled. "This is only the start of our celebration. Wait until this evening." He pulled out my chair. "An evening to remember."

"Where are we going?" I took my seat and scooted closer to the table.

"Dinner at the steakhouse we visited on Wednesday so you can order a steak."

I sat straighter. "I like that idea."

He pulled out his chair and sat. "And I have a special request of you because tonight's dinner is semi-formal."

I touched the base of my neck.

"Will you wear the orange dress from our

wedding?" His face beamed, and he gazed into my eyes.

At that moment, I would have done anything he asked.

We chatted and finished our breakfast. After cleaning the dishes, he hid himself inside his office while I threw in laundry and tidied the house.

He found me before lunch while I cleaned the downstairs bathroom sink. "Got a call from Pastor Young. He wants us at the church at 2:15 p.m. today."

"Any sign of how things may turn out?"

He shrugged. "We'll find out soon." He took the cleaning cloth from me, put it on the vanity, and took my hands in his. "No matter what happens, God will see us through."

I agreed.

"Let's eat lunch and get ready to go to the church. And then tonight, we celebrate you."

After lunch and primping, we headed to the church.

I clutched my middle when we pulled into the parking lot. "My stomach is in knots. How are you doing?"

"Other than a pounding headache, I'm fine."

"May we pray before we go inside?"

He held my hand and prayed for God to guide us in what to say and what not to say and to give us strength no matter what happened.

We stepped inside the church hand in hand and walked down the hallway, which led to the conference room where we were to meet. We peeked inside, expecting to find the room filled with board members, but only Pastor Young remained.

"Come in and have a seat." His eyes drooped. "Chairperson Frank Harden will be here in a minute. We sent the remaining board members home." He rested his elbow on the table, closed his eyes, and rubbed his forehead.

Ben and I glanced at one another. Things didn't look good.

Frank entered the room and closed the door behind him. He spoke in a booming voice. "How are the love birds today?" He grinned. "I saw the two of you on Tuesday at lunch. Looked like two honeymooners to me." He sat across from us and next to Pastor Young.

I eyed Ben. Had he noticed Mr. Harden before he took a seat next to me in the booth? Was it all a show?

He peered at me and then at Frank. "That's kind of you to say, Sir. I didn't see you there or I would have stopped by your table to say hello."

"No problem."

So, he wasn't putting on a show? He'd paid much attention to me since then at home with no one around. I believed him.

Pastor Young cleared his throat. "Frank, tell Ben and Becca how the Board ruled."

Ben squinted and frowned. "Ruled? Hearing nothing more from us?"

Mr. Harden laughed. "Now don't get your feathers ruffled. The Board met with Keith at noon today and agreed on how to proceed." He folded his hands on the table. "The truth came to light, and you two are in the clear."

I opened my eyes wide and placed my hand on my chest. "That's wonderful."

Ben agreed. "Can you share any details with us? What did Keith say?"

Pastor Young leaned back in his chair. "Doris's

recording from Wednesday evening told us what we needed to know. Keith confirmed it when he addressed the Board today."

The two gentlemen told us the full recording included incriminating information from Keith. The story he shared at the meeting of what happened at our party differed from what he'd told Pastor Young in private. Information he shouldn't have shared at all.

In addition, Pastor Young and Mr. Harden commended me on how I handled myself when I spoke at the meeting. I didn't condemn Keith, and they said that spoke well of me.

Pastor Young picked up a pen from the middle of the table and rolled it between his hands. "My daughter, Ellie, doesn't know what's happened today. She went into labor while Keith met with the Board. She and Keith arrived at the hospital a few minutes ago. We need to finish here so I can join them. Keith will tell her after she delivers."

"Tell her what?" Ben reached for my hand.

"We terminated Keith this morning." Mr. Harden spoke to Ben. "His motive wasn't to destroy your marriage. He wanted the two of you to leave Hart Fellowship. He thought if he fed lies to you and Pastor Young, you would quit, or we'd release you from your duties. When that didn't work and you married Becca, he assumed if he made her miserable, she would convince you to leave. That's why he left the fake gator in your yard, sabotaged the Good Friday service, and made advances at the party."

"But why? We were friends?" Ben pulled his hand from mine and raised his palms.

Pastor Young exhaled a deep sigh. "Envy. Greed.

He wanted your position. He tired of the youth ministry, loved filling in for you and leading mission trips since Annie's death, and he plotted to take it from you."

I had trouble comprehending what all of this meant for Ben and for me.

Ben stood and paced. "I should have seen this. For the past six months he's told me things." He faced Pastor Young. "Told me that you doubted me. My abilities. My attitude. And that my position was in jeopardy. He said people talked about how I was mean and hateful to them." Ben shook his head. "I should have come to you and asked you for myself. They were all lies, weren't they?"

Pastor Young confirmed. "In recent months, he fed me the same information about you. But I'd seen improvement and ignored what he told me until I heard from Ellie about Becca's supposed ill behavior."

I gasped. "What? Until this week. Ben's position. Wasn't in jeopardy?" My heart ached and my throat thickened. Where did I fit into the mess? Ben never needed to marry me.

Ben grabbed my hand and whispered into my ear. "Everything's fine. We're okay."

Pastor Young apologized for believing Keith and confirmed that before his lie about Becca there was no threat of Ben losing his job. Keith and Ellie's account of what happened at the party caused Pastor Young to reconsider the other recent allegations Keith had brought to him.

Frank Harden smiled. "We'll need the two of you to join Pastor Young on stage Sunday morning during the first part of each service. He'll clear up the rumors going around about Becca and make sure everyone understands

Ben is a pastor in good standing. We'll also address Keith's termination."

Pastor Young looked at Ben. "I'm thankful I only have to tell the church that Keith was envious of your position and not that he wanted your wife too. That would kill Ellie. I hope Keith will get the help he needs to right this wrong and keep his marriage intact."

Ben rubbed the back of his neck. "Are you certain Keith hasn't behaved in an unprofessional manner with other women in the church?"

Pastor Young rose from his chair and stared out the window at the parking lot. "I suspected he hadn't. But after hearing Becca's side of the story, we emailed anonymous evaluation surveys to youth, college-aged young people who were once a part of the youth group, and our assistants. All evaluations were due back by 11:00 a.m. today to be counted, and the company conducting the survey sent us immediate results. The worst comments were about his practical jokes. Parishioners have described some as mean-spirited."

I could attest to that. "How were these questionnaires explained to everyone?"

"Evaluation surveys are common around here. We conduct them every two to three years." Frank stood. He apologized for needing to stand and stretch his legs. "We note who is being evaluated, send the surveys out to those most likely to have worked with that staff member, and ask a few general questions." He walked around the table. "We omit questions regarding specific behaviors but leave a response area where parishioners can comment with compliments or concerns."

Pastor Young explained the Board requested the church send out the same evaluations for Ben, Vince, and

Lindsey. They assured Ben the comments about him were good, and he had nothing to be concerned about.

Pastor Young rose, shook our hands, and apologized again.

Ben clung to my hand on our way out to his car. He'd said everything was fine and we were okay. I gazed up at him. But would he have written to me had he known his job wasn't in jeopardy? I grimaced and swallowed hard. Did he regret he married me?

Fifty-three

Ben opened the car door for Becca. "Can you believe that? Lies and deception. All because he wanted my position." He shook his head and strode to the driver's side. Greed. Envy. Ben started the car and backed out of his parking space. "I considered him my best friend. And to think he's lied to me all this time."

Becca ran her hand down Ben's upper arm and spoke in a compassionate tone. "What happened six months ago that caused Keith to covet your position?"

Ben pondered her question. "He came back from a mission trip to Ecuador that changed his life and the lives of many who went. We always pray for that kind of trip, and God moved in a miraculous way. Revival broke out."

"We should all want God to move in our hearts, but not at the expense of others."

Ben nodded. "Let's put this behind us, go home, and get ready for a great evening. The two of us."

Her voice quivered. "Are you sure? We can wait." She wrapped her arms around her. "I feel bad about celebrating when Ellie is about to hold her precious newborn and then be told her husband no longer has a job and why."

Ben stopped at a traffic light and reached for Becca's hand. "Tonight, is about us. Not Keith. Not Ellie. But us. You and me. A night to celebrate—"

A car horn blared. Ben stepped on the gas.

"Us?" Becca raised her eyebrows. "You said we were celebrating me tonight."

"And you are a part of us."

~

Ben didn't sound like he regretted marrying me. I wanted to shout, hallelujah.

When we arrived at the house at 3:10 p.m., I rushed upstairs. Our reservations were for 6:00 and Ben planned a forty-five-minute drive to get to the restaurant. Traffic was horrific at that time of day. I didn't need two hours to get ready, but this was important to Ben. After I relaxed for several minutes, I showered, took extra time with my makeup, wore my orange dress, per his request, and fixed my hair in long waves. I tried to fix my hair in a loose bun like I'd worn at our wedding, but that didn't go well.

With five minutes to spare, I called Jill. "Ben has something special planned for tonight." I giggled and covered my mouth. "He said he wanted to celebrate me and then changed it to celebrate us. Isn't that sweet?"

"Glad the two of you are doing better." Jill sounded as excited as me.

"I have much to tell you about what happened today and want to get the scoop on you and Doc, but Ben's waiting for me. I'll talk to you soon."

"Have an exciting time, friend." She sounded giddy. "I know you will. I love and miss you."

What was up with her? "Same here."

We ended our call.

I grabbed my purse and stopped at the top of the stairs.

Ben waited at the bottom in his black suit and bow tie. Reminded me of what he wore for our wedding. He lifted his hand toward me. "You look stunning."

My knees wobbled. His gaze caused my heart to leap. "You look charming yourself."

I reached the bottom of the stairs and took his hand.

He kissed my cheek. My first disappointment of the evening. I hoped for a real kiss.

Ben reached inside his jacket pocket and pulled out a long, slender gift wrapped in orange paper. "For you."

I widened my eyes. "What's this?"

"The first of three surprises to celebrate you." His eyes twinkled mischief. "Open it."

I tore off the wrapping paper and peeked inside. "Oh, my. Beautiful." I peered at Ben. "I love it. Will you put it on me?" I handed the gold chained, orange and blue butterfly necklace to him. "Is this the one I eyed at the butterfly conservatory in Key West?"

"I went back and bought it for you while you were in the photography store." He opened the clasp, pulled my hair away from my neck, and snapped the clasp in place. After a quick kiss to the nape of my neck, he released my hair. Chills ran down my spine.

That was his first kiss on my neck. "Was that surprise number two?"

He jerked his head back and narrowed his eyes. "The necklace was number one. Are you okay?"

I laughed. "Yes. Thank you for the lovely gift."

He took my hand and led me out the front door, which was odd. Had he gone somewhere while I got ready and left his car in the driveway?

I gawked. "A limo?"

He chuckled and led me to the car door where a chauffeur met us. We climbed inside. I sat first and expected with all that room he'd sit across from me.

Instead, he took a seat on my left and wrapped his arm around my shoulder. "Nothing but the best for you."

"So, this is surprise number two?"

"Still a part of number one. I'll inform you when it's time for number two."

Fifty-four

We arrived at the restaurant at 6:03 and hurried inside. The hostess seated us at a romantic corner table for two. We sat shoulder to shoulder on a round bench. We hadn't waited long before an older gentleman approached with a violin and serenaded us with a beautiful soft melody. As soon as he finished his song, a young server took our order. We both ordered the filet mignon.

After we chatted for fifteen minutes, I glanced around the dining room.

"Do you see someone you know?"

I shook my head and focused on Ben. "Checking out the décor. This place looks different in the evening."

"They lower the lights and play softer, romantic music for couples in love."

The skin on my arms tingled. He selected the restaurant and time of day knowing that?

Our server delivered our food, and after a brief prayer, we ate a delicious meal.

"The best steak I've ever eaten." I thanked Ben for bringing me.

"Let's order dessert."

I clutched my stomach. "I'm stuffed, and I don't

dare eat another bite, but I'd love to know about surprise number two."

His eyes glowed. "I haven't told you everything about Pleasant Springs and Pastor Oldham."

I squirmed in my seat. "Hurry and tell me."

"Pastor Oldham is retiring."

I leaned away from him and searched his face. "That can't be. Jill would have told me."

"The congregation doesn't know he's leaving. Only the Board has been told. They've asked us to come. Pastor Oldham will tell the church on Sunday."

"He's leaving that soon, and the Board asked you to fill in for one week?"

"Or more." He grinned. "Pastor Oldham said they've already considered a short list of possible candidates but believe we'd be a perfect fit as the new pastors of the church."

I wrinkled my nose. "Wait. What?"

Ben chuckled and held my hand. "We'll meet with the Board in two weeks on Saturday, the day before I preach. If they agree, they'll ask the congregation to vote after I preach."

I squealed and hugged Ben's neck. "Are you considering this? I mean, if they vote you in, will you take the position?"

"We need to pray in earnest about this and agree. Not just because you want to go back home, but because it's where God wants us." He spoke in a teasing tone. "Will it be too much of a sacrifice for you to give up the gators you've grown fond of?"

I hugged him again. "I can't imagine what surprise number three is. You're going to have a tough time beating this one." I kissed his cheek.

He frowned. "Now you've made me nervous that I can't deliver. I hoped you'd find number three better than number two."

Ben texted the limo driver that we were ready and paid the server. When we got outside, our chauffeur was waiting in the parking lot.

Joy bubbled inside of me. The possibility of going home to Pleasant Springs. I couldn't wait to call Jill and tell her the news. Ben tried to calm me. We had to wait until the church learned they would soon lose their pastor. How could I keep this quiet from my best friend?

We sat next to one another in the limo and chatted about the possibilities of moving back to Pleasant Springs. What a wonderful place to live, but nothing like Orlando. Ben appeared excited too.

"But are you sure? Pleasant Springs Community Church is small and traditional. Hart Fellowship is huge and contemporary."

"That's why we need to pray and make sure this is what God wants." He pulled me toward him with his arm wrapped around my shoulder. "After big church politics and what Keith put us through, I'm ready to move back to Tennessee and enjoy a simpler life with you."

Hadn't he figured out yet that nothing was simple with me? "What will Riley think? Won't she be disappointed you're leaving Florida?"

"She'll be fine. Pleasant Springs will be a wonderful place for her and our grandchildren to visit."

"Grandchildren?" I lowered my eyes to the floor. What about children? Our children? We never discussed that possibility. Although I suffered two miscarriages with Michael, the doctor told me it wasn't impossible for me to have children. I peered at Ben. How did I bring up a subject about children when we weren't really married?

"You're the one who said Riley and Jeremy may talk marriage soon. When they have children, they'll be our grandchildren. Not only mine." He rubbed my shoulders.

I swallowed hard. "May I have a bottle of water?"

He opened the cooler and gave me a bottle. "Are you okay? Did I say something wrong?"

I shook my head. "Everything's fine." I faked a smile and held back tears. He was finished having children. I hoped for a house full. A topic for another day.

Fifty-five

Ben wasn't sure what to do. Should he forge ahead with surprise number three? Becca had gone from ecstatic to sadness within moments at the mention of grandchildren. Had he made her feel old?

"Did I tell you how beautiful you look this evening?"

She nodded and leaned her head on his shoulder.

Ben nuzzled his nose into her hair. Fresh berries. Strawberries to match her strawberry blonde hair? He could get used to this closeness. His heart rate climbed. He wanted to continue with surprise number three. He hoped she was ready to hear what he longed to tell her.

~

We arrived at the house at 8:30. I thanked Ben for the beautiful evening and moseyed toward the stairs while he sent a text.

"Wait. You can't go upstairs yet."

I turned back to him. "I'm exhausted. Been a long day. A wonderful evening, but I'm beat."

"I still have one more surprise for you."

And how important was it if he took the time to text someone? "Can't it wait until tomorrow?"

He rushed to my side. "Please." He raised my hand

to his lips. "The surprise is in my office."

I released a long sigh. "If it doesn't take long."

Ben grimaced and lowered his head. He spoke in a defeated tone. "I'll try to hurry." He led me to his office door, opened it, and flipped on the light.

My face lit up. "This is beautiful." Three vases of orange, white, and yellow gerbera daisies sat on his desk. "This is a surprise." But how could he think this was better than moving back to Pleasant Springs? I kissed his cheek and thanked him for the lovely evening. "I'll move the daisies into the kitchen and living room tomorrow morning."

He placed his palm on my back and nudged me toward his desk. He spoke in a frustrated tone. "You appear to be in a hurry, but I'm not finished." He pointed to the items on top. A Bible lay opened to 1 Corinthians 13. He'd propped his iPad on top of four thick books behind his Bible.

He lifted his iPad, dropped it, and asked me to hang on for a minute while he fiddled with it.

I rolled my eyes and scanned the verses in his Bible highlighted in yellow. The same verses I read on Wednesday evening at the missions meeting. Verses four through the first part of eight.

I stared at Ben and his iPad. What was he up to? He punched a number on his Facetime app. Why did he bring me into his office to show me flowers, his Bible, and to make a call?

"Hi, Ben. Hi, Becca." Jill's voice boomed with excitement. "Thanks for texting me a minute ago. I was afraid you'd forgotten me, and I dressed up for nothing."

I gaped at her and then at Ben. "What?" She was wearing the bridesmaid dress from our wedding.

"And thanks for inviting me to join you for this special occasion."

"I thought a witness would be nice." Ben chuckled. His hand shook when he returned his iPad to the top of the books. He faced me. "I want us to read Bible verses and thought you might like to have Jill join us." He gazed at me with a silly grin on his face. "I'll go first." He read aloud in that smooth tone of his but with a little quiver in his voice.

"Love is patient, love is kind. It does not envy, it does not boast, it is not proud. It does not dishonor others, it is not self-seeking, it is not easily angered, it keeps no record of wrongs. Love does not delight in evil but rejoices with the truth. It always protects, always trusts, always hopes, always perseveres. Love never fails."

I tilted my head to the right and peered into Ben's eyes. Was he doing what I thought he was doing?

He flipped back to Genesis 2, turned his Bible toward me and held it somewhat steady. "Please read the highlighted verse."

I clasped my hands in front of me to stop their shaking. "Verse twenty-four. 'That is why a man leaves his father and mother and is united to his wife, and they become one flesh.'" I searched Ben's eyes. My heart pounded. "Does this mean . . .?"

He placed the Bible on his desk and turned toward me. "What I believed would take at least a year took only a couple of months. I love you more than I ever thought possible."

I brought my hand to my chest. "Really?" I cupped his cheek in my hand. "Surprise number three is way better than number two."

Without taking his eyes off mine, he stepped closer and took my hands in his. "I Benson, take thee Rebecca, to be my wedded wife. To have and to hold from this day forward, for better, for worse, for richer, for poorer, in sickness and in health, to love and to cherish till death do us part."

Jill giggled. "You may kiss your bride."

Dear Reader,

Thank you for reading *An Odd Request*. If you enjoyed Ben and Becca's story, please leave a review to help other readers discover it.

Would you like a gift? When you sign up for my newsletter and monthly blog posts, you'll receive a free short story: www.luannkedwards.com.

Connect with me on Facebook.

Where to follow me.
Amazon
BookBub
Goodreads

Other books by LuAnn K. Edwards.

Love Comes Again
Only A Glimpse
Let Him Go
Charm And Perfection

An Undeserved Gift (a novella)

I hope you enjoy the first chapter from my novella, *An Undeserved Gift.*

One

"Again?" I plopped my phone into my purse and muttered. "The third time this week he's stood me up. Is this how our marriage will be?" I sagged in my chair at an outdoor café. "I can't believe this." My fiancé, Dillon Montgomery, couldn't keep his word.

"Excuse me, Miss." A good-looking guy, a few years older than me, stood and stared from the other side of the table. "I kind of overheard you on the phone. Sounds like you need a friend. Perhaps I can help." He took the seat across from me. "May I join you?"

"You already have." I frowned, leaned back, and crossed my arms.

"Free counseling. How can you pass on a deal like that?"

I leaned toward him, a sneer on my face. "If that's what you're dishing out, I'm out of here." I raised my right palm in front of his face. "I don't need counseling." But Dillon sure did.

"Friendship then from an understanding listener?" He grinned. His dimpled cheeks radiated warmth and kindness. "I'll get straight to the point. My fiancée dumped me thirty minutes ago. You don't seem much better off than me." He glanced away for a moment and took a deep breath. "I'll treat you right. Marry me instead. You won't be disappointed."

I jumped up and knocked over my chair, causing a bird pecking at crumbs to fly off. "You're crazy." I bent to pick up the chair, but the man with the odd offer bolted from his seat and beat me to it.

"Let me get that for you."

I spun on my heels to leave and darted through the parking lot to my car.

A hand brushed my elbow when I unlocked my door. I flinched, looked up, and again noticed his warmth and kindness. This time beaming from his dark eyes.

"You don't give up, do you?" I pulled open my door and threw my purse onto the passenger seat.

He pleaded with me. "I'm a good guy. I am. Please. One minute."

I narrowed my eyes. "Doesn't matter how good you are. I refuse to marry you."

"Be my date tonight? One date." He lifted his index finger and pushed his shoulders back.

I tilted my head, gawked at him, and raised my hands. "Are you for real? I don't have time for this."

"But I need a date. Tonight. My grandfather expects to meet my fiancée, but like I told you, she dumped me. Let me introduce you as her. Tomorrow I'll tell him we broke it off, and I'll be gone from your life."

I gazed into his eyes. "Why can't you tell him tonight she called the wedding off?"

"He's throwing me an engagement party. Huge. He's proud of me. Offered a promotion and marrying a good woman from an outstanding family. Only I'm not." He looked down, studied the ground for a moment and looked back up. "Neither."

I shook my head. "I don't understand. What do you mean, neither?"

"I work for a family-owned business. My boss won't promote me until I'm married and settled down. Now that won't happen."

"And you told Gramps you already got the promotion?" I pursed my lips and opened my eyes wide.

He crossed his arms and rested his backside against my Oldsmobile Cutlass Ciera. "Yep."

I placed my hands on my hips. "Who do you think you are leaning up against my car? You don't know me, and I don't know you."

He straightened and looked behind him at my car then back at me. "Name's Jarrett."

We shook hands and I softened my tone. "I'm Lyn. I can't help you. Even one date. But let me give *you* some advice. You're living a lie. I'm all about truth and honesty." I nodded. "Confess to Grandpa. That's the right thing to do."

He sounded desperate. "My offer still stands. One date. After you talk with my family and friends, *you'll* be begging *me* to marry you."
I glowered, climbed into my car, and said goodbye to mister warmth, kindness, and cocky.

Thank you for reading, and God bless!

LuAnn

Acknowledgements

First, I'd like to thank the Lord for Ben and Becca's story and for His guidance in writing it.

To my husband and family who love, support, and encourage me in my writing, thank you.

I appreciate each beta reader who gave of their time and shared their ideas with me. I'd find this difficult to do without your help. You are amazing. A big thank you to Judi, Julie, Kim, and Moss.

Thanks to Larry J. Leech II for your thorough critique and assistance. Your insights and expertise are a blessing.

Finally, I'm grateful to Winged Publications, Forget Me Not Romances for the opportunity to publish this novel and series.

About the Author

LuAnn writes Christian contemporary romance for women who enjoy a wholesome love story that inspires faith and hope. She grew up in Ohio, lived in New Mexico for several years, but calls Tennessee home. Seven years ago, she attended her first writers conference. There, a spark she'd pushed aside for over forty years to write fiction reignited. When she's not writing, you'll often find her flirting with her husband, who after forty-six years, doesn't mind. LuAnn is Mom to three children and Nana to three grandchildren. She's a former mathematics teacher and administrative professional who enjoys reading, hiking, traveling, and spending time with her family. She holds a bachelor's degree from Lee University in Cleveland, Tennessee, and is a member of American Christian Fiction Writers. Find her online at www.luannkedwards.com to learn more about her and her novels.